THAT'S THE WAY THE
CASTLE
CRUMBLES

LUNA RYDER

Editor: Crystal Lee Wren, COL Proofreading
Designer: S.J. Gautreaux, Night Witchery

PO Box 873543
Wasilla, AK 99687

AUTHOR'S NOTE

I love a big adventure, but I have a pretty short attention span. Perhaps it's down to my neurodivergent brain or perhaps that's just the way things are in this digital age.

Either way, I didn't want my need for perpetual amusement to stop me from slaying monsters, facing down bad guys, and saving the world. And that's why I wrote *When Life Gives You Legends*.

As an avid reader, I love for the high points to just keep coming and never stop. I don't want to sit through a five-page description of an old forest, thank you very much. I want to know what's going to happen once our character wanders in!

And hey, maybe you're like me.

If so, you'll find yourself happily at home in the world of Verandel

with the likes of Tilda Quickthatch and her misfit band of chosen family.

I've kept the chapters short and fast-paced—once you get past the first one, that is!—and I've employed a cast of characters that are far more than imaginary. They represent people in my real life, in our real world, doing super awesome, high fantasy things.

This isn't a book to be taken too seriously. It's all about finding yourself and having fun while doing it.

And I hope you will,

Luna Ryder

1

The dank stone walls felt like they were closing in on me. As a halfling, I didn't often find myself feeling claustrophobic, but I supposed there was a first time for everything.

True, I'd been here before, trapped within the same cell in this underground prison, but it had been many years. I thought I'd left this part of my life behind. I thought I was free...

But now I felt more trapped than ever, not just behind these bars but by the circumstances that had landed me here in the first place. I'd retired. I was done, safe in a small town.

Until I wasn't.

Now, I was back on the road in a life-or-death quest I'd tried for years to avoid. My new adventuring party was composed almost entirely of headstrong and hapless kids, and those same kids had introduced me to many unwanted firsts since we'd taken up our journey together. Honestly, it had only been a few days since we'd set out, and I now marveled at how much had gone wrong in such a short time: near-death encounters, painful injuries, an unexpected capture, and nearly constant bickering from my companions.

I'd been so focused on moving forward despite these problems, on hiding from the necromancer who wanted me dead, that I'd somehow forgotten I also needed to evade the tanuki crime boss who saw me as his child and wanted to wield me like a well-honed weapon, one he believed he created.

Such was life. Or at least such was *my* life. Little body but big, big problems.

I shifted on the uneven stone flooring and pressed my back against the weathered wall, desperately attempting to find some sliver of comfort so that I could enter slumber. Finnian Sly had made it clear that he'd return in the morning and come bearing a sizable —and most likely, a stupid—mission for us.

Ah, Finnian Sly.

The closest thing I had to a mentor but also the one person I hated most in all this world. I generally kept everyone at arm's length, seeing as my list of friends had proven far more paltry than my list of enemies. Finnian and the aforementioned necromancer Maltherius topped the latter of those two lists, with my old adventuring partner Gaaron and small-town waitress slash secret beloved Brynlee leading up the former.

This ill-fated adventure was for them—for Gaaron and Brynlee—the two good guys who took up an enormous portion of my battered and bruised heart. They'd known each other many years ago and even had a child together, and now the teenaged version of that child was my most competent ally in this pity of a party I found myself leading.

But that would be getting ahead of myself...

Our quest was supposed to be relatively straightforward. It was also one I'd meant to take on alone, but the kids had mostly blackmailed their way into their first attempt at adventuring. And, well, when sweet Brynlee batted her long eyelashes and begged for me to take care of her thrill-seeking progeny, I just couldn't say no.

So off we went to meet with Maltherius at his lair clear on the other side of the map. It would be a long journey but a straightforward one—at least, that's what I had mistakenly assumed. Our enemy had made two clear and simple demands in the short, written summons he'd sent by way of an undead servant. The first was to bring a particular artifact in exchange for Gaaron's freedom, and the second was to ensure we arrived before the solstice. I had no idea what he had planned for the big day, and I hoped to never find out. I fully intended to take what I wanted and refuse to deliver on my end of the bargain. It seemed simple enough, right?

By the time the tanuki called Finnian Sly caught up with us, our journey had already been plenty fraught. But that's just what happened when you took three untrained youths and one unconscious elder celestial to face down the most powerful villain in all of Verandel. Of course, I knew it would be hard. That's why I hadn't wanted to bring them in the first place. And that's also why I was in a near-constant state of abandoning them to carry out my mission alone. Only my devotion to dear, sweet Brynlee kept me from acting on this specific desire.

I knew very well that our weak and conflicted party would be its own undoing. If we didn't pull ourselves together by the time we reached Maltherius, we were as good as defeated. And also dead. Can't forget that part. Because when you're fighting a necromancer, dying wasn't even the end for divinity's sake.

We'd finally started to make a small peck of

progress when, lo and behold, Finnian showed up just in time to make our lives infinitely more difficult.

He was always doing things like that, and it's precisely why I both hated and respected him in equal measure.

When I'd first found myself in this cell, it'd been part of his devious plan. A guard on the take had busted me for picking someone's pocket and dragged me here, where Finnian, disguised as another skinny scrap of a child thief, had been waiting. He talked to me and actually listened. His interest gave me a yearning that might have been called hope. That got my attention and made me feel like I was more than just some troublesome urchin nobody wanted. Maybe I could have a family. My parents had died so long ago I couldn't even picture their faces anymore.

Finnian revealed his true form to me and invited me to join his "family." Then, he released us from prison.

And sadly, that's all it took. Already, this was far more than anyone had ever given me before. It took me years to realize that he'd played me like a well-strung lute. By then, it was too late to leave him.

I was a quick study under his tutelage, a fact that caught and, unfortunately, kept Finnian's interest.

I'd foolishly assumed he was done with me after

Gaaron and I left Mirathane to strike out on our own. I thought he was busy enough with all the other orphans and petty thieves he held so tightly in his black-fingered grip, but no. Whether near or far, he'd never stopped watching from the shadows. Waiting for his chance to move into the dappled light.

Ten years ago, he'd set everything into motion, although I hadn't known it was him until last night. Indeed, it was Finnian Sly who'd anonymously posted the original quest that sent me and my bard friend to Maltherius's lair to retrieve a mysterious artifact known as the Genesis Crest. I'd scored the loot but lost my companion in the process.

And ever since then, I'd believed that Gaaron was dead and that it was all my fault. But that wasn't the case at all. Maltherius and Finnian revealed in turn that my former partner and dearest friend was still alive and imprisoned within the necromancer's lair. He'd been waiting all this time, and I hadn't known to come.

But now that I knew, nothing could keep me from Gaaron. Not even these stupid prison bars.

Both Maltherius and Finnian Sly wanted the Genesis Crest, and up until a few hours ago, I'd been keeping it nestled safely between my bosoms. The pendant possessed some peculiar powers, none of which I understood. I understood enough, however, to know that it most definitely should not end up in either set of bad guy's hands.

Except that Finnian already had it...

He just didn't *know* that he had it.

Yeah, I was pretty confused about that part too. Upon taking us captive, he'd rid our party of all our weapons and other valuables, including the artifact. But sweet divinity, how did he not recognize the treasure he'd sought for years?

And if he was indeed so eager to get his grubby paws on the Genesis Crest, why did he insist on forcing us to take care of some lengthy side quest first? Whatever the case, I felt sure he'd tell us at length when he returned in the morning. With the way that tanuki I'd once called "Pa" loved listening to his voice, we'd be lucky to start on this new mission before sunfall tomorrow.

That's why I needed whatever rest I could manage. Unfortunately, my middle-aged body was alive and alert with varying aches and pains to protest its discomfort. The worst part was that my skin felt inflamed.

"Will you cut that out already?" I snarled, not even bothering to wedge open my eyelids. I knew exactly who I wanted to yell at and where he'd positioned himself in the cell. If he were any closer, I'd whomp him right over his big, stupid head.

"Suh-sorry," Rurik mumbled for probably the thousandth time that evening. "It's just... I ca-can't give up now."

"He's making some real progress, Tilda. The bars are getting thinner." was way too full of pep considering the late hour and precarious situation.

"I would also like to sleep," Tulip huffed. "If that's even possible with these wretched accommodations. Zero stars. Do not recommend."

And that was my party, minus the elder celestial named Amariel, who was being kept in a separate anti-magic chamber somewhere within this same dungeon. Amariel had joined us as a chaperone for Tulip—a spoiled small-town princess with anger issues. Also a centaur. Tulip had joined our adventure because she'd deemed it a fun thing to do at the time. Learning that she wasn't "the main character" had put a bit of a damper on her spirits, along with eventually figuring out that this wasn't all fun and games and that she could actually die.

The other two kids were both half-human, half-something else. And the ones who started this whole mess in the first place. By figuring out my secret past and blackmailing me into training them, they'd allowed Maltherius to uncover my hiding spot and issue the ultimatum that had set us on this journey. I would've even been impressed if we weren't in a cell right now. Because of them, I now knew Gaaron was alive, but it was also because of them that we probably wouldn't be all that much longer.

Truth be told, though, I knew very well that the weird, cloaked figure who'd assaulted me at the Mystic Mug was probably one of Maltherius's undead scouts. And I also recognized that he'd found me out before the children had ever gotten involved. Still, I was enjoying blaming them for all my problems. It was just easier that way.

Rurik grunted in exhaustion and put out his magical flame. The half-orc was born to a family of fierce barbarians, but he had a heart for magic and insisted he was a wizard despite all evidence to the contrary.

"Keep going," his best friend Calina urged him, her voice now a bit softer than usual. She was a half-elf aspiring ranger, an excellent markswoman, and the daughter of the only two people I'd ever really loved. Yes, she's the same child turned teen I mentioned earlier. I hadn't figured out her parentage until recently, given that Gaaron had never told me of his past loves, and Brynlee preferred hiding her broken heart.

In fact, I'd only figured it out right before we set off on this journey, and I hadn't been able to confirm it with either Brynlee or Gaaron—but still, *I knew.*

Finnian realized the truth of the situation right away and then gleefully revealed it to the others, spotting it as a ready and easy method to control the girl.

We still needed to hash things out, Calina and I, now that she'd discovered that I had kept this massive secret from her. For a while there, I'd thought I'd lost her, that she'd decided Finnian was a better ally in rescuing the father she'd never really gotten the chance to know.

But she was still on our side, working with Rurik in an ill-fated effort to burn through this jail's iron bars. Maybe she trusted me less now, or perhaps she understood why I'd made the choices I'd chosen. I wouldn't know until we found some private time to talk it out. And that was not something I was looking forward to very much.

Still, I'd promised the girl's mother, Brynlee, that I would keep her safe, and that was a promise I would die to keep if I had to. I would do anything for sweet Brynlee because I loved her. Not because I ever expected her to love me back but just because the very act of loving her gave me a reason to persist. I missed her then, just as I missed her often, but it comforted me to have a piece of her with me. To have Calina. Provided she didn't now hate me.

The kid was so much like me it hurt. Really. Sometimes, I physically wanted to slap myself when having to deal with her. But I resisted that urge and many others toward violence, as I was meant to be the mentor in this situation.

Whoosh!

Rurik's flame burst back to life brighter and stronger than before. I kept my eyes closed but could sense the shift in the lighting. As irritated as this whole thing made me, I was proud that the kids were working so hard to free us. I knew we wouldn't get out until Finnian stuck his key in the lock and twisted, but I admired my recruits for trying to find their way.

When he'd first captured us, Finnian Sly had taken our powerful magical cleric to another holding cell so she couldn't break us out, but he hadn't realized that Rurik also had magic. To be fair, orcs were never, ever anything other than barbarians. But Rurik was half-human and wholly committed to breaking down stereotypes—so long as he didn't have to do it with his fists.

I was supposed to be retired. For ten years, I'd lain

low in Briarhaven, tending the bar, pining after the local waitress, and hoping I would never be found out.

So much for that plan.

"Can you please just cut it out?" Tulip whined and thumped a hoof on the floor. "I'm starting to sweat. And we cremellos burn very, very easily, so, you see, it's only a matter of time before your fun and games get me hurt."

The flame snapped off with a dying hiss.

"Rurik, what are you doing? You have to keep trying." That came from Calina, of course.

"Nuh-no. Tulip is right."

"So what? We're just going to sit here and twiddle our thumbs until that raccoon guy comes back and puts us to work on some stupid suicide mission?"

"He's not a raccoon. He's a tanuki. And I don't think we should twiddle our thumbs. We should prob-ably try to get some sleep." Always so literal, this one.

I eased open my eyes just in time to see Rurik shrink from the iron bars and turn back with a baleful expression.

"Besides, I don't want to hurt Tulip," he murmured as a strange, ruddy blush lit his cheeks.

Calina shoved him hard, but Rurik remained rooted to the spot. "You are infuriating, you know that? You only just stopped gushing blood from your mouth after your freaking tusk was ripped out in cold blood, but you're worried about little miss perfect having to deal with a little bit of sweat on her brow?"

"It's on my neck, actually," Tulip piped up. "My mane keeps the sweat from dripping on my face, but my neck is starting to... to itch. And if my flank is exposed, then—"

"By Sylric, who cares about your precious little flank?" Calina always invoked the elven trickster god when she found herself frustrated, and so far, he'd never bothered to answer her call. That could be because he owed Amariel five coin or because he'd never existed in the first place. But who really knew or cared about such things? Definitely not me.

"I care," Rurik mumbled, raising a hand to the injured side of his mouth and wincing as if expecting Calina to hit him again. The only thing worse than the half-orc's mastery of magic was his poor understanding of social cues. Calina was her best friend, but some-where along the way, he had inexplicably developed a fondness for Tulip, her sworn enemy.

Tulip, believing that everyone should admire her at all times, didn't seem to notice, but Calina sure had. And to say this upset her would be a pretty drastic understatement.

"The flame stays off," I snapped at them. "And our mouths stay shut until morning."

"But—" one of them started.

"But nothing. We have no idea what tomorrow's going to throw at us, and we need our rest."

"Actually, we do know that—"

"Shut up, Rurik. Go to sleep. I mean it."

I waited for more arguments to come barreling at me, but the children remained blessedly—and shockingly—quiet. Perhaps their exhaustion finally caught up to them once they took a moment to be still, or maybe they were finally beginning to accept my authority as party leader.

In any case, I was grateful for the silence and soon found myself dozing off, dreaming of better places.

2

"Wakey, wakey." Soft, furry fingers caressed my cheek—before giving me a firm back-handed slap.

I refused to give Finnian the satisfaction of seeing me shrink away. I could handle the pain, especially if my doing so threw him off his game.

"What do you want, *Pa?*" I spat the old moniker at him like a curse. He'd never been a father to me, despite the fact he saw himself that way. In Finnian's mind, he was not just a parent but a savior. In my mind, he was nothing more than a simple, painfully straightforward villain.

My eyes snapped open and took in the unfamiliar figure before me. The discolored skin around the gangly dark elf's eyes gave Finnian away in an instant.

His magical race allowed him to quickly and easily shapeshift into any person or creature he chose. Still, he couldn't hide the tell-tale thief mask of the tanuki without the help of carefully applied face paints. But he generally used his powers for dramatic flair more so than as actual disguise, so he didn't often take the time to hide this giveaway.

As a dark elf now, the shading around the eyes was a bright, almost bioluminescent shade of purple. Sharp, glowing eyes, a pointed chin, and an aquiline nose rounded out the rest of the face he wore. It was handsome despite the garish addition of the mask Finnian couldn't hide.

"I know, I know. I'm hideous. Hmm?" Finnian grabbed a long black lock of hair, stroking it between his fingers as he sighed. "It's truly painful that you must see me like this, but it's important that you familiarize yourself with the target of your mission. This is Eldrin Grimlock. Much like yourself, he was once a friend and ally, before betraying me in a manner so unspeakable that the only just outcome is his rather timely demise. Yes, yes, it is the only way. Of course, that's where you come in."

I stretched my legs in front of me to force him back and snorted. "In case you've forgotten. I'm a thief. Not an assassin."

Finnian hopped to the side, his eyes never leaving mine. "Come now, Tilly, what *is* murder if not the stealing of life? Or time. Yes, yes, that's more apt. Think of it like stealing his clock. You're simply taking away his time. Hmm—"

"I'm not killing anyone for you," I cut him off before he got lost in metaphors. "I'd rather rot here in your stupid dungeon."

"That can always be arranged, should you prefer it." Just like in my youth, the joyous gleam in his eyes had turned to the deadly glint of his other nature. So often in the past, people had underestimated the tanuki because of his rather foppish mannerisms— never truly seeing the deadly schemer that lay hidden behind that smile. Finnian shook his head and then turned away from me. His hollow voice ricocheted off the stone dungeon walls. "Simply put, my little Tilly, you need me *far* more than I need you right now. But I am not unreasonable. I can, of course, accept a compromise if that's what it takes to get things moving swiftly along."

That was rich. He thought I needed him? Well, I didn't. I never had. His words made me wonder at his sudden desperation, though. If he wanted someone dead, then why had he waited to find me first? As I'd told Finnian, I was no assassin. I also hadn't seen him for years and years. Why had he not gotten someone else to carry out his vendetta? Why now, and why me?

Finnian spun back to face me, eyes glowing with malice, though not for me, it seemed. "Kill Eldrin. Painfully, if you'd please. In truth, I'd far prefer his death to any other solution you might concoct. A painful death would be the best for everyone, really. With perhaps a touch of the dramatic for my sake? But if you've really developed a ghastly new set of scruples in our time apart, I suppose I'd be amenable to any other solution that would remove Eldrin from my city. Permanently. Hmm. I do have to wonder if perhaps one of your young prodigies is more amenable to carrying out my orders as instructed, hmm? Yes, I do wonder. Although, it ultimately matters not, just so long as he has gone far away from here. And that he is gone for good."

"I can do it," came Calina's voice. "Scruples are stupid. Actions are the only things that do any talking at all."

She rose and slunk forward from wherever she'd been resting before Finnian entered. She narrowed her eyes and reached a hand toward Finnian's sharp, elven ear—and then, as if thinking better of it, withdrew and touched her own instead. "Why do you hate him so much?"

I already knew that the tanuki would not give us straight answers. The more we tried to understand his motives, the more defensive he became, the more he evaded and concealed.

He tutted at her question. "Why, I already told you last night, my dear. This scoundrel has stolen my most valuable treasure."

"Your pride," she stated with wide eyes as if this were a perfectly reasonable scenario.

Finnian's dark lips curled in a strange smile. "Among other things. Yes, yes, but it is the pride that matters most. After all, even the largest pile of gold is nothing if you aren't proud of how you gained it. And it is the pride that you will recover for me."

"I've killed some giant locusts and at least two kobolds, but I've never killed a person. And I'm not sure I want to." Calina was often bold and ready for a fight, but she was still an innocent kid. This comment proved that.

"Luckily for you, Eldrin Grimlock isn't much of a person. So it'll be almost the same. You could even think of him as two kobolds in a dark elf disguise." Our captor chuckled, then sighed. "And as I told Tilly, his banishment, while not exactly preferred, would at least be an acceptable compromise. Just pick a method to get rid of him and carry it out. Once you do this teensy, tiny favor for me, You'll be free to go back to your other quest. Why, I'll even help you get there. To Maltherius, was it? Indeed, indeed. I can teleport you to his lair and even ensure you have the weapons to defeat him, too."

"If you have a way of defeating Maltherius, why don't you just go after him yourself?" Rurik piped up. He sat cross-legged on the uneven stone floor with his hands on his knees, taking us all in with his usual combination of shrewd intellectual focus and emotional detachment.

Finnian growled, not even turning to look at the half-orc. "Child, I'm not some petty gambler. I don't bet on dice that I haven't loaded myself, and I certainly don't shoot an arrow that could fail to hit its target. Think of me as the puppeteer, not the marionette. Or better yet, keep me out of your oafish brain altogether. Hmm. Also, this next part is incredibly important, so commit it to whatever you use for memory. I am not now, nor will I ever be speaking to *you*."

Interesting. Finnian didn't like Rurik, though I had no idea why. Still, his disdain for the boy may come in handy later if I could figure out how to use it to our advantage.

Tulip thwapped her tail and ran her hands up and down her arms as she hugged herself. "Enough with your dumb metaphors already. I'm cold. And hungry. And frankly, I'm very uncomfortable, thanks to these poor accommodations. I demand you let us go at once."

Finnian chuckled to himself, not speaking as he turned to examine our centaur friend. He studied her keenly, quiet besides a few odd bursts of laughter. I knew what was coming next, but that didn't stop the squeezing in my chest when our one Tulip became two.

"Eeeeew!" the real deal shrieked. "How dare you mock me in this way? When my mother hears of this, she..." Her words fell away, likely because she realized her mom's position as mayor of the small town Briarhaven held no sway with big-city criminals.

"Ah, yes. That was good fun," Finnian said through wheezing laughter before changing back into his copycat version of Eldrin Grimlock. "But back to business we go. To understand the importance of your mission, you need to hear a story. It is a grand tale of friendship and betrayal, of fallen heroes and risen villains. Pray tell, are you ready to listen?"

He paused for half a breath, not giving us a lick of space to argue.

"Very good, very good. The story shall commence, and it begins with a younger yet equally handsome me on the road from my homeland, wandering the great wilds of Verandel in search of a place to call my own."

"Wait a sec, why did you leave your homeland?" Rurik asked plainly. "Were you exiled?"

"Bah! Such questions are not pertinent to the story. I've already warned you, have I not? Now, I'll remind you once more to be quiet and stay focused." Finnian shifted again, this time taking up a female human form. This new version of Finnian wore the flayed skin of a griffin over her armor and had only one working eye. I knew this woman, and so did Rurik; she was the one who had ripped his tusk out before bringing us to Finnian on a bounty.

Rurik gasped and stumbled back in an awkward crab crawl.

Finnian suppressed a sinister giggle. "Next time you interrupt my narrative, I will not hesitate to take your other tusk as a trophy."

Poof! Finnian turned back into himself, fur and all, and began to pace the cage, chuckling cruelly with each step. Meanwhile, Calina rushed to Rurik's side and sat beside him with one hand rubbing small, soothing circles on his back.

Tulip just looked uncomfortable and bored. It was as if Finnian's return to the dungeon had made no difference to her at all.

I continued to do my best to stay focused without outwardly reacting to anything Finnian said. The master thief had always fancied himself a great orator, talking far more than was necessary. And right now, he had a captive audience. *Literally.*

Most of his words were a grand display meant to amuse himself and impress his listeners, but now and then, he dropped a little nugget that I might be able to use in besting him later. Like his disdain for Rurik, for example.

"Go on," I said, since he appeared to be waiting. "Tell us about Grimlock so that we can get this over with."

It was best to play along. The sooner Finnian finished his story, the sooner he'd release us. Then, we could decide whether to tend to his errand or run off in the other direction. Of course, we couldn't do either while stuck in this blessed dungeon.

"I found Eldrin Grimlock on the outskirts of Sandsibar. Or rather, he found me. I'd been wandering the desert for many long days and nights by then, wearing the skin of a beautiful orcish maiden I'd met many moons ago in a small coastal village. Eldrin, for all his guilelessness, saw straight through my disguise. He asked who I was, allowing me to take my true shape for the first time on my long journey through Verandel. We became companions after that. After all, Eldrin and I were both outsiders looking for a place to belong, so it made sense that we could belong to each other for at least a little while."

"You were lovers?" Calina asked, scrunching her nose in deep thought as she attempted to fill in the blanks.

"Not in body, no. But in heart and spirit and every way that mattered. Yes, yes, yes. It was Eldrin who suggested we settle in Mirathane and build our rank by recruiting street urchins to the cause. And before you can ask, yes, the cause was to amass as many riches as one could possibly hope to amass in a single lifetime. We worked well together for many years. And then..." Finnian paused and drew in a sharp breath before shifting to the visage of an old man, a halfling by the look of him. "This next part is very painful, so I shall remain sparse on the details."

This was very unlike my former master. I hadn't even known the word "sparse" was in his sometimes shockingly large vocabulary. Also, I thought that maybe I recognized the man Finnian was describing as a king. He wasn't someone I'd ever met, but I believe I'd seen his likeness in the odd portrait or history book. That made sense if he'd once been the king of this area.

I wasn't well-schooled—or really, schooled at all—but I had eyes and a reasonable working memory.

Finnian sighed and held a hand to his chest, still speaking to us as the vaguely recognizable former political figure. "Then the king grew ill and died, leaving Mystwood Keep's rule to his sole heir. A daughter."

He transformed into a beautiful, red-haired halfling girl briefly, flickering in and out between the two royal guises before finally settling back into his own skin. "But she was young and inexperienced, unready to rule. Seeing his chance, Eldrin left one night, taking as many of our riches as he could carry. He wooed the young soon-to-be coronated queen, forced her hand, and stole his most valuable treasure yet. The power of the crown. And this, my dear friends, is where the story ends. And now I must have my revenge. It is the only way to make things right again."

Finnian hung his head and heaved a dramatic sigh, announcing the end of his narrative. As far as stories went, it was a poor one. I ventured a glance toward my fellow prisoners to see if I'd missed something. He'd given us very little to go by, meaning he had intentionally kept many details back. This wasn't the Finnian Sly I had come to know and loathe.

Petty revenge, now that was like him. Long-held

grudges, too. But glossing over the details? I'd never seen him go off a topic so quickly, not in all the years I'd known him, which amounted to almost my entire life. There was a lot more to this story than he was willing to reveal.

Everyone remained quiet until inevitably Calina spoke up, "Um, I'm failing to see what he did wrong here. Maybe help me out? Was the problem that he stole from you? That he left you behind?"

"Yes, yes, all that and more. So much more." He sighed again. And then sighed a third time.

"What more?" Calina pushed.

Finnian flapped a hand in the air and then began to pick fastidiously at his claws. "I grow tired of this sojourn into the past. And what good would dwelling on the past do us? The rest of our story is one for the legends, but you now know enough to carry out my bidding. I'm sure you're eager to be back to your quest, almost as much as I am eager to be rid of this plague upon my city. You will find the scoundrel in Mystwood Keep, where he remains regent to this day. Infiltrating his castle will not be easy, but I'll leave the simple rather trifling details to you of the daring do and so forth."

None of this was simple. It may have been if Finnian shared the true nature of his feud with us, but as it stood, we were more-or-less going in blind. Provided we went in at all.

"Oh... kay," Calina drew out the two short syllables for several beats before asking, "So, um, what now?"

"So you leave me, my dears. There's a dark elf to deal with. There's no need to teleport you, because the keep is not far from our city center. Teleportation magic is very costly, you do understand. You don't even want to know what it cost for me to pay off those scouts who brought you here. It was quite ridiculous. Hmm. But no price is too high when it comes to reuniting with my dear, prodigal daughter."

"Sorry it cost you so much to rob us of our freedom," I snapped, more than done with him by now. "But if you want us to take out this regent for you, we're going to need our stuff back."

"And you shall have it. For this task, at least." Finnian continued picking at his claws, focusing on his hands rather than any of us.

"What's to stop us from running away once you free us?" Rurik asked pointedly, drawing fresh ire from our captor. Suddenly realizing his mistake, Rurik raised both hands to shield his mouth and protect his one remaining tusk.

Rurik's question told me a lot. For one, he didn't recognize the king or his history. Otherwise, he would have spoken up immediately to ask more clarifying questions. That made sense, given that Briarhaven fell under another ruler's domain. Why should he know of the regional sovereign in Mirathane, especially one who had most likely died before Rurik was born?

The tanuki sighed and shook his head, finally glancing up at us again. Gone was the gleam in his eyes. Replaced again with the dangerous glint. His words remained cordial, but I could feel the ice in his voice. "Now, you wouldn't do that to your old friend Finnian, would you? Besides, as you witnessed with the scouts, I have eyes everywhere, inside and out of this city. Betray me, and you will be the target of my next errand. Is that simple enough for you to understand, you unspeakably lopsided boar?"

Rurik nodded, finally understanding that it was better if he didn't speak while in Finnian's presence.

Finnian frowned, which was another unusual behavior from him. "I shall leave you then. You'll find your things at the end of the hall stacked neatly along the corridor. I'll send in the celestial to meet you there. Yes, yes." He snapped his fingers, then pointed at Calina. "You, elf girl. You're in charge, which means you're the one who will receive both the glory and the pain, should either come to pass."

Calina twisted her hands together. "Really, I think

Tilda should be the leader. She's the only one with any experience and—"

"Experience means very little in this world, child. Loyalty is a far more valuable and also a far rarer commodity. Little Tilly has proven time and time again that it is something she lacks. First, she abandoned me, and then that dear sweet bard. But I know that you won't let me down. You're so close to finding your father after all this time, hmm? It would be such a shame if you were to fail him now." And with that last little dig, Finnian became a rat and skittered out of the cell. A moment later, the cell door swung outward, granting us our freedom—or at least the permission to begin the next phase of our imprisonment.

3

Calina was the first to step outside of the cell. It seemed she took her role as our newly assigned leader quite seriously. Either that or she was just the most impatient of our group. Probably both, if I was being honest.

Rurik and I followed her out, but Tulip hung back, shuffling her hooves over the loose stones of the floor and even going so far as to nudge one loose from its pavers and send it skittering past me into the corridor.

Tulip winced at the clatter. "What if it's booby-trapped?" she said, continuing to hang back as she flipped her braided mane to the side and looked down her nose at the rest of us. "Like, I know it's not great to be in this dingy little jail, but at least I know I'm safe."

Nope, we didn't have time for this. I growled under my breath and stomped back into the cell, fully prepared to push that giant horse's butt with all my might.

"Fine, then we'll just leave you there." Calina marched off without a backward glance, which, again, could have been because of her budding leadership abilities... or her well-established hate for Tulip. Whatever the case, I liked her no-nonsense style. Saved me from being the bad guy for once.

For all his faults, Finnian always had a way of seeing right through a person. He'd once considered me his most prized pupil, and Calina thought and acted much like I had at that age. It was a small wonder he liked her so much. I liked her, too, even though she drove me nuts more often than not.

Rurik glanced rapidly from Tulip to Calina and back before finally shrugging and following his elven friend down the hallway. I followed after with quick steps, needing to take two or three for every one of his lumbering paces.

"Wait, wait! You can't just leave me!" Tulip insisted, finally trotting out of the cell but still remaining several paces behind the rest of the group. If traps or an army were lying in wait, she wanted to be sure that the rest of us would be the ones to suffer such an attack. Caution was not a trait I admired in a front-line fighter, but I didn't have the strength or patience to beat it out of her just then.

One thing was for sure: I needed to train these kids for real.

Luckily, Mirathane would be the perfect place to do it. After all, I'd grown up on these streets, learned all my skills here, built and maintained a network of contacts, even though I hadn't spoken to most of them in over a decade.

First, we'd get our stuff back, and then we could take our dear, sweet time getting to the castle and carrying out Finnian's errand. He'd already promised to teleport us to Maltherius's lair once we disposed of Eldrin Grimlock however we saw fit. And while it usually didn't pay to rely on the paltry promises of villains, I knew my former master inside and out.

Time can change a lot, but it doesn't change people.

This mission was important to Finnian and related to his plans for the Genesis Crest. I was sure he'd get us to Maltherius because it furthered his private goals. Of course, this meant it was in our best interest to carry out his request.

We could make Finnian Sly an ally in what came next by scaring off his old nemesis, or we could betray him and wind up with two bad guys on our tails. Finnian had never let me go, not even when I'd assumed I'd long since escaped. And now that he had us, he wouldn't just let me walk away, especially since he seemed to believe he was close to completing some long-held goal.

I still didn't know why he wanted the artifact. I also didn't know the true nature of his feud with Eldrin Grimlock, but I chose to side with the tanuki master thief because I at least understood him, even if I neither liked nor agreed with most of what he did.

I knew I could ultimately win when it came to Finnian, even if it meant losing something along the way. This whole intermediary mission would provide good practice for the kids, and by the divine, they needed it—sorely.

Yes, this was all quite irritating, but it could also be a boon for our ultimate quest, the one where we saved Gaaron's life. I smiled to myself as I continued down the corridor.

By the time I reached the fork at the end of the hall, Calina and Rurik had already completely emptied the supply crates left by Finnian's goons. The contents lay spread out on the floor as they both took stock.

"It's all here," the girl said, joyfully looping her bow and quiver onto her back.

"What do you mean it's all here?" Rurik moaned as he picked up the crate and turned it upside down. "My books! They're all missing!"

"This is a stealth mission. We can't carry a little library with us, Rur." Calina tutted and shook her head, a gesture she seemed to have copied from Finnian in their short acquaintanceship. I didn't much care for that. It meant he was getting to her, which meant he could get to her some more. Which could spell trouble for our primary alliance.

I'd have to keep a close eye on the situation, which meant initiating the dreaded talk. She needed to understand my motives if I was to regain her trust. But how could I explain what I had yet to fully understand myself?

Bah, this was all way too complicated. Unfortunately, I couldn't wish the needed conversation away, no matter how much I wanted to do just that.

Rurik remained fixated on his pitiful predicament; his singular tusk jutted out from quivering lips as his eyes searched the floor, hoping to see something they'd already determined wasn't there. "How am I supposed to get better at magic if I don't have my books?"

Nobody answered. It wouldn't have mattered if we

did. The big guy had to feel his feelings to let them go, and none of us could do that for him.

At last, Tulip caught up and knelt to pick up a medium-sized burlap sack. She undid the drawstring and peered inside, wrinkling her nose in disgust. "Ew, no, thank you."

"What is that?" I demanded, not recognizing it from our earlier cache of supplies. "Hand it here."

Fearful no more, the centaur strode over to me and dropped the sack straight into my waiting arms. Unfortunately, it was much heavier than it first appeared, and I did a poor job of catching it.

I fumbled the bag, and it crashed to the stonework floor, spilling its contents everywhere.

Rurik bent down and retrieved one of the strange spotted discs that had rolled toward him, stopping when it collided with his boot. He sniffed it once, twice, and then took a bite.

"Rations," I said with a shudder. "It's a special recipe from Finnian's homeland. They're filling but vile. Far too sweet."

"I like it," Rurik said, finishing the other half of the food disc with one big chomp. "A lot," he added with a contented grin, the missing books forgotten—hopefully for good.

The saccharin scent invaded my nostrils, taking

me back to an earlier time. One that was simpler but not nearly as happy. "For years, this was the only thing I had to eat," I explained, scratching at my nose as if I could dig out the aroma and its associated memories. "They're cheap, easy to stow, and remain fairly edible even when they go stale. Finnian calls them cookies."

"Cookies?" Calina asked before reaching down to grasp one from the floor. "That's a funny name."

"Tanuki cookies," I said with a glum nod. My throat grew dry just thinking of them.

"I'm not eating anything that touched the floor," Tulip said, kicking at the discarded rations with a delicate yet very disgusted hoof.

"Then I guess you're not eating," I said with a shrug. Nah, the cookies weren't so bad, especially considering I was nearly starving. I grabbed one of the blessed things and began to crunch away. Once my belly was full, I would think clearer—and so would the others.

Rurik reached for another, but I stopped him. "One in the morning and one at night. That should be enough. After all, they have to last."

"But if Tulip's not having any, can't I take her share?" he said, his massive hand moving toward the cookies again.

"No, you cannot." I slapped him away. "Besides, she'll come around."

Tulip expelled a long breath that ended with a muted trill emanating from her throat. Then she seemed to remember that none of us spoke horse and said, "As if."

Calina picked up the rest of the scattered cookies and shoved them back in the bag while I finished my quick morning repast.

As soon as I swallowed the last soggy mouthful, I brushed the crumbs off my fingers and turned to examine the weaponry and supplies Calina had laid out on the floor.

But in doing so, I almost crashed right into Amariel, who had rejoined us without so much as a word in greeting. "Sweet divinity, you scared me!"

The old celestial nodded and smiled slightly but did not utter a word.

"Amariel, there you are!" Tulip cried, thundering over to embrace the elder in a tight hug. "I was so worried when we were separated. Are you okay after sleeping on that horrible, dingy dungeon floor? Oh my me, wasn't it just the worst? So disgusting."

Amariel smiled and patted Tulip on the side before turning her attention to the supplies on the floor. It seemed she didn't have much to say, but at least she was wide awake. That was better than I could usually say for the old girl.

I spotted my daggers gleaming on the ground and scooped them up. Oh, yeah. I felt much better now that I had one tucked at my side and the other into my boot. Even though Rurik's books had not been returned, thankfully, all of our equipable accessories had. I yoinked the gem-encrusted bracelet Brynlee had given me and the Genesis Crest from the floor and situated them on my person with great relief.

"C'mon," I told the others. "Let's get out of here before Finnian changes his mind."

I knew he wouldn't, but fear seemed to be as good a motivator for these kids as any—especially for Tulip, who appeared to be the most hesitant of the group.

Rurik handed the centaur her pink bedazzled battle axe and then took up his shield, still muttering about the missing books. At least we were now on our way.

"Can you heal him, like make his tusk grow back?" I heard Calina ask Amariel as we wound through the underground dungeon, looking for a way out.

Rurik interjected before Amariel could answer. "I already told you I don't want it back. My dad gets by just fine with only one arm. I can survive with a single tusk."

"But—"

"It wasn't just a trophy for the scout who took it. It is for me, too. Each battle wound is a badge of honor for my people. And this was my first. I am proud to have faced a foe and lived to tell the tale."

"Okay, then suit yourself." I couldn't see either of their faces but imagined that Calina was probably rolling her eyes.

"I think it's really brave," Tulip said softly. "That you don't care about being ugly and disfigured if it means your people respect you." Strangely, this was one of the nicest things I'd ever heard Tulip say to anyone.

Rurik grunted, but I didn't understand orcish culture well enough to know whether he was pleased or offended. And I also didn't care enough to ask. He was probably still more upset about the books than anything else.

"Oooh, look! Over there!" Calina shouted, racing ahead on quick feet and disappearing around the corner. I had to pump my legs hard to catch up with her, but a moment later, I reached the narrow staircase that wound upward in a tight spiral and eagerly began to climb.

We hadn't even been in the dungeon a full day, but

I desperately missed the sunlight and couldn't wait to feel it upon my cheeks again.

A loud stamping from below startled me enough to make me pause mid-step.

"Excuse me!" Tulip wailed. "Are you just going to leave me and go about your tiny, merry way?"

I turned back and found her staring up from the bottom of the slim staircase. She couldn't get her hefty horse's rump up, not with the many sharp twists and turns.

"Hang tight. We'll find another way," I promised, but the rest of our party had already finished their ascent, vanishing through a small trap door on the ceiling —another space Tulip wouldn't be able to fit through.

As a halfling, I was not accustomed to things being too small. Usually, the world was way too big.

"Well," Tulip demanded with another stamp of her hooves. "Are you coming back or not?"

I popped my head through the trapdoor but couldn't spy the rest of our party. Ugh. Where had they gone? And why had they not waited?

Once we were reunited, I'd have to give them a stern lecture about the first rule of adventuring: *never split the party.* I wouldn't be too hard on them, given that I had failed to relay this information to them in the first place. But still, would common sense never prevail with these kids?

"I'm coming, I'm coming," I called, taking quick steps back down the staircase. "C'mon, there's got to be another more centaur-friendly exit." I just hoped that by the time we found it, we wouldn't be too late to catch up with the others.

4

It took a good ten minutes of searching the dungeon level before Tulip and I eventually found another more accommodating set of steps that led straight outside into the lush greenery of a small, overgrown garden area. Plant life was not abundant in Mirathane, at least not so close to the city center, and its presence here gave me pause. Had things changed so much since I called this place home?

"Calina! Rurik! Amariel!" I called, hoping they were somewhere nearby. Unsurprisingly, nobody answered. A part of me doubted they were even looking for us. But, uh, they had at least noticed that Tulip and I were gone, right?

Yeah, training would be our top priority once we

smushed the two fractured halves of this party back into one irritating whole.

"Ick, ick, ick! There are bugs everywhere!" Tulip cried, screamed, thrashed about, and let out a full-blown neigh. The one thing she did not do, however, was make any effort to remove herself from the tall, insect-infested grass.

"Follow me. We'll go around to the front!" I jumped and waved both arms overhead, which is precisely how far the grass came up on me—over my head. Tulip may have had bugs nipping at her legs, but I had them crawling into my figgin' mouth. And that was more than enough motivation to get me moving.

Granted, I was not the best navigator, even under ideal conditions. Our current predicament was extra difficult, given that I couldn't even see where we were going. Still, it was up to me to chart an escape. My centaur companion had already proven herself to be more than useless, too busy throwing a fit to help us find our way out of there.

After a few minutes of fruitless wandering, I walked smack dab into the side of the building we'd just exited. I rubbed my hand over my sore nose—not bloody or broken, good. Reorienting myself, I trailed one hand along the wall that had inadvertently attacked me until, at last, I rounded its corner and came upon a clean opening to the streets. Tulip, for her part, had at least managed to stick with me while she continued her hysterics.

It was good to be out of there. Somehow, the grassy knoll had been even worse than the dank dungeon.

I shook off like a drenched pack beast, flinging the last of the pests from my tiny, agitated body as fast as possible. Then, I helped pick them off Tulip's knees so that we could move on.

"How could Calina just leave us like that?" she complained, but even I could tell her heart wasn't in it. The encounter with the insects had taken much of the fight out of her.

"It wasn't just Calina," I pointed out, squeezing one exceptionally resilient bloodsucker that clung to Tulip's leg between my fingers, pulling and pulling until it finally yanked away clean. "Rurik and Amariel left too."

"Amariel wouldn't leave me." Tulip sucked in a sharp breath, making me wonder if I'd hurt her with my indelicate insect removal methods.

I shrugged, then dropped the fat tick to the street and stomped on it with my boot. "Well, I don't know what to tell you because that's exactly what she did."

"Rude," was all she had to say to that.

"I agree, it was. But now you have to get over it because, like it or not, we need to work together. Not just you and me, but all of us."

Tulip let out a breathy sigh. "Yeah, yeah, I know."

Once I was sure we weren't harboring any more stowaways, I glanced up and down the busy city street in an attempt to find the best way forward. But I couldn't see much of anything through the bustling crowd of people, vendor stalls, and carts.

Mirathane was Verandel's capital and its most populated city. As a street orphan, it had once been easy for me to disappear into these vibrant throngs. It would probably also be easy to move about unnoticed now—or at least it would have been without a massive centaur stuck to my side. It wasn't just Tulip's size that drew attention; everything about the girl commanded notice. And she wouldn't have it any other way.

"You have a better vantage point than I do. Can you see them anywhere?" I asked, after trying to dart through the foot traffic but failing to make any real progress toward the intersection.

"Um, let me see." Tulip stretched even taller than her usual eight feet and craned her neck in a valiant effort to find our missing party members. "I think they're—*hey!*" she screamed suddenly, making me jump out of my own blessed skin.

A small, hooded figure zipped past, clutching a bedazzled pink battle axe to its chest as it dodged vehicles and pedestrians alike.

"That's mine!" Tulip roared, immediately giving chase. She bent at her waist and held her arms crossed protectively before her as she charged headlong down the street. All who intersected her warpath were quickly and carelessly shoved aside. A flurry of carts, bodies, and assorted handicrafts went flying out of the way as she continued to tear after the cloaked thief.

All this made it easy for me to follow after, now that Tulip had cleared a rather lovely path. I had no doubts we'd just encountered one of Finnian Sly's child thieves. Of course, Tulip's sparkly "weapon" had caught immediate notice. I liked seeing her get mad; even more than that, I loved seeing her do something about it.

There was hope yet that the spoiled princess could transform into a skilled battle companion, and I clung to that hope with everything I had in me.

Unsurprisingly, it wasn't long before Tulip intercepted the fleeing pickpocket and grabbed him tight, pulling him off the ground and into her arms. I was still sprinting to catch up when she flung the hood away to reveal not a small child but rather a large kobold.

"Forgiveness! Forgiveness!" it chanted, drawing out that sibilant syllable each time, but there were no others of his kind to join him in this plea. Kobolds never survived long when separated from their pack. A group of kobolds was more commonly referred to as a confusion, an apt title if ever there was one. And if a group of kobolds was a confusion, a lone lizard would be best described as a pity. Seeing this one on its own twisted something in my heart. How could it even exist here without its kindred?

A bit winded myself, I finally caught up, but Tulip was so focused on intimidating the would-be thief that she didn't notice my returned presence at her side.

Tulip, it seemed, was unmoved by the poor solitary creature. Now that she had him clutched firmly in her arms, she slowly started squeezing the life out of him. "You stole from me! You wretched thing! I should have your head!"

"Take back! Take back!" the thing cried as big reptilian tears splashed down onto the stolen axe, which the creature held fast while Tulip held him.

"Who do you work for?" Tulip demanded as she shook the little guy ferociously. "I shall be repaid for this insult either with your life or with favors from your boss. Your kind never works alone, so take me to your leader. And take me right this instant!"

"Need... ground. Nee...d gr...ound." The kobold's voice came out hoarse and ragged, like he couldn't breathe, desperately needed water, or both.

"I will set you down now, but if you try to run off, I won't hesitate to smash you into the ground. Do we understand each other?" Her blue eyes shimmered with an unfamiliar green overcast as the rage continued to overtake her.

"Understand! Understand!" Gagging noises followed. I'd have to intervene if Tulip didn't let him go soon. I hoped she'd do the right thing on her own, mostly because I still wasn't sure she'd even listen to me if I were to issue any orders.

Her white knuckles turned red, suggesting she'd loosened her grip. "Tell me what you understand, not just that you do."

Okay, enough was enough. "Tulip," I said gently, touching her side. Gentle was best, given that my anger would only amplify hers.

"He's a kobold," I explained, hoping she understood what I was getting at. "They can't do what you're asking. They only speak in—"

"I will take you to my boss. There will be no running, no tricks. Have I understood your wishes correctly?"

I blinked hard, rubbed at my eyes, and then

double-checked that the glib voice interrupting me belonged to the kobold thief. When I saw that it did, I swear my jaw dropped to my chest. Never had I heard a kobold speak in complete sentences before. Unless... "Are you honored?"

"I was at a time but have since fallen from grace. Now I must roam the streets to—

AAAAAH-ha-ah-ha!"

Tulip yanked the axe from the kobold's grip and held the sharp blade to his throat. "Less talking and more taking us to your boss. Nod if you understand."

Crying once more, the creature nodded his narrow head. The gesture was slight but enough to pull forth a bead of blood from Tulip's blade. The red life force trickled down his equally red scales, disappearing beneath the cloak.

Tulip wore a simpering and self-satisfied smile. "Very well. Off you go. And make sure it's slow enough for the little one to keep up."

When she set the kobold back onto the street, I'd expected him to run away in terror, but he surprised me by standing his ground. The creature offered Tulip a deep bow, then slowly turned and led the way down the street.

The gawkers and bystanders who had gathered to observe the exchange had already cleared out of the way, apparently losing interest once it was clear that nobody was going to die during our heated exchange. A petty attempted theft wasn't big news in such a big city; it was just part of life. Regardless, the kobold's expert guidance and Tulip's enormous backside made the path clear for me to follow.

"We have to find the others," I called ahead to the determined centaur. She'd used both rage and intimidation with impressive zeal, and I was incredibly proud of her. Still, I was more concerned by our missing companions than I was excited by the prospect of meeting this strange kobold's crime boss. What were the chances that it was Finnian? Might we be serving the same master? No, not likely.

"Then go and find them yourself," Tulip called back without even turning to look at me. "I'm not letting this thing get away until it repays me for its blatant show of disrespect."

"Oh, no, you don't!" I yelled, picking up my pace even though my little legs already ached from the dizzying pace the lizard and horse had set. "It's bad enough our group is already split in half. I'm not letting you wander off on your own, too."

"Well, I'm not letting this stupid lizard get away. Besides, Calina is the one who abandoned us, not the other way around."

For one so easily offended by racial stereotypes, Tulip was laying it on real thick when it came to our new kobold accomplice. Then again, she knew he could hold a rational conversation despite his attempts to convince us of the contrary. I couldn't put her improbable assumption down to ignorance, not when her mother worked so closely with the kobold guard back in Briarhaven. The ordeal made me wonder what she knew that I didn't. Might the spoiled girl have even more undiscovered skills that I could use to our party's advantage? That thought excited me more than anything had in a long time.

Together, our new trio wound through the crowded streets that zigged and zagged to form my old stomping grounds. Every last one of my senses was assaulted with memories both cherished and reviled. I wish I could say it felt good to be home, but Mirathane wasn't home for me. Not anymore.

I longed for Briarhaven, for Brynlee, for my peaceful existence as an unassuming tavern wench. I could have it again. I *would* have it again.

We just had to get through this quest and then the next. After that, I'd be home, no longer in hiding. I'd be safe and seen for who I really was, all the parts of me. Even the ones I'd once worked so hard to keep hidden.

I looked forward to being wholly myself, surrounded by all the people who mattered. Provided we managed to survive Finnian's quest and then Maltherius's.

I once again envisioned Brynlee's sweet smile as she spotted me marching back into town with the kids in tow when something big and green caught me by the corner of my eye. "Tulip, Stop! Wait!" I shouted and spun on heel to find Rurik and the others standing beside a vendor's stall as they each tucked into a big, meaty drumstick.

"Young man," I boomed, charging right over to him. It didn't matter that he was more than twice my height; I could still evoke the fear of the divine in him. "Where have you been? And why didn't you wait for me and Tulip before wandering off?"

"Relax, it's not his fault," Calina murmured through a mouth full of bird. "It was my idea to grab a snack while we waited for you and Tulip to find your way out of the dungeon. And look, now you're here."

That explanation would have made sense were it not for one crucial point.

"But we're many hundreds of paces away from where we started," I pointed out with what I hoped was a stern expression etched into my face. Calina was harder to intimidate than the other two, so it took some added work on my part. "How were we supposed to find you all the way over here?"

She shrugged as she continued to make quick work of her snack. "I don't know, but you did, so it's not really worth arguing about. Is it?"

I once again found myself wanting to smack a child. Was Calina acting this way because of the truths Finnian had revealed when I had not? Would the heart-to-heart I had planned be enough to quell her growing disrespect? I didn't know the answers, and that had me pretty miffed.

I was still trying to figure out what to say to diffuse the situation when Tulip came storming over.

"How did you pay for that?" she demanded with a hooked brow. She had the kobold grasped tight to her chest again, apparently not trusting him enough to allow him to remain on his own two feet.

Calina guffawed as she took in the scene. "Did you find a pet? By Sylric, we were only separated for a few moments at best."

"I'm not talking to you. I'm talking to him." Tulip narrowed her eyes at Rurik. "How did you pay for that?"

The half-orc didn't know to be afraid. He simply answered the question he'd been asked. "Well, I was carrying all our things, so..."

"With my money, I knew it." Tulip stomped one of her front hooves on the street and then the other as if she was revving up for a battle against her party mate. "That is not okay. You will pay me back. Promptly and in full. With interest even."

Oh, sweet divinity. Everything was two steps forward and three steps back with this group—and that kind of math just didn't add up in our favor. Once again, I tried to be gentle so as not to further spook or enrage the horse girl. "Um, Tulip, Rurik doesn't have any money. C'mon now, be reasonable. The supplies your parents provided were for all of us, right?"

The centaur huffed and tucked the kobold under one arm while using the other to yank the drumsticks away from Rurik and Calina's hands. She let Amariel keep hers.

"Mine now," she said before tossing the meat to the ground and stomping it under hoof. "Don't you ever take my things without asking. Not ever again."

Calina rubbed her greasy fingers on the seat of her pants and groaned. "Fine, whatever. Now, are you going to explain the kobold?"

"No," Tulip said dismissively, putting the scaly thief back on the ground and urging him to continue our rough city tour.

"Rule one of adventuring: never split the party. No

matter what," I told the kids with a firm voice. And if rule number one was don't split the party, then rule number two should be don't ever, under any circumstances, steal from the centaur. I'd be sure to remember that one for later.

5

After a little more wandering and a touch of meandering to go with it, our kobold guide stopped before a tall Y-shaped crack in a lonely wall tucked partway down some shadowy alley. "This is the best entrance," he said with a quick nod before ducking through it.

"Whoa, did that kobold just use a complete sentence?" Calina exclaimed without so much as hesitating to dart in after him.

"He must be honored," Rurik surmised before launching into full-on professor mode despite his lack of knowledge and experience. "An honored kobold is one that has completed its five years of conscription, surviving hundreds of battles and skirmishes to receive

LUNA RYDER

an exalted place in society. It is a most remarkable accomplishment."

"I don't know. None of this seems very exalted to me." Calina's voice came out muffled and far-off sounding before she popped her head through the fissure and started shouting at full volume. "Are the rest of you coming or what?"

Amariel nodded and then squeezed past Calina into the crumbling edifice.

I, however, remained standing with Rurik and Tulip, one of whom appeared pensive while the other was downright furious. I felt a bit of both at the moment. Why hadn't the old celestial played the grownup card and instructed Calina and Rurik to hang back rather than venture away from the dungeon without us?

Amariel was one of the most magical beings I'd ever met, yet she was also one of the most useless. Her healing powers had come in handy a time or two, but she never helped in any other way. Like now, was she really going to leave our larger party members out on the street while we lither folk followed the kobold to who-knows-where?

Honestly, what even was the point of her?

I had to pinch the bridge of my nose to fight off a rapidly approaching migraine. "Calina Starbrook, is it that hard to tell when a doorway or stairway or what-ever-way is or isn't accessible to our entire party?" For now, it was easier to appeal to the rebellious half-elf than try to reason with the oblivious elder. At least Calina was still in my line of sight.

She smiled brightly at me, then levied her gaze at her sworn frenemy. "So Tulip's got a wide butt. That's not my problem."

"Oh, that does it!" The centaur released a fearsome snort and dragged a hoof across the ground, kicking up a sizable cloud of dust.

Rurik raised one finger, somehow drawing every-one's attention to him. "I have two counterpoints. First, I won't fit either. And second, it *is* your problem, seeing as Finnian Sly appointed you as party leader. That means looking out for the interests of the entire party, including Tulip. And also, as a third bonus point, I think Tulip has a rather lovely butt."

I couldn't suppress the lengthy groan that ripped from my throat. Rurik was growing bolder in expressing his romantic intentions, and that wasn't a complication our party needed. I mentally added this topic to my list of uncomfortable conversations I would soon need to initiate. Unfortunately, I'd still need to speak with Calina to ensure she was on our side after Finnian revealed the major secret I'd withheld from her. At least Tulip remained a relatively simple creature by comparison—or, perhaps more accurately, she'd become a bit easier to predict.

Calina's violet eyes narrowed, and one of them grew twitchy. "This is ridiculous. Tulip can find another way into this place, just like she found another way out of that basement dungeon."

"We go all together or none at all. Besides, the only reason we have this whole kobold boss lead is because of Tulip." After delivering this decree, I marched through the Y-crack and dragged our kobold friend back onto the street. I didn't know whether what came next would help us with our quest, but it was worth the effort required to find out, especially since we'd already come this far.

"We'll need a more accessible entrance, big guy," I said, nudging him.

"Apologies. This is the master's preferred route, but there is another. Follow me." The kobold delivered these words while bowing deeply in reverence. He dipped so low to the street that his snout brushed the cobblestones, making me wonder about the keenness of his sense of smell. From where I stood, the swirling scents of dung, days-old vegetables, and dust were practically an assault.

"Is it true you're honored?" Rurik wanted to know

as he indelicately pulled the creature back to his feet. "If so, I've got a lot of questions."

The kobold tensed and rose high on his spindly legs. He spoke fluidly but refused to make eye contact with our orcish friend as he did. "I'm incredibly intelligent for my species, but pursuing two conversations simultaneously is still difficult. The angry one wants to meet my boss, so I will focus on that for now. If we remain together after that transpires, I shall answer your questions then."

Rurik seemed satisfied by this response and remained quiet as we returned to the street and journeyed down a separate alley. There, the kobold led us to a solid stone wall, which he immediately began to examine by squinting his gaze mere inches from the facade.

"It should be here somewhere," he muttered mostly to himself. "I don't often take this path to the sanctum. Perhaps it's this one. No. *Ah-ha-ah-ah!* Yes, here it is. Please avert your eyes. This will only take a moment."

The kobold's request made me pay more attention to his actions, not less. I watched with rapt interest as he placed his palm, with splayed scaly fingers, on an unmarked stone and twisted.

The entire wall disappeared with a decisive blink.

The kobold turned to face us, its snout displaying an almost indiscernible smile. "We are almost there. Please, please, proceed inside."

I went first. If this were an elaborate trap, I would be the most likely candidate to escape it. Luckily, nothing terrible happened upon crossing the threshold, which seemed like a pretty good sign to me. The wall had vanished, giving way to a stately foyer with rich upholstery and abundant gold adornments. It rivaled even the grandeur of the famed centaur country club, The Stable.

"I like it here," Tulip said with an approving nod. "Feels like home."

My eyes scanned the room, taking a quick and thorough inventory of the many treasures in the space. What did we have? What was it worth? What could I easily carry on my person? What would the kobold do if he caught me helping myself to this wondrous bounty?

No, wait a minute.

If he were truly this wealthy, why had he tried to lift Tulip's bejeweled battle axe? Didn't he already have enough treasure? Why had he called this the inner sanctum? Were we in some temple? And where was this boss we were supposed to be meeting?

Something wasn't adding up here, but it wasn't my

THAT'S THE WAY THE CASTLE CRUMBLES

value estimations. I'd confidently estimated this room's worth to be a staggering five-point four million coin. *At least.*

I could happily remain here all day were it not for the encroaching feeling that we'd been baited and trapped, and soon, the hunter would come to collect us.

"Well, you promised you'd take us to your boss. So where is he?" Tulip demanded, but she didn't appear anywhere near as intimidating as she'd been on the street. She now stood admiring her reflection in a large oval-shaped mirror with a ridiculously posh frame as she tried on various jewelry pieces from the surrounding treasure heap. A confident smile played at her lips, but it was the gorgeous, ornate mirror that really caught my eye.

Oh, that beautiful, blessed mirror. It would have looked so good hanging over my bed back in Briarhaven. I wanted to take it; I wanted it so, so badly.

But no, I needed to be alert—I needed to keep us safe now and worry about the pretty shinies later.

The kobold bowed again, and I did my best to keep my eyes fixed on our host rather than the glorious, glittering treasure surrounding him. "Our guests must first close their eyes, then the master will join us."

Oh yeah, this was most definitely some sneaky

ploy. But what did this creature want from us? That's what I couldn't figure out. Maybe he was working for Finnian, after all.

Tulip, Calina, and Amariel immediately followed our guide's instructions, while Rurik and I remained suspicious.

"Why do we need to close our eyes? Is it so you can attack us or run away while we aren't looking? That's not very hospitable... or honorable." Wow, he really went there. Well, good on him. It helped when others said the hard things sometimes.

"No tricks! No tricks!" The kobold cried, reverting to the simplistic speech common of its kind. He then skittered across the room on all fours, tossed off his cloak, and rose to a standing position before folding at the waist and bowing deeply again. "I shall not betray your trust. Of this, I can assure you. The master's magic will not work with an audience. Not work! Not work!"

I smacked my forehead. "You know we're still here even if our eyes are closed, right?"

Rurik's expression, however, changed immediately. "Your master is magic? What kind? Can he teach me?"

"The master is a wise—Wise! Wise!—and generous soul, but she cannot be summoned to this realm while outsiders are observing. Look away! Look away! That is, close your eyes until she arrives, then you may later open them and speak with her directly. Speak then! Speak then!" This thing reverted between its base kobold instincts and honored presentation so rapidly it felt as if we were in the presence of a creature possessed. My head throbbed from trying to keep up.

Mmm, I didn't much care for this whole closed-eyes business. Rurik was right. It could be an excuse for the kobold to pull one over on us.

Or...

"Yes, okay. We're closing our eyes. Go get your master." I squeezed my lids shut tight for a few beats and waited for the sound of claws skittering across the marble floors. When I felt confident our host had left us, I opened them again and made a beeline for the heavy golden chalice I'd previously identified as the item I'd most like to steal. It wasn't the most valuable treasure in the trove, but I could easily lift it and knew the goblet would catch a reasonable price without raising too many questions from a buyer.

Yup, my mind was more than made up. I snatched the chalice with well-practiced fingers and then slid it into the bag of tanuki cookies Rurik had agreed to carry for our group. The big lug didn't even notice. His lack of perception served me well now, but I made a note to work on this ability with him later. After all, it wouldn't do us any good to have him carrying the heavy stuff if anyone could take something from the bags without him noticing.

And just like that, the job was done. In the blink of an eye, I returned to my original spot, transforming my face into a mask of innocence.

"Yes! Yes! She has entered this place. Here! Here! You may now open your eyes to greet the master! Master!" the kobold cried with such force that I shivered.

I blinked my eyes open and then rubbed my fists at them. I saw only our same kobold guide; now, he wore an old, dented crown. I couldn't tell what metal had been used to forge it—just that it hadn't been gold.

Tulip appeared not only unimpressed but genuinely peeved-off. "You promised we'd meet your boss. So then, where is she?"

"I am already right here with you, Tulip Thunderhoof. My spirit is tied to this crown whenever I venture into this realm," the kobold answered in a completely different voice than before—the most notable difference being that it was now entirely feminine, soft, and melodic with a resonant authority, not at all like the frantic, slithering speech of her servant.

"Who are you? Where are you, and how do you

know her name?" Rurik asked, his face alternated between awe and angry suspicion.

The kobold had stopped blinking, and now his— her?—eyes began to tear up from the effort of keeping them open at length. "I know a great many things, Rurik Bane, but be careful what you ask of me, for I can only reveal so much before I must once again leave this realm and return to my own."

"Ooh! Do you know my name too?" Calina asked, ducking down to the kobold's height to get a better look at the crown.

The creature took a step back to regain some distance. "Yes, Calina Starbrook. I know you."

"Hold up!" I shouted, thrusting my arms out to the sides to keep the others back. "Everyone stop talking right now." I recognized a prophetic moment when I saw one, and this was clearly one of those situations. I didn't know how many questions this otherworldly entity would allow, but I knew we'd already wasted too many with the children's nonsense.

"No one else says a single word until I give my okay. Not a single word." This conversation would be much more effective if I could get the magical entity to reveal information without directly asking any questions outright. Which meant I had to proceed very carefully.

"If Rurik's questions already count toward our tally, you may answer them. If they do not, please forget them. There are other, more pressing things we need to know," I said, choosing each word with great care.

The kobold spoke again as soon as I'd stopped. "I am Zephyriel, a high celestial. I experience all timelines, all lives, and all possible eventualities simultaneously, which, in turn, makes me all-knowing when it comes to mortal matters. Were I to take a conscious form while visiting your world, I would be chained to that body until its mortality expired. As such, I keep my visits brief and possess this simple object instead of a more complex vessel." The kobold blinked rapidly as if catching up on its quota for the last several minutes, then turned toward me with unseeing eyes. "What is it you would wish to know, Tilda Quickthatch?"

Even though I understood that Zephyriel was an omniscient being, it wasn't any less eerie hearing a stranger speak my name, especially by way of kobold. I paused, attempting to puzzle out how many questions she'd answered just then, but it was a waste of every-one's time, given that I didn't know how many she would even allow.

I glanced toward Amariel, wondering if she might

finally prove useful since we were dealing with one of her kind.

But the old woman just stared straight ahead with a curious expression. I found it funny that Amariel always spoke with musical accompaniment, but Zephyriel used only her words. I wondered if this was down to her possessing the crown instead of a body or if it had something to do with her status as a high celestial instead of the standard variety.

Well, if Amariel wasn't going to provide any guidance, that left things to me and my best instincts. So, I cut right to the chase and asked the most important question outright. After all, it might be the only one we had left. "Our group has embarked on a pretty lofty adventure, and honestly, we're not really equipped to handle it. How can we ensure our victory?"

"Two adventures both inexorably intertwined, both above your skill level to be sure, but also both quests you will ultimately conquer. You asked of one adventure, but I shall do you the kindness by revealing a sliver of guidance for each, for they are one and the same. To emerge victorious, you will need to pay the ultimate cost. Sacrifice what matters most, and you will surely win."

"Oh my god," Tulip huffed and appeared to shrink

in on herself. "Does that mean someone's going to die?"

I elbowed Tulip in the flank. Even if she needed clarification on the high celestial's words, I did not. *Sigh.* So much for keeping the kids quiet through this.

"Yes, the deaths will be swift and unforgiving, but they are needed for your party to persevere. I have answered all that is required of me now. I wish you each well in your journey."

"Wait, wait. No, please don't count that. There's so much more we need to know," I begged. The kobold shook his head, and the dingy old crown began to glow and pulse, preparing to expel the entity within.

"I bid thee farewell, Tilda Quickthatch. Nearly all that you desire shall be yours in due time." The kobold bowed its head toward me before turning toward Tulip.

"Goodbye, Tulip Thunderhoof. You would do well to remember that the most valuable riches are not made of gold but flesh and blood."

One by one, she turned to each of our party and gave a personalized goodbye.

"Go with grace, Calina Starbrook. Family is indeed a divine blessing, but it is not only the family to which we are born that deserves our love."

"Rurik Bane, farewell. You are only just becoming

who you were meant to be. But your heart, not your mind, will get you to the place you need to find. Be open to these gifts of growth even if they go against logic."

At last, she met her celestial sistren. The crown let out a gentle melodic hum as the kobold clasped Amariel by the arm and squeezed. "And Finnian Sly, all your many tricks do not serve you well. You will not obtain what you desire until you learn to request it plainly and without artifice. Goodbye and good luck."

6

The old crown let out a blast of light that enveloped the entire treasure room, temporarily rendering us all blind. When, at last, the stars had worked their way out of my eyes, I glanced eagerly around for the others. I had so many questions but didn't know which I needed to have answered first: How had this summoning worked precisely? Had the high celestial known we were coming? Had she specifically sent her kobold servant to collect us? What did she mean by saying I'd acquire "nearly" everything I desired? Why couldn't I have it all, and what part would I not get?

And Finnian! What had he done with Amariel? Why had I not noticed his presence earlier? Why couldn't he have trusted us to do the job we'd agreed to?

I clenched my fists to keep from throwing them in his stupid face. However, his face—or rather Amariel's —wasn't the first I found when I searched for the others.

The kobold servant had collapsed onto the ground at my feet in an almost lifeless husk. From what I could tell, he was still alive, just absolutely drained from the encounter with Zephyriel. I wondered how long the little dude would be out before regaining consciousness. Would we have enough time to—

"I'm going to rip your head from your body!" Tulip shouted as she charged at Amariel, who had produced a giant sack and was shoving treasure into it as fast as her fragile fingers would allow.

The tanuki in disguise quickly leaped to the side, leaving the centaur to crash face-first into the mountain of remaining treasures. Gold coins, cutlery, and other accoutrements clattered everywhere, creating a terrible cloying ruckus. Tulip fell forward and twisted onto her side in a painful, failed attempt to keep her balance.

"So there's no chance you missed that then. Hmm?" the old celestial asked in Finnian's unmistakable voice.

Tulip pulled herself back to her feet and shook out her limbs while searching the space for Finnian. "Give her to me right now, you no good dirty trickster, and I'll consider allowing you to live."

Finnian abandoned Amariel's skin and went back to wearing his own. He now held a sword in one hand, aloft and pointed straight at Tulip, while he continued to clutch tight to the bag of treasures with his other. "Come now, we don't want any trouble. No, no. I only acted the part of a good businessman, didn't I? I had to make sure my little investment got started on the right path. That is, I had to make sure you'd follow through on your end of the deal."

"Where's Amariel?" Tulip demanded as she flipped her thick braid back over her shoulder and stamped a hoof several times in quick succession.

"The celestial is safe. Comfortable, even. Let me take my leave with a bit of this treasure, and then you shall have her back at your side." He made a swishing motion with the sword, a clear sign he hadn't even the slightest idea how to use it. And why should he have to learn, seeing as he always sent an army of hand-selected children to do his most dangerous bidding?

The centaur stopped stamping but stood her ground. "You're not going anywhere until I know she's safe."

Finnian chuckled and hung his head in apathetic resignation. "You leave no room for argument, it seems." He set the sword he'd lifted from the treasure pile onto the marbled floor and reached into his breast pocket, pulling out a small and shiny black stone, which he then raised to his face and pressed his lips against. "Yoohoo, Levvy. Bring the celestial to me at once. I'm in an alley off Shadowmere, after its cross-section with Moonlily, but before it hits Elderwood. I expect to see you within five clicks, tops."

The tanuki pulled the stone from his lips and dropped it back into his pocket with a shrug. It glinted with shades of blue and green as it caught the light, making it a wonder to behold. "Very well then," Finnian ground out dramatically, drawing my focus back to him. "She'll be here before you can even realize she's been gone. A terrible situation, this. If that Zephyriel hadn't revealed my presence, I wonder if you'd have figured out my little ruse on your own. Hmm. It does make me doubt your ability to outwit Eldrin Grimlock. He will not be an easy foe to fell. No, not at all."

Finnian shook his head as if disappointed in us, then resumed filling his bag with treasure. He hadn't let it go during his confrontation with Tulip, not even briefly. That, more than anything, showed what he valued in this life. Finnian's laughter grew more robust and confident with each new prize he secured. "Calina, my young apprentice, I know you will not disappoint me. At least not again, hmmm? There's far too much you could lose. Not just my respect."

Calina swallowed hard but said nothing. When did the girl not have a quick comeback ready to fire like one of her steel-tipped arrows? No, this was not good. Her silence showed how accurately Finnian had hit the mark with his jabs.

I had to stop him from talking. His words held too much sway over her, especially since I had not set things right with Calina.

I glanced to Rurik for a bit of help, but he was wholly focused on the kobold's discarded crown, studying it with each of his senses, one by one. Sight, touch, sound... Gross. What did he even gain from dragging his tongue across the dirty headpiece? If this was what academic pursuit looked like, I was glad I'd never been smart enough to worry about school.

Tulip kept her arms crossed over her chest as she watched Finnian's every move, ready to tackle him if he stepped out of line. I wondered when she would finally realize that the battle axe made for a far more potent threat than a simple glance.

Having filled his sack to bursting, Finnian dropped

it on the floor with a grunt. "Full already. Such a shame. I really should have brought a second. Hmm. There will be swift and severe consequences for that fellow when he awakes, I'm afraid. Mirathane is my city. We simply don't have space for rival crime rings."

"Cut the crap, Finnian. Tell me why you really sent us on this quest." I slowly stepped toward the bag of treasures, knowing this was the best way to ensure his attention remained on me.

Sure enough, his shiny black eyes followed my every move, just as I'd intended. "You mean the quest you have yet to start?"

I prickled at his implication that I would give any mission less than my best. I hated him, yes, but I also took tremendous pride in what I did—or what I once did and now found myself doing all over again. My word meant more than any trinket or treasure as far as I was concerned. I'd assumed Finnian knew that, too, but maybe not. "Yeah. That would be the one. Why are you really out to get Eldrin Grimlock?"

True to form, Finnian chuckled. Either he found everything amusing or nothing at all. I couldn't say which. "Is the betrayal I already described not motivation enough?"

"We both know there's more to the story." I took two quick steps toward his overflowing bag, but

Finnian immediately leaped to block my path, dropping his sword in the process.

"What does it matter?" he asked, grabbing the sack again and holding it tightly so I could not take it from him. I went for the sword.

Finnian inched away carefully as his words stumbled out haphazardly. "You know the high points and that Zephyriel-being said you'd be successful. The finer details are of no significance regarding the final outcome." He hoisted the heavy bag off the ground and then moved toward me, ignoring the sword as he loomed tall in an unspoken threat. "Get it done, then we'll talk about what happens next."

I leaned forward to meet his threat, keeping the sword wedged between us as I whispered, "I'll do what you've asked, but leave the girl alone. You'll deal with me and me only."

He laughed and flapped a hand between us, batting the steel weapon away as if it were a mere plaything. "You do realize you're the least intimidating creature on earth, do you not?" he asked as the sword clattered across the stone floor.

I glanced longingly at the sword that now lay just out of reach. I didn't need it to stand up to Finnian. I had never planned to use it, anyway. "That may be so, but you need me," I hissed, which wasn't a sound I made often. I much preferred to growl. "You made that clear by sending those wing scouts. How much did that bounty cost you, I wonder."

He tsked and shook his head, still clutching tight to the sack. "Little Tilly, this is no way to speak to your pa."

"Then it's a good thing you're not my father."

"Tilda, I'm hurt. Truly. You—"

A trumpet blared, cutting his sentence short as it announced Amariel's much-anticipated arrival... I leaned to the side, eager to welcome our missing member back to the party.

Only I couldn't spot her anywhere.

The only movement came from a two-headed serpent as it slithered out from behind a tapestry. Presumably, this heavy fabric wall hanging covered the other end of the alley passageway that started with the Y-shaped crack we'd abandoned. That was the only functional entrance to this space since the magical wall had reconstituted itself shortly after we passed into the foyer. And now it gave way to this strange serpentine's arrival.

The left-most head tasted the air with a hiss and another blast of brass, making its way to the center of the grand room. It stopped beside Finnian and me, then raised both heads and began to increase in size. A part of me wanted to run for cover, but curiosity kept me rooted in the spot, especially since the tanuki didn't seem worried about the strange display.

The two-noggined creature kept growing until it was far taller than me, and then—*poof!*—a burst of magical smoke enshrouded its form, falling away to reveal Amariel and a young boy who couldn't have been much older than twelve.

"Levvy, thank you for bringing my quarry, but the display was unnecessary."

The child thief, who I realized must have a strong, natural aptitude for the druid arts, shrugged. "She wouldn't come willingly, so I improvised."

Tulip rushed to Amariel and put an arm around the elder celestial. "Amariel, are you okay? I'm so sorry we left you. We didn't know you weren't with us. That-that thing tricked us. But I promise it will never happen again." Now that Tulip had what she wanted, she was losing her edge. I half-expected her to fall apart in relieved sobs, but the centaur somehow managed to hold herself together.

Amariel smiled in greeting, then nodded off to sleep, summoning her snoring metronome the moment her eyes shut. Ah, of course. We should have realized that the Amariel who'd joined us in Mirathane was an imposter. She'd spent too much time conscious and alert, even if she had remained silent.

"Wow, that spell was amazing! You brought a second person into your shapeshift? Phenomenal," Rurik crowed, leaving the crown so that he could examine the boy. "Can you teach me how to do it?"

Levvy looked the half-orc up and down, then scoffed. "You? No."

Finnian wagged a finger at his underaged underling. "Now, now, my child. We must always be kind."

The boy scraped a filthy hand through filthier hair and winced. "Even when we don't mean it?"

"Why, yes. Especially then." Finnian scampered over to his rucksack and dragged it across the floor before handing it off to Levvy. "Here. Take this back to base. I'll follow along shortly."

I watched the young lad struggle with the great weight of the sack until he disappeared behind the tapestry. Yet another of Finnian's young victims. I wondered if one day he'd manage to escape like I had. My heart fell when I realized that I hadn't ever really escaped at all. Not really.

"You can go too," I snarled at my former master. I'd had just about enough of him and his refusal to surrender any semblance of control. "You asked us to complete your quest, and we agreed to do it, but we can't do a single blessed thing with you hovering over us. So get."

"Such angry words for the one who raised you, Tilly. Use that anger as power to get the job done." He plucked the magic stone from his pocket and pressed it into my palm. "Take this. Keep it. The stone will give you a direct line to me."

I wrapped my fingers around the cool igneous and nodded curtly but refused to smile. The last thing I wanted was to carry a piece of Finnian around on my person. Well, at least the magical item could fetch a good price at market. I'd spent too long being poor and hungry to throw away a gift, even if it was one I had never asked for. "Fine" was all I managed to say.

"Then I shall see you on the other side," Finnian sang out before dropping to all fours and transforming into his rat self. The rat had always been his preferred form for sneaking around. It suited him.

Before scurrying after Levvy and the heaping bag of treasure, the little masked creature sat on its hind legs and twitched its whiskers. "Oh, and Tilly?" it squeaked. "Don't pawn off Pa's gift. Hmm?"

7

"I don't like that guy," Calina mumbled through clenched teeth once Finnian had taken his leave. But I knew better than anyone just how shaky the boundary between love and hate could be. I'd once considered Finnian a savior and happily called him Pa. And it was that same love I'd once felt for my former master that caused me to revile him so much now.

Even if Calina claimed to dislike Finnian, she'd played right into his greedy little hands. She'd even adopted some of his mannerisms, a cause for growing concern.

Now that the shifter had tried to supplant one of our party members, we knew to be on the lookout. Or at least I did, though I shouldn't have needed this blaring reminder to stay alert. Really, I was more disappointed in myself than any of the others. How could they have known what we'd be up against? They were a bunch of small-town kids who'd grown up in the comforting embrace of parents who loved them, even if some of them had odd ways of showing it.

This whole distraction with Finnian was my fault —and mine alone. I was to blame for everything, including the fact that Maltherius had even called us to our adventure in the first place. I hated that these kids might one day have to pay the price for mistakes I'd made many moons ago.

What had the crown-wearing kobold declared?

That we'd win but pay a significant cost. If someone was going to lose their life on the battlefield, I'd make sure it was me. I'd already lived well past what was expected of either an urchin or an adventurer, and I was grateful for that. Really.

My job now was to set as much right as possible before my time was up. And when it was all over, I wanted the kids and townspeople of Briarhaven to remember me fondly, to say nice things in memoriam. That's better than most got and probably more than I deserved.

I shook my head to free it from this tragic line of thinking. I'd always survived by living in the moment, by not planning too far ahead. That kept me ready for anything, a necessary skill. Right now, our group was stuck in a hidden treasure room deep within the bowels of Mirathane. They needed me to be present. *Time to snap back to it, Tilda.*

"It looks like we're trapped in here," I said as I searched the space for a more accommodating exit. We already knew that the alleyway crack couldn't fit Tulip or Rurik. "Unless we can find a way that fits everybody, we'll need to wait for that kobold to wake up and help us."

"That summoning ritual looked pretty potent. He could be out for days. But maybe..." Rurik's words trailed off as he moved to Amariel and gently nudged her awake. "Hey, hey," he said until finally, her eyes fluttered open. Do you, by chance, know a high celestial named Zephyriel?"

Our celestial's answer came with an underlying woodwind cacophony. It felt frantic and unmoored, strangely stressed, coming from our genuinely calm companion. "Zephyriel? I haven't seen her for many centuries, not since I entered the mortal realm. Where is she? Is she here?"

Rurik handed her the old crown. "She spoke to us through this. Well, this *and that.*" He nodded toward the out-cold kobold.

"What exactly did Zephyriel tell you?" Amariel insisted the brass she usually reserved for marching into battle flared with this statement. "Tell me every single word. Exactly as she said it."

Rurik's eyes took on a glossy appearance as they drifted toward the far corner of the sanctum. I knew this meant his sight had turned inward to search his mind. Yes, I was getting to know the kids for all their quirks, and Rurik was the quirkiest of them all. Being able to read and sometimes predict their behavior was good; I could use this newfound ability to make sure they were well-trained and ready for the battles ahead. But my growing understanding of their idiosyncrasies also meant I was getting too attached, that they probably were too. Another worrying observation I preferred not to think too much about.

Luckily, Rurik's memory bordered on magical, even without training to hone it further. If there was any fault with his recounting of the high celestial's prophetic phrasing, I couldn't find it.

"I see," is all Amariel offered by way of response when he had finished, this with two big booms of a drum. "I see." *Boom, boom.*

"It sure would be nice if someone would help find a way out of here," I muttered as I continued my search for an alternate escape route.

"I'm on it," Tulip answered before clopping across the room and yanking the sleeping kobold into her arms. She gave him a good, firm shake and proceeded to shout in the poor thing's face. "Wake up, you little jerk!"

"Dear sweet divinity, not like that," I swore, but I should have seen this coming from a hundred paces away. Maybe I didn't know them as well as I thought, or maybe I was just too flustered to think straight.

"Anyone else have any less violent ideas?" I had to admit requesting less violence was a new one for me. Generally, too much was better than not enough, but that poor little creature had already been through quite enough torment on our behalf.

I turned to the other adult in the room for backup.

But Amariel failed to pick up on my plea for assistance. She just held the crown artifact in shaking hands, saying nothing. Tulip's parents insisted on sending the weathered old woman along as a chaperone, but I still couldn't figure out why. Yes, she'd healed Calina and Rurik when they needed it, but so far, Tulip had avoided any hostile action unless she was sure she could emerge without so much as a scuff on her hoof. The centaur family had also assumed my serious, life-and-death quest was some kind of guided tour for bored youth. So why would they have even thought to send a healer along?

I briefly wondered if they had just needed a break from their child. Had they considered my big adventure a good opportunity to distract her for a few weeks?

"Tulip, put the kobold down. Calina, Rurik, what have you got for me?" I appealed to the others, raising my joined hands and shaking them emphatically. "Any ideas on how we can get out?"

Rurik patted Amariel on the shoulder, then crossed the room to where we'd entered. What had once been an open passage was now a solid stone wall. It didn't fit the rest of the space, appearing far too plain by comparison. "When we entered, the kobold had to put his hand in a specific spot and turn approximately seventy-five degrees to the left. Since we're now on the opposite side of the door, everything should be reversed, which means we need to look around here." He gestured broadly at the right side of the room.

Calina jogged over to join him. "I'll help you search. What are we looking for?"

"I duh-don't nuh-know," Rurik confessed, his confidence shattered at the first request to clarify it.

As our party's resident rogue, I was supposed to be the one to unlock doors, but magic had never really been my thing. I did at least have one small tidbit to contribute, however. "It will need to be the kobold's hand. The magic is attuned to him, not any of us."

"Excellent point, Tilda," Rurik said with a one-tusked smile. And just like that, he was back to his more balanced demeanor.

Tulip yanked the kobold from the floor, forgetting my earlier request to be gentle or perhaps just not caring. She said something in horse, then trotted over to join the other kids at the wall. "How about right here?" she asked before smashing the lizard kin into the wall face first. Oh, that poor, blessed creature. I hoped his master could offer him a bit of healing when next he summoned her because the little dude would sorely need it.

"It needs to be his hand. His right hand," Rurik pointed out.

"And, last reminder, you either need to be a bit gentler or let someone else hold the key. He is a living creature, after all. And, if you'll recall, he helped by bringing us here."

Tulip huffed and shoved the unconscious kobold at Rurik. "He also stole from me, remember?"

"I think that was just meant to get our attention. It seemed like Zephyriel wanted to talk to us and told him to find a way to get us here," I thought aloud, but it all made perfect sense.

"I agree. They knew we were coming," Rurik said with a nod as his eyes continued to roam the wall for any markings or indentations that might indicate the secret latch. "You know Zephyriel better than any of us. What do you think, Amariel?"

Amariel just kept holding onto that crown without saying anything. I took her lack of argument as either agreement or inattention. Well, at least the kids were actively helping now. That was definitely progress.

"The kobold is way shorter than you or Tulip," Calina said. She seemed excited to have something to contribute to solving this puzzle. "If the magic is attuned to him, then the handhold would be closer to the ground, somewhere he could easily reach without drawing too much attention to himself."

"Good thinking." Rurik smiled brightly at his best friend. It was easy to picture them back in Briarhaven, putting their deviant minds together to cause a ruckus at school. They were a good team when they wanted to be. Would that easy camaraderie eventually extend to encompass me and Tulip as well?

"Let me get down on my knees and hold him in a

standing position while you and Tulip move his hands around," Rurik said, assuming the position.

I hung back and watched the three kids work together to overcome the obstacle. This was a proud mentor moment, even though I couldn't take credit for it. What I could do was watch and rest up for whatever came next.

After a good long while of sitting back and watching as the kids groped about the wall and smashed our unconscious host's hand up against it, the magical door finally blinked open.

Calina, Rurik, and Tulip all cheered before rushing outside.

Even I did a small fist pump when I was sure nobody was watching. Then I realized I had a small problem: I'd gotten so wrapped up in watching the youth problem-solve that I forgot to filch more treasure.

Oh, well. At least I had that chalice. And I looked forward to drinking my wildflower tea from it at the very first opportunity. Yes, that would be quite lovely indeed.

We started moving down the alley, but Tulip abruptly forced us to halt. "Where's Amariel?" she asked with a breathy rasp. Sure enough, the old lady hadn't thought to follow us outside.

"She's probably sleeping," I offered before sprinting back to check on her. Figging fig, I hoped that the magical door hadn't sealed itself shut again.

Okay, thankfully, it had remained open, but I worried that crossing the threshold would slam it shut again. I stayed in the alley and called out to Amariel, who I found exactly as we'd left her. She stood motionless in the treasure room, apart from her violently shaking hands that clutched the old crown in a death grip.

"Yoohoo," I called and waited for her to glance up at me before saying any more. "We're going now. Do you want to bring that with us?"

Amariel shook her head and looked at me with watery, pale eyes. "No, Zephyriel must remain with her servant. Come, let us proceed with our adventure." I didn't recognize the music that underscored her words, and I didn't much care for it either.

Instead of setting the crown on the ground reverently, she tossed it to the side, where it noisily collided with a mountain of coins.

"What was that?" Tulip called from farther down the alley. "Is Amariel okay? I'm coming!"

"Child, I am fine," the elderly celestial rasped, then marched straight through the open magical door to join me in the alley. Once out, she raised both arms and swept them down, resealing the entry.

Huh, it sure looked like she could have done that any time she wanted to. Maybe, like me, she was trying to get the kids to figure some of these things out for themselves. But somehow, I doubted that.

"Amariel, there you are. You had me worried," Tulip cooed upon joining us at the now-hidden entry, then swept the old woman onto her back. No one was ever allowed to use the centaur princess as a mount except for her beloved chaperone. I allowed this double standard because it sometimes saved us time and headaches.

"Where to now?" Calina asked, falling into step beside me as we turned onto the main road.

"Where else?" I asked with a beleaguered chuckle. It seemed Finnian was rubbing off on me as well. "To Mystwood Keep."

Calina's violet eyes widened at my declaration. "We're just going to barge straight in there? Don't we need at least a little bit of battle training first?"

"I won't know how to train you until I know what we're up against," I explained. While inwardly summarizing, *That she and I needed an honest-to-blessed heart-to-heart before we entered into any more collectively life-threatening situations. I needed to know I could trust*

Calina and knew she needed the same from me. After all, the two of us had always been quite alike.

"That makes sense," she said, once again making me question whether these kids could somehow read my thoughts. I'd undoubtedly seen crazier things in my day.

That's when I realized, with a shocking start, that "my day" had ended. It was now a "new day," and this one belonged to the kids. I'd been the one to start this series of quests—well, me, Gaaron, and Finnian—but it would be up to them to put a proper end to it. Once and for all.

8

Mystwood Keep stood high above Mirathane on a rocky plateau about an hour's journey from the northern city border. The appearance of the expanse beneath the castle compound made me wonder if there had once been a mountain here and some mythical giant had simply sawed off the top half. Where nature had once risen tall and proud into the sky, claiming its rightful domain, now a sprawling and decadent complex of various military and merchant dwellings existed. This was all punctuated by a single tower that climbed so high past the clouds that it appeared the blessed thing might very well topple over at any moment.

What even was the point of all that height? Height did not translate to power, especially considering that the previous ruler had been of halfling stature like myself. I wondered if the keep had always been so tall or if its new regent had erected additional levels since taking over the castle. If it was the latter, I could easily see how he and Finnian had once been good friends.

Our hike to the top of the plateau was difficult, even with a paved path to aid us. The angle of the ascent was steep and challenging for little legs and big ones alike. And it was immediately apparent that this positioning gave Mystwood a significant advantage in times of war. But I hadn't come for war, regardless of what might happen after I disposed of the regent here.

I didn't want to kill Eldrin Grimlock, at least not currently. That might change after I had the opportunity to meet him, though. Time, great enemy that it was, would tell. Until then, I'd just have to take things moment by moment, day by day.

"This place is amazing," Calina gushed as she skipped ahead of the group. She had the easiest time traversing this—and, really, any—terrain. Rurik's clumsiness, combined with his continued careful examination of the castle ahead, often caused him to stumble over his own feet. Tulip, meanwhile, was weighted down by carrying her passed-out chaperone on her back. As for me, I always took up the rear in any situation, given the relative shortness of my stride compared to the others.

Calina glanced over her shoulder, then skipped back toward the rest of us, pumping her arms as she pranced playfully. "Do you really think they'll just let us in? Because to me, that doesn't seem very likely."

"Our chances of success are less than one percent," Rurik said between taking deep gasps for air as he stumbled up the slope. "And even that's optimistic."

"I don't expect this to work, but we still have to try. If nothing else, it will give us a closer look at the place and whatever defenses it has in place." I felt like I'd already explained this more than once. In fact, I was sure of it.

"So this is a reconnaissance mission? That's the most boring kind. When do we get back to the exciting adventure stuff?" Calina grabbed her bow off her back, nocked an arrow, and then pointed her weapon at a series of imaginary opponents, making various sound effects as she played out her pretend battle.

I rolled my eyes but otherwise held back a response. Calina was already busy occupying herself, which I liked far better than having her focused on me —especially if that meant her asking even more questions that had already been answered. We still needed to talk, but we also needed to do so privately, given the delicacy of the matter.

"Are we there yet?" Tulip asked with a huff.

I shot ahead on the path just so I could stare daggers at my whiny, entitled charge. And, let me say, as an expert dagger-wielder, this particular stare packed a punch. "Why are you even asking me? You have eyes. You can see that we're not there yet. I think you just want something to complain about, but you know, nobody is forcing you to be here. I can turn this party around and take us right back to the bottom of this hill if you don't improve your attitude. Is that what you want?"

Tulip's head jerked back at my snappy retort, and she blinked hard. "Nuh. No. Sorry." Yeesh, she sounded more like Rurik than herself now.

"Yeah, you are. You all are. This is why kids don't go on quests," I muttered as I fell back to a more comfortable pace.

"You keep calling us kids, but we're not really. Are we?" Calina piped up, lowering her bow to focus her shrewd gaze on me. "I'm old enough to get married if I want, which I do not, but that's beside the point. Just because we're not old like you doesn't mean we're children."

"Fine," I said through gritted teeth. I made a

mental note not to call them kids anymore, at least not aloud. It wasn't worth the argument, especially since I knew Calina rarely backed down when issuing even the smallest challenge.

We continued up the incline for about ten minutes of blessed silence before one of my *youth-gifted* companions raised a fresh complaint.

"It's too sunny. I'm going to get a burn." This came from Tulip.

"We can pat you down with mud if you need some protection," I rasped, my throat dry with thirst. Still, I relished the image of our resident princess covered in filth. Rurik would happily assist with such a task if she needed a hand or two.

"With mud? Are you serious? That's disgusting. I'd rather risk the burn."

"Good," I said, then hummed a few beats in tune with the dozing Amariel's ubiquitous metronome. I already had a hard time keeping my cool, and soon, I would lose it entirely if the kids—yeah, sorry, I couldn't think of them as anything but—continued to nag at me.

That's when I got an idea I rather liked.

"Hey, Rurik. Teach us something," I demanded as sweetly as I could.

He immediately picked up the conversational

gourd I'd lobbed his way. "What would you like to learn about?"

"Anything. Just pick a topic and talk." I couldn't show my irritation if I wanted this to work. Otherwise, one of the girls would complain at me. Probably Calina.

"I'd be happy to enlighten you, but I'm going to need more direction than that, Tilda." Rurik shook his head, tripped over a pebble, fell to the ground, and pushed himself back onto his feet. It all happened so quickly that it almost looked like it was on purpose. I knew better than that, though.

"Uh, uh... How about the history of Verandel, the life cycle of a spruce tree, magic theory..." I started spitting out any topic that came to my mind, hoping he'd latch onto one and start soliloquizing, thus forcing the other two to remain quiet. "Orcish history," I continued, "Barbarian battle tactics, Tribal—"

"I never did finish showing Tulip how to use that battle axe," he interrupted with a lopsided grin and a quick glance toward the centaur he was growing increasingly enamored of with each passing day. This was all very cute, but I had to ensure Calina was also included in his lecture. Otherwise, the distraction wouldn't work.

"Yes, and we'll work on that soon," I promised. We did need to work on that. Now that I had a better idea of how to motivate Tulip, we needed to ensure that she knew how to carry through on her threats of violence when appropriate. Rurik would be instrumental in that. Just *later*.

"Right now, I need more of a talking lesson," I explained patiently. "What can you teach Tulip—and the rest of us—about barbarian battle tactics?"

Rurik tripped again, but this time, he caught himself before falling. "I don't think Amariel wants to learn about that," he said smoothly despite his janky movements. Apparently, he was so used to tripping over his own feet that he hardly noticed anymore.

"She's sleeping, so it doesn't matter," Tulip pointed out. I didn't expect Tulip to argue on my behalf, but I was incredibly grateful for the assist. "Besides, I would like to learn what you know. I mean, you obviously know way more than me about this stuff."

I watched Rurik's cheeks turn from green to a muddy pink. Was Tulip starting to notice his affection, or was she just becoming... nice?

It was weird but also precisely what I needed to shut the kids up, so I didn't worry too much about it. I half-listened as Rurik expounded on the various schools of barbarian thought. I didn't even point out the oxymoron in that. Mostly, I enjoyed the relative peace, and Tulip and Calina seemed to be learning something while Amariel enjoyed her rest.

And with that last unwitting aid from Rurik, we finally made it to the outer gates of the complex at the top of that ridiculous plateau with no further grievance.

"Okay, let me handle the talking from here," I whispered to the others as we drew near.

"But I'm not done explaining how to find and make use of improvised weapons in the woodlands," Rurik argued with a frown and a furrowed brow, but, hey, at least he didn't trip again.

"You are for now, buddy. You can tell the other ki —" I glanced toward Calina and saw that she had one eyebrow raised in challenge. Her lips were parted and ready to spew a few enflamed syllables my way.

"You can tell the others about it later," I course-corrected to avoid any further arguments while we needed to stay focused.

Even though my little legs were aching and tired, I jogged ahead of the group and raised a hand toward the gates in greeting. "Good afternoon, my good sirs!" I called to the uniformed guards standing at the entrance. "Lovely weather we're having, isn't it?"

"What do you lot want?" a curly-haired half-giant who reminded me of Pat asked. He stood tall, holding a pointed spear, and stared straight ahead, his chin titled up in a stoic pose that didn't quite mesh with his lower city accent.

"We would like to enter," I stated simply. Don't provide any information that's not explicitly requested. That was a rule I often played by. I wouldn't get caught in this ruse if I didn't give away any clues.

The half-giant lowered his chin and studied me with curious eyes before raising his face toward the sun and saying, "No."

This was about what I'd expected, but now that the guard had sized me up, he was no longer paying close attention. I could use that to my advantage.

"We'd like to pay our respects to the regent and offer him a proposition," I said vaguely as I searched the compound's tall stone walls for hidden entrances or accidental footholds.

The guard scoffed at my declaration. "You? What can you offer a king?"

"If I'm not mistaken, he's a regent. Not a king. And don't be deceived by appearances. There is much that my companions and I can offer. Unfortunately for you, the opportunity we've come to present is for Eldrin Grimlock's ears only." As I spoke, I glanced at each of the guards in turn. Did we have any weak links? Any that could easily be swayed with the right bribe?

The big guard's lip curled. "You will leave. And you will leave at once."

"Okey dokes, buh-bye!" I waved at him decisively and headed back down the plateau, motioning for the others to follow.

"That's it!" Tulip exploded. "We came all that way up that stupid hill for that?"

I nodded and drew a finger to my lips. I didn't speak to the kids again until we'd been walking for a solid ten minutes. And when I was confident we were out of earshot of the guards, I stopped and motioned for them to come close.

"Okay, huddle up," I said and then waited until they complied with the order. "There's a hobgoblin guard. He's going to let us in. He was stationed to the right, so we're going to head back up there, but we can't approach from the main road. We have to catch him at shift change when the others aren't paying attention."

"What? How can you possibly know that?" Tulip demanded with a stomp. This was why I'd waited until we were far from the gates. If there was one thing I could count on from my companions, it was that they were always, *always* loud, whether or not the situation called for it.

I simply smiled. "We all have our areas of expertise. And this is mine. I'm telling you, that guard can be bought, so let's go find out what the price is."

9

"Psssst!" I hissed while crouched inelegantly behind a bramble bush. The kids waited a few hundred paces back where I'd left them at the forest's edge. Our earlier exchange with Zephyriel had proven they couldn't keep quiet, so I decided it would be best to keep them out of the way entirely. Calina, of course, had griped and moaned, shouting at the top of her lungs while insisting that she could be very sneaky when she wanted to be.

Somehow, I hadn't been convinced.

So I'd made all three swear up and down that they would wait exactly where I'd left them—never once straying even a single step until I returned to collect them. I had no idea how long I'd have to wait to get my targeted guard on his own, and I didn't need the added complication of playing babysitter on a stealth op.

Amariel slept through all of these negotiations because, of course, she did. This had all gone down a while ago, but I felt confident she hadn't stirred in the time that had passed since.

I wasn't normally patient, but I rather enjoyed this blessed solitude away from my charges. By the divine, I could wait all night if that was what it took.

When the sun had begun its official nighttime descent, I watched my chosen hobgoblin break rank and march purposefully toward one of the side entrances on the keep's perimeter.

"Hey, over here," I whispered hoarsely when my first attempt to get his attention failed. Sweet divinity, I could use a drink when this was all over. My parched throat made me long for my home at the Mystic Mug more than ever. But that's why I'd committed to this quest in the first place—to keep everyone back home safe so the kids and I could join them again and live happily ever after. Or something like that.

"Helloooooooo!" I called a third time, raising my voice as loudly as possible without risking the other guards' attention. For one with such large ears, this hobgoblin seemed to have difficulty using them.

"Oh, goodness," a feminine voice exclaimed as the

hobgoblin brought a dainty hand to her chest. Okay, so this was a lady hob. It was nearly impossible to tell the difference between the genders at a glance, but I still felt guilty about mistaking her for a male. Luckily, hobs couldn't read minds, so she'd stay blissfully unaware of my slip. However, she was proving far more concerned about my presence in general.

"You gave me quite the fright, wee one. Are you that same halfling from earlier?" she asked, dropping her hands back to her sides as she peered at me with bright, unblinking eyes.

I pulled a twig from my curls and tossed it aside. "Yes, now keep quiet and come here. I want to make a deal."

"I simply have no idea what you're getting at," she said while glancing toward places I couldn't quite see from my current vantage point. "I don't make deals with..." Her words fell away as she joined me behind my bramble. Wow, she was a terrible actress. Good thing she already had a job as a guard.

"Okay, you've got my attention. Now, what do you want?" she whispered, cutting the act.

"What'll you need to sneak my companions and me into the keep?" I jumped straight to business, even though I was still huddled in a low crouch. Semantics.

"The regent pays generously. I don't need money."

Pah, like I believed that. Still, I played along. "I don't have money either. I trade in favors. What can I do for you so that you do something for me?"

That last bit got her attention. Her eyes widened, and she looked at me like she was finally seeing me for the first time. "I do need a favor, actually. But it's no trifling thing. How do I know you're up to the task, wee one?"

"You don't. You'll have to trust me. Besides, I can't get into the castle until I keep up my end of the bargain, right? So let me ask again, what do you need?" This was already taking longer than I wanted. Despite the kids' promise to behave, I knew that the longer I left them, the more likely they were to wander off and find trouble we most assuredly didn't need.

Plus, there was always the chance that the lady hob and I would be discovered by one of her fellow guards, and none of them seemed the sort that could be bought off with pretty words and secret bargains.

The hobgoblin glanced around again, sniffed at the air, then narrowed her eyes. "You travel with an elf," she said with a sneer that didn't surprise me. The two races held a long-seated animosity. Due to her small-town upbringing and kindly mother, Calina had no idea of their rivalry, but this guard clearly knew the full history.

"And you serve one." I pointed my chin toward the keep as a reminder.

Her voice grew reverent, almost haunting. "Eldrin is a dark elf. He, too, has been shunned by the light."

"Shunned, eh? I'd say that there is one impressive-looking castle. Eldrin seems to be doing okay by my standards. And besides, my girl is only half elvish." I shrugged and pulled another twig out of my hair. "Now, I'll only ask one more time before I take my offer off the table. Can we help each other?"

I watched as she thought my proposition over. Her red skin reminded me of my infernal friend Insy back in Briarhaven, but that's where their similarities ended. While Insy stood tall and confident, the woman before me was hunched in on herself. Her long hair reached halfway down her curved back, and the sharp widow's peak of her hairline acted like an arrow that pointed toward her oversized leonine nose. Her ears were pointed, eyes small, and brow heavy. She was not an attractive creature; none of her kind were. I guessed that was at least part of why she had such a strong adverse reaction to seeing Calina, who was stunning to behold.

"Aye," the hobgoblin said at last. "I'll accept your help, though I'd prefer you leave the elf out of it."

I jumped at the chance to close the deal. "Sorry,

she's part of my party, which makes us a package deal. Now tell me your terms."

"It's my brother." She sighed heavily and raised her face skyward, looking off into the distance as she continued her tale. "He worked his whole life to earn out his indentureship. His former master made good and handed over the estate, but a short while later, it fell to some wayward spirits. They drove him out so that they could freely haunt the place. All those long years of service were for nothing, not if my brother can't even enjoy his hard-earned retirement."

"So you want us to get rid of the ghosts?" I summarized. It was not what I expected, but it was not much of a problem either.

"Aye." She lowered her gaze to meet mine and nodded curtly. "Drive out whatever haunts that place, then return to me with proof of a job well done. Ask my brother for a letter and have him affix the family seal—that way, I'll know you've made good. You do that, and I'll let you into the compound."

She offered her hand, and I clasped it to seal our bargain. "Deal. How will I find your brother and the estate?"

"Wait there a moment." The lady hob said before disappearing through the door in the outer castle wall.

And I did as I was told, which resulted in my

waiting there for many tense moments. The sun finished setting, the moon took over the night watch, and still, I stayed there, fearing I would soon be discovered—or worse, arrested. The longer I waited, the more I doubted that my hobgoblin associate would ever return to me. As stressful as the situation had become, it was still better than dealing with the whiny teens. Amariel had the right idea, sleeping every moment she could get. My eyes grew heavy, and I was so tempted to let myself drift off.

Of course, that's when the guard finally returned, clutching a rolled map as she hurried toward me.

"Here," she said, pressing the scroll into my hands. "It's all marked on the map. My brother's name is Brugnor. There aren't many of our kind around these parts, so he should be easy enough to spot."

I tucked the map into my pocket for safekeeping, but it was so big that it rose past my hip and up to my navel as it jutted out from that pocket. "Thanks. And what's your name?"

"You don't need to know that to complete the favor. I'll see you once it's done. Return to this here bush at the same time. I'll check each evening as I end my shift. Good luck to you."

By the time I unrolled the map and took a look, the hobgobliness had already vanished. I cursed under my breath when I saw how far off Brugnor's estate was from our current location. It was not a quick day's journey as I'd hoped—especially not on foot.

And that was only one of the problems with this plan.

I still had no idea how we'd get rid of Eldrin Grimlock once we'd gained entry to the keep. Beyond all that, Maltherius had a deadline he'd made very clear from the beginning. Either I made it to him by the solstice, or I needn't bother coming.

I wasn't sure how much time we had left, but I knew every second was precious. And now we had a quest within a quest *within a quest.* The whole thing was getting ridiculous, but I didn't have time to find another way. We just had to get on with it.

And so, with my frazzled mind made up, I returned to the kids in the forest. Much to my surprised delight, they'd managed to stay put. I didn't spot any new injuries either. We were genuinely making great progress here.

Of course, Calina was the first to notice my return with those keen elven eyes of hers. "So, how'd it go? Tell us everything!" she shouted, skipping over to meet me.

I waited to answer her, making straight for the supplies that sat at Rurik's side and rummaging around until I found a bladder of water. After taking a good long drink, I wiped my lips and gave them a quick summary of our new objective. "We've got to hunt some ghosts that are haunting the estate of the guard's brother, but then she'll let us in."

"Ghosts aren't real," Rurik said flatly. Whatever pedantic thing I had expected him to say, it wasn't this. "Something may be causing trouble at that estate, but I can guarantee it's not a ghost."

I took another long drink, resealed the bladder, and placed it back with the other supplies. "Of course, ghosts are real. How can you not believe in ghosts?"

"I've never seen them, so..." He shrugged and reached up to touch the tip of his one remaining tusk as if to say, *See this point? I have a point too. With my words.*

"So?" I challenged, more than a little miffed.

"So then the evidence I've gathered would suggest that they aren't real." He touched the tusk again. This was a new gesture, and already I hated it.

"Rurik Theodore Bane," I scolded, even going so far as to wag a finger at my charge. "There are many things you've probably never seen in your short, small-town life, but that doesn't mean they're not real. You believe in Maltherius, don't you? You've never seen him."

"My middle name is not Theodore," he griped, glancing at Tulip, who didn't appear to be paying attention anyway.

"It is now, sonny. And if you keep smack-talking ghosts, we're going to have a problem." Honestly, I didn't know why this was so important to me. In truth, I wasn't entirely sure I'd ever seen a ghost before either, but I'd seen many real and terrifying things in my day. And, frankly, I was sick of all the arguments plaguing our party since the beginning.

"Yeesh, Tilda. Calm down. Why do you like ghosts so much anyway?" This came from Calina as she munched on a tanuki cookie.

"I don't like ghosts. They're pretty terrible actually." I yanked the rest of Calina's cookie away and took a giant bite. "But the quickest way you can give something power is by saying it doesn't exist. If we go in expecting nothing, we'll be prepared for nothing."

"Which will make it easy for the ghosts to overpower us." Finally, Rurik got it. Praise divinity.

I finished the cookie but needed the water bladder again. Multitasking while I was famished was difficult, but we were too busy to take a proper break. "Exactly. So let me hear you say it, Rurik. Say ghosts are real."

"But they're no—"

Calina jabbed him in the ribs. "Just say it. Tilda's

right. We have to go in with our eyes open, right? Maybe it's not a haunting, but maybe it is. And if there are ghosts, we'll need our magical expert to help dispatch them. Yeah?"

"Yeah, okay. Fine, ghosts are real. Now let's go kill them dead." Rurik smiled, making me think the last part was probably meant to be a joke. Good on him.

"Uh, you know what? Yeah, sure. Let's go. Just one problem. It's pretty far away and we no longer have our conveyance, so..."

"We'll need mounts," Rurik said, casting a lovelorn look toward Tulip.

Tulip gasped and crossed her arms over her chest to hide herself. "That's offensive," she spat.

"Yeah, I get it. Everybody hates everything, but we've still got to go forward with the plan, so get over yourselves already."

"Rude," Tulip huffed again and flipped her braided mane dramatically over her shoulder.

"I agree about needing mounts, but don't forget, Tilda." Calina placed a hand on my shoulder and squeezed. Hard. "Finnian put me in charge. He trusted me to make the decisions for us. So far, I've given you a lot of free rein, but you'll need to remember who's in charge here. Okay?"

This made me so mad I saw stars—okay, it wasn't

rage stars that danced before me, but the literal stars in the night sky above us. Still, the day was done, and so was I. I glared daggers at Calina while fingering the hilt of the one I now kept tucked into my waistband.

"I'll take your lack of argument as compliance. Thank you, Tilly. Now it's late, and we need sleep. We should get a bit of distance from the keep to avoid attracting anyone's attention, but then we'll need to bunk down for the night. Tilda, can I trust you to pick a good spot and get the fire started while we set up camp?" Calina's whole manner changed upon directly challenging me for leadership—not just the words she chose but also how she said them. I didn't like it. I didn't like it one bit, but I just nodded my agreement and kept my honest thoughts to myself. I was exhausted after our long day and just wanted to get to bed.

I could deal with the children, the ghosts, and whatever else this blessed quest threw at me... tomorrow.

10

Even though we were all exhausted by this point, we retreated farther down the hill before setting up camp. I figured it would look suspicious to bed down anywhere near the castle walls, but I also knew it would be difficult to find a safe place for our group within the city. When we finally found a good spot somewhere between the two, I got to work making a campfire, even though Rurik could have done it just as quickly with his stupid dinky flame.

I hadn't spotted any good wildflowers for my tea, which annoyed me more than it probably should have. But I wanted to use the fancy new chalice I'd snatched from the high celestial treasure room, for one. And I also craved the comfort of my routine, now more than ever. Our group had been through a lot since leaving Briarhaven, and that was putting it mildly.

Amariel didn't wake up when Tulip gently removed the old celestial from her back and placed her onto a soft bed of grass. I wasn't surprised. Amariel had spent almost no time awake and alert since we'd left that treasure room. I was used to her sleeping a lot, but this was ridiculous.

She'd probably rouse herself if we needed help with something important, like if Rurik got his other tusk ripped off or Tulip lost her cool and maimed Calina a second time. Probably, but not for sure.

Eh, I decided not to worry about it.

There were plenty of other, better things to fret over. And, unlike my other companions, Amariel was an adult and thus could look after herself.

As a cool breeze ripped through the night air, I sat huddled at the fire, sipping hot water and wishing it was my tea. It was better than nothing, but not by much.

Once again, Rurik had given up his tent for Tulip and then disappeared somewhere on his own. He said he didn't need much sleep, but I still worried he might not be getting enough. We'd need him in fighting shape for whatever tomorrow threw at us.

As for me, my mind needed rest even more than

my body. And so I intended to sit alone with my thoughts while the others slept before finally nabbing some shuteye. Of course, that plan was quickly foiled when Calina crawled out of her tent to join me at the campfire.

"Is a little peace so much to ask for?" I groaned and cupped my face in my palms. They were warm from the fire, and it felt nice to press them against my exposed skin.

"Yes," she answered, then pointed at the scroll jutting from my pocket. It was the one the guard had provided to direct us to her brother Brugnor.

I sighed and shook my head, too tired to deal with her wild machinations at the moment. "We can go over the plan tomorrow."

Calina pointed even more sharply, then raised a finger to her lips to indicate I should be silent. What was she getting at? Ugh, the quickest way to find out would be to play along, and I did want this over quickly so I could get back to my solitude. With another pointed sigh, I grabbed the map and unfurled it on the ground between us, keeping it safe from the flames.

Calina nodded, pulled the scroll toward her, and then grabbed a small item she'd kept tucked behind her ear. I hadn't even noticed the quill until it was already in her hand, further proof I needed my rest. Calina, on the other hand, looked bright and alert as she flipped the map to its backside and quickly dragged the pen across the parchment.

I remained quiet as I watched. Calina wrote for a long while before finally giving it a rest and pushing the map and quill toward me. The quill, I realized, had come from the supplies Tulip's parents had provided us. As such, it was enchanted to never run out of ink. Very handy for travelers on the road.

I stifled a yawn as I gripped the feather and held the scroll near the fire to read what the elf girl had written. The first thing I noticed was how beautiful her script was, with big swooping letters all drawn in a uniform size and style. My writing was coarse by comparison. I'd never been formally instructed but had picked up what I could while on the road with Gaaron or scribbling down notes about inventory at the tavern. The quill had never felt natural within my grip, and I was far too old to change that now.

I glanced up at Calina, and she pointed at the map and urged me to actually read the message she'd painstakingly spelled out for me. So I did, and it said:

I'm not mad about my dad. I know you must have had your reasons for not telling me. I also know you care about him and are trying to do the right thing by rescuing him from Malfair—

She crossed out this attempt at the necromancer's name and replaced it with *M* before carrying on with her message.

I also don't want to be in charge, but FS is listening through that rock he gave you. He expects me to take the lead. I don't know why, but I figured it would be better to act out a little for his benefit. If he suspects we aren't doing what he wants, he'll spy on us some other way. And it will probably be worse than this. Like he did by pretending to be A. At least with the rock, we can still write out our thoughts to keep them private.

Calina was right. Of course, she was right. I'd completely forgotten about the stupid magic rock Finnian had imposed upon me, but he was most definitely listening whether we wanted him to or not.

The stone felt heavy in my pocket now that I had remembered its presence. Dear sweet divinity, I wanted to chuck it off the side of a mountain now that I realized Finnian was using it to listen in on our every move. But as Calina had pointed out, he'd probably find another way to keep tabs on us—a worse one.

I spread the map back out on a flat patch of dirt and gripped the quill indelicately in my fist as I wrote:

> I know you're not mad, but I'm still sorry. I didn't realize it at first, and when I found out, I didn't know how to tell you. You are right about Finnian. That's really good thinking. I should have known myself, but I'm proud of you for figuring it out and finding a way to tell me.

I set the quill down and waited for Calina to read my message. When she had, she pressed the paper between us and then lay on her belly, propping herself up by her elbows as she wrote.

> When did you realize that your old partner and my dad were the same person?

She turned the paper so that her words faced me, and I mimicked her posture, dropping to my belly to write.

> *The old journal you gave Rurik. I recognized his writing. I had no reason to suspect before then. You look so much like your mom. I thought you were a full elf.*

I spun the map toward Calina, and she nodded before taking her turn with the quill.

> *How did you and my dad meet? And how did he meet my mom?*

Those were both excellent questions. The first I knew well and thought of often, but the second I could only guess at. Still, I did my best to scribble out a satisfactory answer for the girl:

> *We were both in Finnian's guild, neither by choice. Finnian had me since I was very young, but your dad only joined up when he was a bit older. Finnian wooed him with big promises about finding an audience for his art and ensuring his name would be in the*

history books. It was all talk, but your dad wanted to share his music with the world, even if it meant keeping bad company on his way to the top.

I stopped writing and thought for a moment before continuing.

Your dad wasn't a bad guy, but he had a big heart and trusted too quickly. By the time he realized what Finnian stood for, he was already too deep. He wanted out, so we made a plan together. We took a couple of others with us, but they didn't last. For years, it was just me and your dad. And it was wonderful.

Calina scrunched up her nose as she read this, as if she were trying to hold in a sneeze. She thought for a long while before writing the next part.

What about my mom?

I wished I had the answers she so desperately craved. All I had was the truth as I knew it, and I would do my best to convey that to her in its entirety.

There could be no more misunderstandings, no more wedges for Finnian to gleefully wedge between us. We had to set things right—right here, right now.

I envisioned Brynlee's beautiful face as I wrote, how her petite nose pointed up just slightly, the way her cheeks always wore a sparkling rose, the ever-present smile that tugged at her full lips. Calina shared all these same features. She was so much like her mother in appearance but nothing like her in nature. She was like me, but also, I now realized, very much like her father. She would be a good adventurer if she got a better handle on her attitude.

He must have met her before falling in with Finnian. I don't know, and I'm a bit confused. We traveled a lot, and the ladies loved him everywhere we went. I hadn't known he had someone special.

All the flirting and carousing that was one area where they were markedly different.

Did you ever visit Briarhaven with my dad?

No, but he did talk about it often. I decided

to go there when I needed to hide. I missed him, and he had loved that little town so much. Now I know why.

I wish I'd have gotten the chance to know my dad.

You will. If there's one thing I can promise, you will. I'll make sure of it.

Our eyes met briefly after that. I thought I spied a tear shimmering in the pale light of the fire, but before I could tell for sure, Calina grabbed the quill, hopped to her feet, and returned to her tent, shutting me out.

But that was okay. I was ready for sleep too.

The following day, I awoke to trumpets blaring. And I was on my feet, even before I'd fully opened my eyes. My daggers were ready, one clenched in each fist, as I prepared to face whatever threat had wandered into our camp.

"Good morning, sleepy head," Amariel said, still blaring brass. Strange. I thought she only reserved this type of instrumentation for battle.

"You're chipper today," I muttered, resheathing my weapons and placing them back on my person now that I knew there was no threat to dispatch.

"I've had a good rest," she said before pointing to the two tents that sheltered the slumbering youth. "Wake up! Wake up!" she tooted brightly.

Well, at least it seemed she'd be helpful today. That was, if the old girl didn't wear herself out by making this rather intense wake-up call.

I used water from the bladder to wash my face and hands, then grabbed a tanuki cookie for morning rations. There was no time—and there were still no flowers—for my tea, so the cookie would have to be enough.

The kids grumbled as they pulled themselves together. And, honestly, I was happy that their grousing was directed at someone other than me for a change.

Calina was ready first. Once again, she had the enchanted quill tucked behind her ear, a good reminder that Finnian was always listening.

Rurik stumbled over next, his flame held aloft. It looked bigger than the last time I'd seen it on display. He must have spent the midnight hours practicing his craft.

Tulip didn't emerge from her sleeping quarters

until Calina started to disassemble the tent with her still inside. She kicked and screamed but eventually cut the tantrum and came to join the rest of us around the fire.

When everyone had gotten the chance to eat their morning rations—yes, even Tulip was hungry enough to deign to join us—I nodded toward Calina to take charge.

She hopped to her feet and rubbed her hands together. "Okay, guys. Big day. We have to go to Brugnor's estate and get rid of the ghosts. That all needs to be done today to remain on schedule. Tomorrow, we'll return here and offer the guard proof of our completed job so she can let us inside."

"What will we do then?" Rurik wanted to know, always thinking several steps ahead—or behind—the rest of us.

Calina wagged a finger at him. "That's a problem for tomorrow. Our problem for this morning is that the estate is a good distance off. We need to secure at least two more mounts to get us there."

Tulip prickled at this. "What do you mean *two more?*"

"Well, you're carrying Amariel," Rurik answered in place of his friend, unaware that Tulip wasn't simply asking for clarification; she was upset. "And I assume

Tilda and Calina are light enough to ride together. Still, I think three would probably be better."

"This is offensive," she snorted but didn't attempt to leave. "I'm not going to listen to another word."

Calina rolled her eyes and made a dismissive gesture at the centaur. "Then don't listen. Cover your ears or something. It doesn't concern you anyway."

Tulip whinnied, stomped, and ultimately raised both hands to cover her ears as she glared at her rival. Wow, I couldn't believe she'd actually listened. She must have finally realized she was stuck with us and that her theatrics didn't hold any real sway.

Calina smiled triumphantly before turning back to the rest of us. "Right, so for those of you who are still with me, I figure we can get our mounts one of two ways."

"We can barter, or we can steal," I supplied. Finally, things were getting interesting in the way I liked.

Calina pointed at me and grinned. "Very good, Tilda."

"So, which will it be?" Rurik asked with an open mouth and quivering tusk. He didn't like either of our options, obviously. But if he had a better idea, he would have offered it already.

Calina just shrugged. "Eh, let's see what the day brings us. C'mon, crew. Let's go find us some horses."

11

As it turned out, the day brought us to a little farm on the outskirts of Mirathane. We found it almost immediately upon descending the plateau, making me wonder how we'd missed it on the way up. Maybe we'd gotten turned around somewhere, or maybe we'd been so fixated on the keep that we'd failed to notice anything else.

Another black mark for our perception skills.

I had to teach the kids how to look out for themselves, and in the meantime, I needed to make up the difference. I opened my eyes wide as I surveyed the farm, as if this would help me see it better.

The property was unimpressive. I'd take our makeshift camp over this destitute set up any day. It did have one thing that might be useful, though.

A lone mule stood grazing in a scraggly patch of grass just outside a weathered shack. There was also an old wooden cart stacked with what appeared to be empty crates.

In the distance, a withered-looking man tended to a grain field with slow, jagged movements. Every time he swung the scythe to hack at the stalks, he paused, winced in pain, and sucked in a stuttering breath.

"We can't steal from this guy," I told the others as we all stood and watched from a few dozen paces away. The farmer hadn't noticed us, and I wondered whether he even would. Even from this distance, I could tell he was quite old. Maybe not as old as Amariel—humans didn't live that long—but he was decades past his prime. Certainly too old to be engaged in such strenuous physical labor.

Stealing from him would be easy, but it would also be wrong. As a practiced thief, there weren't many situations that gave me pause. This one did.

"But it would be so easy," Calina argued half-heartedly. "He's not even paying attention." The girl had a rebellious side, but her mother had also raised her to be kind and compassionate.

I shook my head. "Yeah, but he hardly has anything to begin with. If we took his animal, it would devastate his farm. Maybe even kill him. Besides, even if we took this mount, we'd still need another."

"Wait. I have an idea," Calina murmured before charging ahead and calling out to the farmer. "Hey, you there!"

The rest of us hung back. If we all came charging at him together, we'd probably give the poor man a heart attack. I turned toward my remaining companions to make sure they'd stay put.

Tulip paid no attention to me. Instead, she snorted and eyed the mule suspiciously. "Whatever that thing is, it's no cousin of mine."

"It's a mule," Rurik said, moving forward to pat the animal on its flank. "Half-horse, half-donkey. It's a pretty good combo. They're stronger, hardier, and easier to take care of than—"

"Say one more word, I dare you," Tulip seethed.

"Obviously, the human-horse hybrid is far superior," the half-orc said with a studious nod, diffusing the situation if only by mistake. "It seemed like you wanted more information, so I gave you some. Nothing I said reflects my own opinion. In fact, I think that centaurs are *always* superior, not just when compared to horses or mules but when compared to any race."

Tulip smiled and reached for the feathered end of

her braid, stroking it delicately as she asked, "Including orcs?"

"Most definitely." Rurik's expression remained serious.

"What about half-elfs?"

He gave a one-tusked smile now. "Do you even have to ask?"

Tulip let out a breathy giggle and stroked at her hair faster than before. "Go on, big guy. Tell me more."

I rolled my eyes but didn't interrupt them. This was good. Rurik could distract our resident princess while Calina and I bartered away some of her supplies, and Amariel did... who knew what? I briefly glanced toward the old celestial and was surprised to find her missing.

Bringing my gaze back to the distant field, I spotted her floating forward serenely, halfway between our group and the crops. Wait, was she actually going to help with something?

I nudged the supply sack away from Rurik and snuck out to join the others in the field. He was so taken by Tulip's attention that he didn't notice me *taking* away our supplies. The cargo was heavy and slowed my gait considerably, but we would need it for barter.

I fell into an awkward step-step-heave combo and

put a dozen or so paces behind me when Calina came jogging back to join me.

"Do you have the chalice?" She held out a hand and motioned for me to hurry up.

I blinked at her, disbelieving.

"The chalice, do you have it?" she echoed. "The farmer is willing to lend us his mule and secure a second mount in exchange for that fancy cup you took from Zephyriel's room."

"But I thought we were going to barter away something of Tulip's." I'm not proud to confess this, but I whined those words.

My companion shrugged. "The cup was the first thing I thought of, so it's what I offered, and he agreed, so give it here."

I hesitated. I hadn't even drunk my tea once from this splendid vessel. Not one blessed time.

"Tilda," Calina ground out. "It's not like it matters. You've had it less than a day. Besides, this way, we don't lose anything important we might need later."

She had a point, but that didn't mean I liked it. Begrudgingly, I offered my prize.

Calina accepted it with a triumphant smile. "See, easy. You know, this leader stuff isn't nearly as hard as you make it look," she added before jogging back to the farmer.

My heart sank as I watched her go. As Calina had already completed the trade, there didn't seem to be any need for me afield. I left the heavy cargo and returned to Tulip and Rurik at the cart.

"The best part is how your flank looks white in some light and golden in others. It's like magic." Rurik was practically drooling now as he openly admired the regal centaur. What a pair these two made.

Tulip shuffled her hooves and... blushed? Yes, she actually blushed. Oh, sweet divinity, somebody save me.

"It's just you and me, bud," I said to the mule as I rubbed his grayish-brown snout. "The rest have gone crazy."

This was confirmed when I noticed a blast of light surrounding the farmer. Amariel had joined the man to heal his aches and pains, which was sweet but would also require far more time than we had to waste right now. We still needed to secure our second mount.

Calina jogged back toward us, stopping momentarily to retrieve my abandoned supplies. "He told me where to go to get the second horse."

This misinformation was enough to draw Rurik's attention away from Tulip. At last. "Actually, this is a mu—"

Calina rolled her eyes. "Yes, yes, this is a mule. The

other mount will be a horse. You guys wait here. I'll be back in two clicks."

I stopped petting the mule and put both hands on my hips. "What about rule number one of adventuring? Have you forgotten it already?"

"Never split the party," Calina moaned in a strange voice that I think she meant to be an offensive—and wholly inaccurate—impression of me. "I know, Tilda, but I won't be gone long. Besides, Amariel needs time to finish her healing ritual or whatever it is she's doing. Can you please just trust me on this?"

Could I trust her? Yes.

Did I want to? Now that was another matter entirely.

Calina was true to her word. She returned to the farm before Tulip and Rurik had even noticed she'd left. Okay, they'd noticed her departure, but they definitely didn't care. Rurik had become far more confident when speaking with his crush, and Tulip had finally realized that the best way to get her ego stroked was to engage the smitten half-orc.

I did my best to tune them out by replaying some

of my favorite tavern songs at maximum volume inside my head. I'd just gotten to "twenty-four mugs of mead on the bar," when Calina came striding back to us, leading a stunning black steed.

Tulip immediately took notice.

"She looks a bit like your mom, huh?" Calina said with one eyebrow quirked. "I wonder if you're, like, long-lost cousins or something."

"She is beautiful, but I hope you know that the centaur race was created by magic, not interbreeding." Tulip practically sounded polite—and when speaking with her sworn enemy, no less. All that flattery from Rurik seemed to be helping our interparty dynamics. Who knew?

"I heard that—" Calina began, but Rurik cut her off.

"I am familiar with the lore." His eyes became unfocused as he reached for a new bit of trivia to share. "Many moons ago, in the Age of Unity, there lived a brave band of warriors called the Centa. They had conquered many lands but soon grew disenchanted by battle and decided to take on a peaceful tribal existence. They were favored by the goddess Equinara for both their mastery of war and their willingness to turn their backs on it. But their former rivals had not forgotten and spent many years seeking out the lost Centa warriors. Once they found them, they planned a siege, falling upon the tribe at night and absconding with all the maidens of the tribe. Seeing this, Equinara became enraged and granted the Centa warriors a boon. She changed their form to give them the swiftness to chase down their foes and the strength to carry the maidens home once retrieved. Over generations, all forgot that the peaceful Centa had ever known war, and eventually the name "Centa warrior" was shortened to centaur." The story had come out so fluidly, it was like Rurik had been reading from a book. Once he finished this recounting, he glanced toward Tulip for approval.

She nodded simply. "That is how the story goes. Not everyone believes it, but I do."

"I do, too," Rurik was quick to interject. When Tulip smiled at him again, he blushed. I wondered if she knew that she was playing with fire—a magical flame, to be exact.

"I don't care about your random lore, Tulip." Calina overemphasized the *P* making a crude popping sound. "I care about getting back on the road and making it to Brugnor's. The sooner we help this hobgoblin, the sooner we can get into the keep. And the sooner we get into the keep, the sooner we can complete our mission for Finnian. And the sooner we—"

"We get it!" I shouted, unwilling to listen to any more of this impassioned stating of the obvious.

The corners of Calina's mouth dropped into a frown, and her brows pinched together. It looked like she was trying to hold something back. Fig, I hope it wasn't tears. I'd hurt her with my outburst, and now I felt bad.

"I mean, we'll get to your dad. I promise." I patted her on the lower back in a way I hoped she found reassuring. "I'm just as eager to see him as you are, remember?"

She appeared placated by this. "Yes, right. So, do you want the horse or the mule?"

"The mule is stronger, so it should take me," Rurik pointed out. "I'm still heavier than the two of you combined, so it only makes sense."

"And are you okay carrying Amariel?" Calina asked Tulip.

"Of course. I mean, it's not like I haven't been carrying her this entire time already. But she's not ready to go." She jerked her chin toward the field where our celestial stood beside the wizened farmer with glowing outstretched hands.

"She'll have to be." Calina took off running toward the field.

"Wait!" Tulip cried. "She doesn't like to be interrupted once she starts her healing spell."

"Too figgin' bad. We need to go." This came from me.

Rurik remained quiet, only caring about facts and information... And Tulip. He rarely interfered with decision-making unless he had a strong logical reason to do so.

"We could just go without her. It may take a while," Tulip offered with a shrug.

But that was not an option I wanted to consider. "And wander into who knows what without our healer?"

Tulip contorted her face in a strange grimace, just as Calina came running back.

"She says she's not done. I think we should leave her," she reported.

I blinked at this show of stupidity from our supposed leader. "You do understand the risks of venturing forth without a healer. Right?"

Calina met my gaze directly, not even willing to consider that she could be wrong. "It's not a big deal. She sleeps all the time anyway. So, really, what's the worst that could happen?"

"We could die," I practically exploded. Our newly acquired horse spooked and let out a frightened neigh. Oops.

Tulip made shushing noises and pressed both hands into the horse's snout, calming it instantly.

"Dying seems pretty bad to me," I continued, this time keeping my volume in check. "In fact, I can't think of much that would be worse."

"You're such a pessimist, Tilda."

"Rule number one, Calina. Rule number one."

"Never split the party," Rurik recited. Well, at least somebody got it.

"Never split the party," I repeated with emphasis, biting out each syllable like it was a delicacy.

Calina pushed Tulip aside and mounted the horse. She did this far less gracefully than most other things and had to climb onto the old wooden cart and then hurl herself at the poor animal to reach its back. "I say we just leave her," she said as she adjusted herself atop the mount.

"No, this is one area where I won't make an exception. I don't care who's leader. Stupid is stupid, and stupid gets you killed." I huffed, marched out to the field, and tugged hard on Amariel's robe.

"We're going," I spat, angry that she'd even put us in this situation to begin with. Did she know how hard it was to wrangle these kids? No, because she never, ever helped.

"Leave me be while I tend to my magic," she sang with a lutist accompaniment. Not this song and dance again.

"No," I spat at her. "You're not here to help random farmers. You're here to take care of our party —or at the very least, Tulip. The clock is ticking, and we don't have time to waste. So let's go." I yanked her by the arm this time, upsetting the flow of light coming from her hand.

As soon as their connection broke, the farmer gasped and fell to the ground in a writhing heap. Uh-oh.

"You absolute fool!" Amariel shouted, then dropped to her knees to tend to the man. "You could have killed him!"

"Well, he's fine," I said once he stopped groaning in pain and grew still. I could see he was still breathing, so it seemed he was fine. "C'mon, let's go."

Amariel shook her head, and her white hair fell loose from the tight bun she preferred to keep it in. "I must begin again. It will take much longer now."

Even I could admit that the poor farmer looked in worse condition than we had initially found him in. His eyes were shut tight, but his mouth was open wide.

He looked like a fish that had been removed from the water, sucking at the air but finding no relief as his limbs spasmed in an unpredictable series of stops and starts.

Okay, maybe Amariel wasn't being dramatic. Maybe she did need to finish her healing rituals once they'd begun. No, not maybe. Definitely.

In the future, the trick would be to stop her from ever starting. For now, though, that left us with two equally unappealing choices: wait it out and lose precious time or proceed without our party's healer.

I glanced toward the young elf girl that Finnian Sly had appointed as the leader of this mission. She sat atop her horse, staring arrows at me. When she noticed me looking, she raised her hands to make a funnel and shouted at me through them. "Tilda, let's go!"

Well, I guess that decided it. We'd be riding into our next mission with no backup and no idea what we were up against. What could possibly go wrong?

12

I didn't claim to be a great rider. I'd spent most of my life journeying on foot—or, more recently, not journeying at all. But despite my severe lack of experience, I'd still have done a much better job piloting the borrowed black stallion.

Unfortunately for me, Calina refused to give up the reins. And I couldn't even argue with her, seeing as it took everything I had to keep my arms circled tightly around her waist as I held on for dear life. I was going to fall, and when I did, I would die in one of two equally horrifying ways. Either I'd break my neck on impact, or I would be trampled to death by Rurik's mule as it struggled to match our horse's frenzied pace.

Personally, I didn't care for either of those options.

I wanted down, and I wanted out. Stupid Finnian

Sly and his stupid side quest. We could have been through Nexara by now and quickly closing the remaining distance to Maltherius's lair if my old master hadn't so rudely intercepted us. Or maybe the fault was my own. Maybe I had missed another disinterested guard, one who could have been bought for a much easier price.

Stupid Brugnor and his stupid sister.

Yup, I hated everyone right about now, including myself. But it was Calina who drew the worst of my ire. She now had the guard's map unfurled before her, completely blocking the view ahead as she tried to puzzle out the best path.

"Dear sweet divinity, will you put that thing away!" I shouted into the wind and got a mouth full of winged insects for my trouble.

"As long as the horse can see, I don't need to!" Calina continued her reckless multitasking, completely unbothered by my panic.

"What's the matter, little Tilly?" Tulip called ahead in a sing-song voice. "Are you afraid?"

"Yes, I'm afraid! And I'm not too proud to admit it!" I ground out through clenched teeth. I didn't want to ingest another bug; that just introduced more ways to die—such as choking on an unwanted projectile.

Nope, no more talking, Tilda. Only holding on for dear life.

Rurik's mule finally caught up, and he smiled at me as he pulled up alongside my insane stallion. He clutched the saddle horn tightly, turning his deep green skin a pale mint. At least it seemed I wasn't the only one afraid. That made me feel a little bit better, though it wouldn't stop me from dying. Death was something you had to do alone. Bringing company didn't make it any less final.

Besides, if Rurik fell from his mount, he'd just have to walk off the hurt.

I would die, plain and simple. And Amariel wouldn't even be here to make my passing any less painful.

I hated this. Surely there was some other way into the castle? Stupid hobgobliness and her stupid side quest. *Stupid, stupid, stupid.*

"What's that writing all over the back of the map?" Rurik asked now. "Something about—"

"SHUT UP, YOU BIG OAF!" I bellowed with everything I had in me, briefly losing my hold on Calina and falling to my death.

No, wait.

I didn't fall.

It just felt like I had.

I was still seated firmly in place. Only now, my head was spinning, and my breaths escaped in shallow gasps. Actually, it felt like I couldn't breathe at all.

I couldn't breathe, but I also couldn't let Rurik read out what was written on that map. Finnian Sly was still listening through the bewitched stone he'd slipped into my pocket, and scribbling notes on the back of that parchment was the only way Calina and I had to communicate in private.

Why did Rurik always say the thing that was meant to remain unspoken? Did he have no etiquette at all?

I guess I shouldn't have been surprised by this behavior from an orc, even if he was a half-breed. Humans didn't have all that much decorum either.

Rurik fell back, and I noticed him clumsily swiping at tears with one fist while desperately clinging to the saddle with his other. "Duh-don't yuh-yell at me."

"She didn't mean to insult you." Calina tried—and failed—to pep him back up. "It's just Tilda's kind of freaking out right now and not exactly at her best. We can't talk about the map, okay? Just trust me on that."

Rurik grunted in response but made no effort to rejoin us at the head of the stampede. Hopefully, he'd fallen in with Tulip. She'd make him feel better.

She'd also keep him from heading off to sulk on his own.

At least, I hoped she would. I couldn't exactly turn back to ensure our party was still together, and I didn't want to risk inhaling another lungful of bug by opening my mouth to shout. I hoped by now the kids had internalized the first rule of adventuring. I'd certainly shouted it at them enough.

Ugh, how much longer would this crazy journey take? I just wanted to get to the spot the guard had marked on her map, so we could finish our business with Brugnor and put this whole thing behind us.

We'd promised to return the mounts to the farmer when we no longer had need of them. That at least offered a modicum of solace. Because, honestly, I'd rather walk across hot coals than spend one more moment than necessary on the back of this blessed beast.

I sure hoped Calina knew how to read a map properly. We had a lot of distance to cover and couldn't afford to go the wrong way. I was useless in my position—not because of my blind panic, but because I couldn't see all that well in general.

Couldn't see. Couldn't speak. Couldn't do anything other than wait and hope that death either took me quickly or didn't come at all.

Hours passed as we galloped across open meadows and along forested paths. My muscles ached from being clenched for so long, but I didn't dare loosen my grip. Not even when Calina complained that I was squeezing too tight. I only had one life and refused to let go of it so easily.

I had almost gotten used to the nonstop terror when Calina slammed the stallion to a halt. My nose bonked into her back from the sudden lack of momentum, and I cried out in pain.

"Shhhhh!" she chastised me while motioning for the others to stop. "Do you hear that?" she asked hardly above a whisper when they'd finally closed ranks.

"Hear what?" Tulip asked.

Calina shushed her, too.

Rurik still wasn't talking to us, it seemed.

Okay, what was going on here? I bravely removed one hand from around Calina's waist, allowing myself to turn and get a better view. But as soon as I did, Calina swore under her breath and urged the horse back into a gallop.

And I fell.

Because, of course, I did.

I knew these kids would be the end of me...

But before I could hit the ground, somebody

swept me into their arms and then proceeded to squeeze the remaining life out of me.

"What is she doing? Is she insane?" Tulip hissed as she set me on my own two feet. "You could have died, and I still don't even know what it was we were supposed to be hearing." Yes, those two things were definitely of equal importance. *Sigh.*

Rurik closed his eyes and held one finger in the air as he listened to the surrounding sounds of the forest.

All was peaceful for a moment until Calina came running straight back at us, shouting at the top of her lungs. "Bandits! Go, go, go!"

All three kids took off on fast hooves, forgetting I only had my own stumpy halfling legs to serve me. I watched in only partial disbelief as they disappeared over the horizon, leaving me to face down a fast-approaching troupe of bandits on my own.

The first of the bandits—a troll—came charging at me, club raised, fangs bared. He was big, strong, and ugly as sin. But also slow.

It was no trouble at all to simply take two giant steps to the side and send him crashing headfirst into a tree. Ha, that reminded me of Rurik with the kobolds.

I chuckled to myself, taking a brief moment to enjoy this small victory. After all, it would probably be the last one I got.

A half dozen of the troll's bandit buddies crested a wooded hill, rushing toward me with an assortment of deadly weapons glinting in the scattered sunlight bursting through the trees. Uh-oh.

An arrow whizzed past me and sunk into the ground a few paces to my rear. Calina?

No, it was another bandit, sniping at me from the treetops—figgin' fantastic.

Well, I'd need to dispatch that one first, so I clenched one of my daggers between my teeth and started to climb. The bigger thugs wouldn't be able to reach me up high, and once I took care of their archer, I'd have a safe distance to plan the next stages of our skirmish.

Right now, however, It was time for less thinking and more doing. My body was a well-honed weapon. It knew what to do.

The ranged tree bandit saw me coming but couldn't get away. I had the goblin archer cornered in the worst possible way—well, for him, at least. For me, this was fantastic.

I smiled around my glinting knife as he inched back on his chosen branch. It couldn't hold us both, and I wasn't planning on falling. Been there, done that. Barely survived.

I hung close to the trunk, keeping one hand out to steady myself, then whipped my blade end over end, flying so fast he didn't even see it coming. He probably noticed my dagger when it lodged right into his eye socket, though. Blood went gushing all over the place as he screamed, grabbed at the hilt, and then fell straight down to the dirt. Dead.

That was one.

How many bad guys did I have left?

Seven? No, eight. The troll had gotten back up and now looked even more menacing than before. He charged at my tree, pressed his palms against the bark, and started to push with all his might. The dude was buff, but not nearly strong enough to take out an aged oak. Unbothered by his display, I stayed put on my perch, surveying the scene below.

"What do you want with me? I haven't got anything worth stealing!" I tried to reason with the horde.

"If you haven't got any treasure, you're probably out to steal some too." This came from a slobbering goblin.

"Not up for a little friendly competition?" I challenged. Wrong move.

"This is our territory, and we don't like to share," the same goblin said—their leader, I supposed.

"What do you mean you don't like to share? Haven't you ever heard that sharing is caring? I mean, I care. And because I care so much, I'm going to let you in on my plan, okay? Let's start with facts. There were nine of you when we started this whole thing. The way I see it, you can either let me go, or we can keep subtracting from that total until we hit zero. There, now I've shared my plan. Your move."

"Raar, we no care! Come down from tree, little half-half!" the troll boomed. Idiot.

The sound of galloping hooves caused everyone to pause and glance toward the horizon. Yay, the kids had come back for me! Now, it was time to really get this party started.

While the bandits' backs were still turned toward my fast-approaching reinforcements, I skittered down the tree and lunged for my missing dagger, dislodging it from the goblin corpse's eye with a squick.

Tilda's fully armed and loaded, baby! Let's dance!

13

The kids burst into the clearing, sending our relatively calm showdown into absolute chaos.

Tulip shouted and huffed as she kicked up a mighty cloud of dust. I don't know what purpose she thought this served, especially since none of her words were ones I recognized, but at least she had shown up. She cut an intimidating figure that was sure to unsettle our foes, and if I could get her angry enough, she might also throw a punch, a kick, or improvised weapon to help us out.

Calina was the perfect picture of silence as she moved with deadly precision, running her horse in increasingly tight circles around me and the combatants and pushing us all together. I hoped she'd eventually remember her weapon or realize that I was stuck in the fray and didn't appreciate being edged in.

It was still progress, though.

The girls had voluntarily joined the battle, and both were focused on the bandits rather than each other. We'd come a long way from that siphon fight in the deserted mountain town. A long way, indeed.

Rurik joined a few beats later, unable to get up to speed on his mulish mount. He pounded to a stop at Tulip's side and slid off his mule in an inelegant heap, landing on the ground with a resounding thud. He was nothing if not resilient, though, hopping right back up and immediately summoning his flame cantrip, which he waved in front of the bad guys with a series of menacing grunts.

The troll jumped back in fright, but the others—a mix of orcs, goblins, and hobs—hung close. Their bodies stuck by me, but their eyes were on Calina, who'd fallen back and begun fidgeting with her bow. She seemed to have some difficulty staying astride the horse while preparing her weapon, so her solution was to stop running altogether and focus on one thing at a time. The seconds ticked away like sands in an hourglass as she twisted and turned in an effort to free one of her arrows from the quiver on her back.

Strategy didn't seem to be a strong point for these

bandits. They should take me out while I'm close, then move on to the others. Couldn't they see I was the leader here?

Tulip continued her inane stomping and let out an ear-splitting neigh that spooked Rurik's mule and sent it running for cover. The orcish bandits stared at her slack-jawed, making me wonder if this strange admiration for the horse girl might, in fact, be a cultural thing.

Rurik also turned to Tulip with a besotted smile, taking a moment to appreciate her presence before bringing a second flame out to play.

The troll cried out as he fled from the group, and Rurik followed with slow, steady steps.

Meanwhile, the hobgoblins and their lesser cousins swished their mix of daggers, cutlasses, and morningstars defensively as they advanced on Calina. Sweet divinity, I hoped that none of these guys were the Brugnor we'd been sent to help. That lady guard probably wouldn't take too kindly to us murdering her brother in cold blood.

Actually, you know what?

My blood was running mighty hot right now. And with Rurik currently distracting the troll, I saw my chance. I lunged after him, then climbed that big boy like the blessed tree, quickly ascending to his shoulders.

What a lovely position from which to slice a throat. *Squip!*

"Down to seven." The troll buckled and fell, and I deftly hopped off my fallen mount, landing with both daggers held out before me and ready to stab some more. "So, fellas, tell me. What comes next?"

"Si—"

I'd have slapped myself in the forehead if both hands weren't currently clutching at my new set of daggers. "Gods, Rurik, so help me, don't answer my rhetorical battle banter. Just focus on the opponent closest to you."

A flurry of activity broke out then.

Calina, still mounted on the ebony steed, circled the group, firing arrows like a maniac. Thank the divine, she'd finally readied her weapon and had even figured out how to use it while moving about on horseback. Of course, many of the arrows missed their marks, but just as many hit. Unfortunately, she'd emptied her entire quiver into a single opponent—one of the hobgoblins—and now she was out of ammo.

An orc rounded on her, sweeping the horse from its feet with his maul. No, no, not good!

Calina soared one way as the horse stumbled the other. Both would survive but were also down for the count. "See?" I shouted. "This is why we don't leave our healer behind!"

"Sh-should I answer?" Rurik sputtered as one of his two flames blinked away. "Because it really seems like you're asking a question, and I don't want to be rude."

We were down to six—two orcs, three goblins, a hob. Even if Rurik dropped the flames and went fully tribal as he had with farmer Dewglen's giant locust infestation, he would still be no match for his full-grown, battle-hardened brethren. Calina struggled to get back to her feet, but she'd taken some serious damage from being thrown.

That left me and Tulip. The orcs were no longer enamored with her and were now fully present in the battle. That meant all her shouting and stomping was only tiring her out—and giving me a bit of a headache. I needed more from her. Much more.

Luckily, I knew exactly how to get Tulip Thunderhoof fighting.

But first, I had to ensure the others stayed out of our way. "Rurik, shield up, buddy. Protect Calina."

He grunted and did as he was told, still hanging onto a flame with one fist. That thing was like a security blanket, which would have been great if he could do any real damage with it. *One thing at a time, Tilda. One thing at a time.*

"Tulip," I crowed. I needed to shout at the top of my lungs to ensure she heard me over her own ruckus. "Tulip, I need you to listen to me!"

She narrowed her eyes and dropped her hooves, standing in impatient silence as she waited to hear me out. Good, good. Shutting her up was the hardest part. The rest would be child's play.

"These guys are bandits," I explained with as much dramatism as I could muster. "They're dirty, no-good thieves, and they're looking to steal any valuables they can get their greedy, disgusting hands on. Hang tight to your axe because you know that's the first thing they will try to take."

She snorted and scraped her hoof through a crush of desiccated leaves. But she also deployed her blessed battle axe. "Nobody steals from me and lives to tell the tale."

Yes, yes, this was the exact right response.

Sure, Tulip had taken some creative liberties with the, uh... truth. She'd never killed a single creature. The other two had at least faced the bugs and the kobold army. But this was Tulip's first real battle, given that the only foe she'd struck during our rumble with the siphons was... Calina.

But she had such a beautiful innate rage. We could use that. I could use that.

I jerked my head to the side, knowing her gaze would follow. "To your right! That orc is trying to sneak up on you. He's going to take it. Don't let him!"

"Oh, like Infernus, he's going to take it!" she stormed, sweeping hard to the right and kicking her hind legs to slam him in the chest. "What's mine is mine, and nobody else's!" she seethed, chest rising and falling rapidly with the sudden burst of effort.

"That's a great start. But he still hasn't paid for what he tried to do!" I shouted. "Finish the job. Show him who that axe belongs to. Show him what it can do. Swing! Slice! S... Seriously injure the guy!" I wished I had a third great S-word to throw at her, but my heart was pounding hard, adrenaline pumping. My body was at its best, but my brain was blurry from the sudden high.

We didn't need poetry. We just needed dead bodies.

"Off with his head, Tulip. C'mon. It's him or us!"

Tulip let out a battle neigh and charged after the orc she'd already hoof-punched hard. Still breathing heavily, she raised her sparkling, gem-encrusted weapon high overhead and brought it down with all her might. His head shot clean off his shoulders, leaving a vicious spray of blood in its wake.

"Great job, Tulip," I cheered. "That makes five. We're almost done here. Take out the other orc. I'll go for the goblins."

Tulip snorted and galloped to her next target, swinging that axe with reckless abandon as she huffed out horse curses. She was covered in blood and gore but didn't seem to notice. Thank goodness for that.

I slit the remaining hob's throat and then went for the goblins, but an arrow zipped past me, making short work of my next target. I jerked my head to the side just long enough to see that Calina had recovered her bow and a handful of arrows. Rurik must have taken it to her on his way to shelter her with his shield.

Great job, team!

"Oh, forget this!" one of the goblins moaned as he and the other last man standing took off at a run. Calina took each of them down with a well-placed arrow.

And just like that, we finished our math lesson for the day.

Nine minus nine equals zero.

14

I yanked the last of Calina's special steel-tipped arrows from their fallen quarry and shoved the lot back into her quiver. The poor girl still sat where she'd been thrown, her legs tucked to the side with Rurik's shield embedded in the ground before her.

"How are you feeling?" I asked gently as I attempted to retrieve the arrows we'd lifted from the bandit archer. They were poor quality and splintered in my hands. Oh, well.

Calina sucked in a sharp breath as she attempted to pull herself up using the shield as leverage. "My leg's hurt," she explained, dropping back to the ground with a wince.

"Can you walk on it?" Rurik asked as he attempted to help her up.

"I think so. I just need a moment." Calina waved off his offer of support. "Ugh, why didn't we wait for Amariel to come with us?"

I practically choked on the groan that threatened to rip itself from my throat. I'd wanted to wait for Amariel. I'd even tried to force her along. It was Calina who insisted we leave without her, and now—big surprise—she was the person who needed our missing cleric the most.

"Take a breather," I muttered, turning my back so she wouldn't see me roll my eyes. It was simply too hard to control my face and my voice at the same time. If I didn't find something else to distract myself with, one of them would inevitably betray me. I cast my eyes around the makeshift battlefield until at last an idea sparked.

"The rest of us can check the bandits for loot," I said with a big smile as I turned back toward the kids. "C'mon, Rurik. Tulip."

Rurik nodded and moved to the nearest corpse to pat it down.

Tulip, however, remained stuck in place.

"Tulip... Tulip, you still with us?" I called with increasing agitation. It looked like she'd fallen prey to some sort of stasis spell, but that was impossible. Our opponents hadn't fought with anything besides their weapons and brute might, and our own wizard only knew how to cast a dinky flame cantrip.

Speaking of... *Whoosh!*

"Suh-suh-sorry," Rurik cried as the corpse before him was quickly consumed by flames. He tried to reach through the blaze to set things right, but immediately learned what a foolish idea that had been. "I... I didn't muh-mean to..."

Rurik tried reaching for the body again, only to hiss and flinch away in pain.

When I saw him rear up for a third attempt, I rushed forward and tugged hard on both of the half-orc's shoulder. "Dearly divine, I told you to loot the bodies, not torch them. What gives?"

I wasn't strong, but he wasn't coordinated. My actions were enough to make him fall back on his butt.

"I cuh-couldn't see, so I thought maybe with a little extra light..." He began inching toward the fleshy inferno once more, but I put my foot down. Literally stomping on his hand so he wouldn't hurt himself again.

"Big guy, I know you love that flame of yours, but can we just be honest here for a moment? That thing has caused us more harm than good at this point. Are you sure you can't—I don't know—fight with a weapon instead?"

He held his injured hand near his chest and rubbed at it pensively. That single tusk of his quivered as he fought back tears. "I'm going to get better. I just need more practice. Practice takes patience."

I shook my head in dismay. "You know what doesn't have patience? A maniacal necromancer with a deadline. I know you want to improve your magic, champ, but we may not have time for that."

"Leave him alone," Tulip said, coming out of her fugue and snapping me back to the present. "I believe in Rurik, so why can't you?"

"I didn't say I didn't believe in him. It's just... We could have used whatever supplies that corpse had on him." The body was still burning, and if we didn't put it out soon, the rest of the forest would catch too. I shuffled over and began to heap dirt onto the flames.

"We have more than enough supplies, Tilda," she snorted, not bothering to look at me as she moved forward to kick dirt at the corpse with her hooves. With Tulip's help, the last of the embers were quickly killed.

"What we don't have is proper training, and that's on you," she said when we were both satisfied with our amateur fire-fighting escapade. It seemed I would not be escaping her disdain, not until she said whatever else was on her mind.

"So you're teaming up on me now? Is that it?" I groused as I went to check the other stiffs myself. The least we deserved for all the trouble with the bandits was a fresh bounty of supplies—and maybe a small peck of treasure.

"I just think things will go better for us if we act like we're on the same team," Tulip said as she watched my every move but made no effort to help. Looting was beneath her, I guessed, given that she always got whatever she desired the moment she wanted it.

Well, her spoiled princess act may have worked on her parents, and it might be enough to win over Rurik too, but it wasn't going to convince me. "Are you kidding me right now? That is what I've been saying this whole time."

"Saying, maybe." Tulip flipped her braid over her shoulder and stared down her annoyingly pert nose at me. "But not *doing."*

"As much as it pains me to admit this, she's right," Calina piped up from behind Rurik's shield. Wow, they really were conspiring against me.

"So what? You and Tulip are best friends now?" I challenged, kicking at one of the fallen orcs when I found he had nothing of value in his pockets.

"More like begrudging allies," Calina said with an alarmingly neutral expression.

I turned toward her with a look of bafflement. There was so much I could say in protest, but also I wanted this—wanted them to get along. So what if they turned on me in the process? It wasn't my favorite thing ever, but progress all the same.

A small smile tugged at one side of Calina's mouth. "Hey, we fought the bad guys instead of each other this time. You noticed that, right?"

"Fine, fine. I yield." This wasn't a battle worth embarking upon. Especially since I was in the wrong here. Maybe. I mean, I'd gotten so used to the kids bickering I hadn't noticed when they'd stopped. Now, the only one with a bad attitude was me.

"He's hurt. He can't bear any extra weight." This came from Tulip, who first coaxed the mule back and then found her way to the injured stallion that had accidentally thrown Calina during the brawl. I watched in contemplative silence as the centaur communicated with her equine cousin—or not-cousin, depending on whether or not you believed the lore.

I still assumed that somewhere back along the timeline, someone had lain with a horse. Humans would mate with pretty much anything, and they did so whenever they got the chance. The fact that our party's other two members were both half-breeds was proof enough of that.

After several breathy back-and-forths with the steed, Tulip summarized for the rest of us. "He wants to come with us to see Brugnor. He's too afraid to be left alone after the whole situation with the bandits. He says he can still carry a passenger, but I think he's just trying to be brave."

"How close are we to the spot the guard marked on the map?" I asked Calina, who was already reaching into her quiver to retrieve the scrolled parchment she'd stashed there.

"Not far. The next settlement is close. Probably why the bandits were camped out here. We should be able to make it within an hour or so."

I chewed on my lower lip, reaching my arms forward. "Can I see?"

"No." She rolled the map back up and stowed it away. "You just have to trust me to lead, remember?"

"How are you going to lead when you can no longer walk, and our mount can no longer carry you?" Logic would prevail. Eventually. Maybe.

"C'mon, Cali. I'll get you settled on the mule. I can walk." Rurik gallantly helped his elf-friend to her feet and then atop the waiting mule. He then turned to me askance. "Do you want up too, Tilda?"

"Only if I can hold the reins. Otherwise, I'll walk."

"You can walk then," Calina told me coldly.

I had to bite my tongue. Literally, and it hurt.

A smile broke out on her face a moment later. "Just kidding. I don't care if you steer. It's better than you squeezing the life out of me from behind. Can you help her up, Rurik? Just be careful of my leg. It still hurts."

I wondered if it was the same leg she'd injured when Tulip hurled her from the conveyance at the start of our adventure, but I knew better than to mention past hostilities when everyone was currently playing together so nicely.

"Let me help," Tulip said, shocking us all by scooping me up and carrying me over to Calina and the mule. "I have a better vantage point." She plopped me onto the mule with ease, then brushed her hands together as if ridding them of something filthy. "There we go."

"To Brugnor?" Calina asked from behind me as I squeezed the reins in my fists.

"To Brugnor!" the rest of us answered in chorus.

Finding Brugnor was not nearly as tricky as I'd feared. The map took us straight to the nearest settlement, and the very first villager we encountered gave us clear and simple directions to his abandoned estate.

As the guard had confided in us: not many hobgoblins held land, which meant Brugnor was well known in these parts. He'd also lived here for years as he carried out the indentureship that had earned him this estate.

It all seemed simple enough, although I did wonder why our kindly peasant helper could barely contain her laughter as she instructed our group on which turns to make to land us at Brugnor's front door.

"Left from here, then right at the abandoned wagon, and right again at—hahahaha, sorry, sorry—right again at the pub. You should be able to—hehehe-hehe—see it from there."

If this entire side quest was a joke, so help me...

But the chortling villager had steered us straight, and the estate was easy to identify. It was the only grand dwelling we'd seen since entering town, which meant it stood out.

And Brugnor's home was truly a thing of beauty. As I surveyed the three-story structure's deep slate walls and enormous windows wrapped in iron trim, I could see why the ghosts had decided to move in. If I could, I'd haunt this place, too.

Oooh. What treasure might we find inside? And would Brugnor be willing to give us any as his way of saying thanks once we'd cured him of his unwanted guests?

Maybe I could get an even better chalice for my wildflower tea.

Yeah, that would be nice.

"Tilda, are you coming?" Rurik said this, standing beside the mule with his arms outstretched, waiting for me to jump into them.

I had no problem dismounting a stationary animal, however, so I resisted his offer of help and hopped down of my own accord. "Yup, I'm ready," I answered with a nod as I continued to inwardly salivate over whatever treasure—and bonus reward—might await us inside.

Rurik moved toward the front door and raised his fist to knock.

"Nope, we're heading straight in. We already know we're invited." Calina pushed through the double-doored entryway, which was rather helpfully unlocked, and our small group ventured inside together.

Tulip needed to bend forward at the waist in order

to fit, but she did so with minimal complaint, which showed real growth, I thought.

Save for the steady clomping of heavy hooves, everything was quiet. Too quiet.

I raised a finger to my lips to keep the others silent as we searched the ground floor. Calina's newly acquired injury caused her to drag her leg in an awkward shuffling gait, but otherwise, we moved as... well, as ghosts.

In search of ghosts, yeah.

I pulled ahead of the group, trusting my experience in dungeons. I might be rusty but it was still—

Thump!

"What the—" I spun around just in time to see a net fall from the ceiling and trap Calina underneath.

"Calina, I'll help you," Rurik whispered and rushed forward when—

Crash!

A suit of armor fell forward and pinned Rurik to the ground. Luckily, he was big and strong and able to wrest the thing aside.

"What's going on?" Tulip asked, taking careful steps back.

Clang! Clang! Clang!

Some kind of hollowed-out bell started to go crazy. It was almost as if Amariel had rejoined us.

"Traps," Rurik moaned, rubbing at the side of his face that was missing a tusk. "This place is trapped."

"You think?!" Wait, wait. I'd promised to be more sociable. "You think... right," I course-corrected a bit awkwardly as an ornate clock began to spin in dizzying circles from its spot on the wall. One of the floorboards also rose up on one end before slamming back down and sending a billow of dust into the otherwise still air.

I stepped up to the rotating clock and yanked it from the wall. Little iron gears continued to churn and spark within the wall. So not ghosts, not magic. We were dealing with a wayward artificer here, and from the positioning of both this clock and that ceiling, I wagered he was someone of modest stature—much like myself. "Definitely traps, which means we're not dealing with ghosts here," I summarized for the kids. "Something living is haunting this place."

"Because ghosts aren't real," Rurik grumbled, crossing his arms over his chest in his closest approximation of a tantrum. "I tried to tell you."

"This time, you were right, but that doesn't mean you're always right, and it doesn't mean ghosts can't exist in other situations. That would be a... what was it? Oh, right. A logical fallacy."

Calina pounded one fist into her chest and then saluted with two fingers. "Wow, Tilda. Respect."

I just smiled as I set the broken clock on the floor to free my hands. "See, I do listen to you when you talk, Rurik. Even when you talk for way, way too long. Now, nobody move while I find and dismantle anything else that might be lying in wait. Stay there and stay quiet. Got it?"

"Got it," the kids answered in a scattered chorus.

I quickly sifted through the surrounding rooms, dislodging and disarming trap after trap. Some were a bit more sophisticated, like the tapping floorboards and windows that open and shut by some invisible mechanical force, but most were akin to the falling suit of armor and the spinning clockface.

All very curious if you asked me.

This place was booby-trapped to the gills, but most of the traps were nothing more than annoying inconveniences, nothing that could seriously injure anyone.

Someone had gone to great lengths to set this all up, but why?

15

"Tilda! Tilda! Come back! Come back!" Calina shouted from below while I was performing a bit of careful reconnaissance on the estate's upper levels.

A hot bolt of fear lanced my chest, and I took off running, moving as fast as I could while artfully dodging the traps I hadn't yet gotten the chance to disarm. Were the kids in danger? Did angry spirits inhabit this place, after all? Or had whoever set those traps come back to check them? Both?

Dear sweet divinity, I hoped it was not both.

I moved as silently as I could, given my hurry, hoping to take any interlopers by surprise. When I soft-footed back into the main entranceway, I didn't find any ghosts or monsters, but rather a gnome in court dress regarding the teens with a curious smile.

"Well, well, well..." he drawled with a regional twang. "So you're the leader of this *misadventuring* party, I take it?" He chuckled at his painfully obvious joke as if he were the royal court jester. He looked like one, too, given his ridiculous dress.

I remained on the bottom step of the stairs to give myself a bit of added height; this enabled me to look the gnome directly in the eye. I crossed my arms and scowled at him. "Are you the purveyor of all these traps?"

"Tilda, I think you may have misused that—" Rurik began, but our gnomish challenger cut him off.

He tutted and shook his head before speaking. "I do not buy or sell traps, but I do make them. And set them. Now tell me, why are you here? It's such a bother to reset these things just because some curious wanderers decided to play squatter."

"We're not the squatters here. You are," Rurik interjected with obvious distaste as he moved between us, standing right in front of me and blocking my view of the others.

"Yeah, this is Brugnor's estate," Calina shouted louder than the situation required.

"What? How do you know Brugnor?" The

gnome's words had lost their previous bluster. It seemed the kids had unsettled him with their bold—and seemingly correct—assertions. This would be even easier than dealing with a legitimate haunting. All we had to do was get this guy to leave and promise not to come back. And intimidation, at least, was one skill my party of amateurs had mastered.

Rurik stepped to the side to give me a better view of the situation.

Tulip and Calina both stood with crossed arms and dangerous glares pointed right at the unsettled gnome.

Rurik's expression remained peaceful, his stance open. But he also did not mince his words. "Let's just say we're here to secure justice for our dear hobgoblin friend. Are you standing in the way of said justice?"

"This was my house before it was his," the gnome answered with a casual sniff, adjusting his dark, steel-framed glasses on his nose. "It is my house still."

"That's not what we heard," I said, eager to put this whole thing to rest. "We heard that—"

"Tilda, please. I've got this," Rurik interrupted, displaying a confidence so uncharacteristic that it left me dumbfounded.

"Pray, tell me, good sir. What is your name?"

What the what? Was Rurik really trying to lean on

his social skills? That was so not his strong suit. Still, I chose to keep quiet to see where this would go.

The gnome stood straighter, fingering his jacket lapels with gloved hands. "Why, I am Lord Pellinick Twiggleby, and who, pray tell, are you?"

"Rurik Bane of Briarhaven by way of Mystwood Keep."

Twiggleby bowed deeply, then straightened and stretched onto his tiptoes, looking all about like a startled prey animal. "Mystwood Keep? So you're here on behalf of... Of the Regent?"

"Yuh-yes," Rurik stumbled, but only momentarily before recapturing that same confident, charismatic veneer from before. "One of his prized guards has been distracted on the job lately, thus endangering the safety of everyone within the castle compound."

Rurik's stutter had shifted some of the power back to his verbal sparring partner. Twiggleby dropped flat onto his feet and jerked his chin up, staring Rurik down from waist-height. "I don't see how that's my problem."

"This guard is worried about her brother's well-being, one Brugnor. I believe you are acquainted."

"What do you want? Get on with it already." Twiggleby crossed his arms to match the girls and gave them each a scowl in turn. He seemed to grind his heels into the floorboards, staking his claim to the property.

Rurik's voice deepened and slowed as he chose each word carefully. "Brugnor fled this estate because he believed it to be haunted. But it's not, is it? It was filled with your traps."

The gnome blinked hard but didn't speak.

Rurik smiled slightly as he continued. The power had shifted back in his favor. "Brugnor earned this estate with years of servitude. It is his by right and by law. The regent would be very unhappy to learn of your shenanigans."

Twiggleby appeared to fold in on himself as he brought clenched fists before him and shook them in supplication. "Please, please, this doesn't need to make its way back to the regent."

Rurik quirked an eyebrow. Good gods, he was really doing this—doing it and succeeding. "So you will vacate the premises at once, correct?"

"I cannot leave." Twiggleby's voice cracked as he fought back a sob. "You must understand. My home is all that I have left."

"But it's not your home, is it? This estate now belongs to Brugnor."

"Yes, yes, I know. But try to understand. I made that deal with him years ago. Back then, I still had everything: my wife, my family, my reputation." He paused and choked on another, larger sob. This was one gnome who didn't want his emotions to show, not that Rurik would have been bothered one way or the other. "I have lost all that in the time since. The estate is all that remains, and I cannot afford to lose it."

"Hmmm. What's it worth to you?" Calina asked, leaning against the hall wall with her arms still folded defiantly across her chest.

Lord Twiggleby turned to her in desperation; his whole body shook as he fought to keep his emotions contained. "You can have anything you can carry. You can have all of it. Just please leave me within these four walls. I have no other place I can go."

Well, this was an interesting turn. I surveyed the foyer, taking a quick inventory of its many riches. This place couldn't hold a light to Zephyriel's treasure room, but it was still nice—very nice.

"You know we can't do that," Rurik answered without even conferring with the rest of our group.

"I do?" Twiggleby squeaked.

"You do. Because deep down, you are a respectable gnome. Titled even. Pray tell me, is this any way for a lord to behave?" There was that "pray" again; it irked me, though I couldn't quite say why.

A shudder racked through me as I raced to speak. "Um, Rurik. Maybe we should discuss—"

"There's nothing to discuss," Rurik cut me off. "What's right is right, and what's wrong is wrong. In this case, *very wrong.*"

"Is that it?" Tulip asked, shuffling her hooves in boredom. Unlike Calina, she'd dropped her intimidating stance almost as soon as the conversation had started. She'd spent the last several moments wandering up and down the hall and admiring whatever bric-a-brac she happened upon. She'd stopped wandering and started playing with her thick braid now as she whined, "Are we done here?"

"Almost, my sweet." Whoa, Rurik was moving from confidence to hubris. I had to put a stop to his role-playing before it landed us somewhere we didn't want to be.

He marched straight up to Lord Twiggleby and raised his finger. The disgraced gnome didn't even come up to his chest. When Rurik saw that, he squatted down so his finger hung in the poor guy's face. "You knew you wouldn't abandon the estate despite the deal you had made with Brugnor many years prior. You also knew that hobgoblins are deeply superstitious. Marrying that with your natural affinity for artifice, you faked the haunting and moved in once you had Brugnor out."

Twiggleby rolled his eyes and sighed. "Yes, and?"

"And it was a miscarriage of justice, which we are here to correct."

"Please don't hurt me." The gnome flinched and took two giant steps away from Rurik, which unfortunately backed him straight into the wall.

Rurik snapped back to his full height in surprise, temporarily forgetting his role. "Wh-what? No, I won't hurt you, but I will ask you to leave."

"No," Twiggleby practically boomed. I was surprised such a deep, resonant sound could come from such a small, prissy body.

"Okay, then we'll just have to report back to Eldrin Grimlock." Rurik turned toward the door, paused, then fixed his gaze on the gnome once more before whispering, "He probably will hurt you."

"No, please!" Twiggleby inched along the wall as if he planned to flee through some back exit, but Calina was there and ready to put the kibosh on any escape attempts before they could materialize.

"Our hands are tied." Rurik sighed and shook his head as if the next words hurt him to speak. "You can leave of your own accord or be forced out. Which do you prefer?"

"Neither?" Twiggleby squeaked a second time.

"That wasn't one of the choices, you dolt!" Calina interjected with great vehemence, shoving the smaller man to the floorboards.

"I can't." Lord Twiggleby's voice cracked as his body heaved and shook with fright. "Please, please, I can't."

"Okay, enough of this." I marched forward, fixing Calina with a stern look as I helped Twiggleby back to his feet. "I'm going to find Brugnor. He should at least be included in this conversation, right? Everyone just try to relax while I'm gone, and for the love of all that is divine, try to keep your hands to yourself!"

I found Brugnor at the local tavern. The poor chap was practically pickled, sitting in a bottomed-out ale barrel he'd obviously emptied into himself. I was tempted to join him, soaking in the scents and sights and thinking back to the beautiful friends I'd left behind in Briarhaven.

But no, needs must.

After a wrestling match to extract the drunken hob from the barrel, I kept him propped up as we stumbled back to the "abandoned" estate. I wasn't sure he understood who I was or what we were doing, but I knew having him present would help yank us out of our standoff with the gnomish squatter.

When we stepped onto the porch, Brugnor jerked away from me and practically threw himself down the steps in a desperate attempt to flee. "No! No! I can't go in there!"

"Yes, you can. It's your house, and I'm here to make sure it stays that way."

"But the spirits! They'll be very displeased!"

"The only spirits you need to worry about are the ones you drank." I helped him to his feet, then shoved him forward with all my might, sending him crashing through the doorway. "Just trust me on this, okay?" I whispered a bit more gently, feeling a sudden rush of sympathy for the poor drunken fool, as I ushered him across the threshold.

Brugnor struggled against me and let out a keening wail, more befitting a child than a fully grown hobgoblin. Somehow, in all the hubbub, he caught sight of his former master, Lord Twiggleby, and suddenly fell still. "Pellinick? What are you doing here? Don't you know this place is haunted?"

The gnome hesitated and glanced at Rurik, who offered a stern nod. "Tell him the truth."

"It's not haunted. Someone placed traps and—"

"Tell him the whole truth," Rurik urged with a tone that left little room for argument.

Twiggleby cleared his throat, then mumbled, "I placed traps to make you think it was haunted."

Brugnor hiccuped, his mouth hanging open as he studied the gnome he'd thought he knew and trusted. "You did? Why?"

"To keep the house, of course." The gnome rolled his eyes, even though he had zero room to condescend in this situation.

"But you promised it to me." Brugnor appeared crestfallen as it all finally connected.

"It's all I have. Please let me stay." The disgraced lord's words should have sounded more sincere than they came across, but the other creature seemed too inebriated to notice.

"But it's all I have, too. That and a huge tab at the tavern around the corner." Brugnor hiccuped again right on cue.

"If you won't share, then we can cut it in half so that you each have a piece," Calina suggested with a shrug.

"Like how? Build a wall down the middle?" Tulip chimed in brightly. "Or I can cleave it with my axe!"

I rubbed at my temples and growled. "That is the

stupidest thing I've ever heard, and I worked as a tavern wench for over a decade."

"No, no. Calina's right," Rurik said thoughtfully. "Well, sort of. They could share."

"How do you mean?" Calina asked, fully invested now that her idea was being actively considered.

"Brugnor served Twiggleby faithfully for many years."

"Twenty-five years," Brugnor slurred.

"For twenty-five years," Rurik continued. "Now I think it's Twiggleby's time to return the favor. Are you in need of a man-servant, Brugnor?"

"But I am titled nobility!" The gnome argued with a new burst of passion.

"Yeah, but you also said you lost everything, including your reputation," Tulip pointed out with a yawn. "And I'd bet you also lost your title as part of that. When do I get to cut this place in half? I still really like that idea."

The gnome didn't speak.

"Do you want to stay?" Rurik dropped to his haunches and looked the lord right in the eye. "It seems the only way you can is if Brugnor takes pity on you. And honestly, why should he? You lied to him. You went back on your word."

Brugnor ambled over and slapped his hand on Twig-gleby's shoulder with a resounding thud. "You can stay, Pellinick. After all these years, I consider you a friend, and I'd have hoped you would think of me the same."

"Really?" Calina balked at this. "Even after the whole trick with the traps?"

"Even then," Brugnor said thoughtfully before ruining the moment with a beer-drenched belch.

"Surely, I could stay as an equal," Twiggleby attempted in a last-ditch effort to receive everything and give nothing.

"You don't deserve to stay at all. Lower yourself or get lost," Tulip huffed and stamped a hoof, which caused Twiggleby to jump and press himself against the nearest wall.

"Fine, fine. I accept."

Rurik nodded solemnly. "Great. Now, please fetch a bit of parchment. We're going to draft a new contract, and this one will be magically bound."

"Meaning?" Twiggleby asked from his safe spot on the wall. The paisley pattern of the paper matched his waistcoat almost perfectly, almost like high-society camouflage.

"Meaning if either of you steps out of line, the fires of Infernus will rain down upon you." Rurik stretched out a palm and sent up a magical flame to further prove his point.

"Yes, yes, of course. Brugnor, go and..." Lord Twig-gleby stopped short. "I mean, I'll just go fetch the papers myself."

"Good," was all Rurik said as the gnome hurried up the stairs and out of sight, and I finally picked my jaw up off the floor. It would take me days to digest what had just happened here, if I ever even managed to figure it out at all.

16

We left Twiggleby and Brugnor in good spirits. Brugnor was still a bit too intoxicated to fully understand what had happened. However, he still happily provided us with his family seal, which was the one thing we needed to deliver proof of our successful mission to his sister, the guard who had set us on this whole ridiculous quest in the first place.

A part of me wondered if I simply could have requested the seal when I first roused him in the tavern. Regardless, it felt good to set things right for this relative stranger. He'd been underestimated and manipulated because of his race, and that was something I could identify with. Folks were always expecting less from me because of my short stature. It's why I made sure my attitude loomed so very large. Nobody looked down on Tilda Quickthatch. Hopefully, Brugnor would also keep his wits about him well enough to fight his own battles in the future. Similarly, I hoped that Twiggleby had learned a lesson he wouldn't soon forget.

The gnomish artificer did appear properly apologetic; he even worked up a mechanical leg brace for our injured horse, which enabled him to carry a rider again. We tried placing both me and Calina on his back, but that proved too much. Tulip still refused to let anyone other than Amariel mount her, so that left me squeezing onto the mule with Rurik.

I had difficulty hanging onto his thick waist, but the journey was more manageable overall with the orcish fellow at the reins. Rurik knew his weaknesses and worked hard to compensate for them. His lack of ability as a rider meant he kept to a slow and steady clip.

This—plus the stallion's injury—meant we had to set up camp for one night before returning to Mystwood. We stopped smack dab in the middle of a beautiful meadow filled with delicious wildflowers. I sent up a prayer of remembrance for my lost chalice as I fixed my tea in a plain metal mug.

Even though my herbal brew wasn't fancy, it was still good—and I felt happy to have it.

Rurik came to sit beside me as I tended the fire. Both girls had already retired to their tents, and I'd assumed Rurik had gone off alone to while away the evening. Obviously, I had assumed wrong.

"Today was a big day," he said, fixing his coal-black eyes on the dancing flames.

I nodded and used a stick to rearrange the shifting wood inside the fire. "It was, and you did great. I didn't realize you knew how to create magically bound contracts. That was very impressive."

Rurik shrugged and rubbed his palms together. "I don't."

I stomped on the stick to ensure it didn't hold any lingering sparks, then tossed it to the side and turned to my companion with wide, unblinking eyes. "But you told them—"

"Twiggleby's already proven once that he can't be trusted. I don't know how to bind contracts, but I figured if he believed I did, he'd be more likely to stay true to his word." He met my gaze head-on and offered a lopsided grin. "Just a little bit of mental manipulation. Sometimes that can be like magic, too."

I chuffed at this. Definitely impressive. "I didn't realize you had it in you."

"I don't think I did either." He chuffed too, attempting to mimic my gesture, but his different anatomy plus the missing tusk made it come out like some poor fool's dying breath. A bit of phlegm also loosed itself from his maw and fell upon his knee. Didn't bother me, but he was lucky Tulip hadn't witnessed this little show of brutishness.

We sat in companionable silence for a while, me enjoying my tea and Rurik lost in thought as he rubbed at his soiled knee.

"All those traps," Rurik mumbled, startling me from my stupor. "They were like magic, too. I've never seen anything like it."

"Well, we don't have any artificers around town in Briarhaven. They're more common in the big cities. Especially ones that host a lot of gnomes or dwarves." I tried to recall whether I had ever met a halfling artificer on my travels, but the answer was a resounding no.

Rurik grunted softly. "But that settlement was much smaller than Briarhaven. Why do you suppose Twiggleby settled there?"

"Well, maybe he's a bit like you. You know, breaking the family mold."

Rurik's lips tightened at this, and I wondered if what I'd said offended him. "His work was masterful," he stated emphatically, even though I hadn't suggested otherwise. "Those traps were silly but impeccably made. But me? I'm not getting any better, no matter how hard I try. I'm just silly." He sighed and ran one thick palm through his hair. "I'm trying so hard, Tilda. Every night, I read, I think, and I work on channeling my innate power. I do everything I can think of, but I never get any better."

So we were having one of these talks. I guess Rurik and I were due. I thought back to the tense words we'd exchanged in this same forest after the dispatching of bandits. "It takes time, right? Patience."

"But you said we don't have enough of either. What if my inability to improve endangers the others? Zephyriel said we'd see two deaths. What if they're my fault?"

I sucked air in through my teeth. "Prophecies are a tricky business. For all we know, those deaths could be metaphorical. Or the first body could belong to Eldrin Grimlock, you know the guy we were sent to assassinate?"

He sighed and leaned back on his palms, his chin lifted skyward as if searching amidst the stars for an answer.

I stood and forced him to look at me. The tea sloshed in my mug, but didn't spill. "Listen up because I don't say this often and can't promise I'll ever repeat it, but, kid, believe me, you're doing a good job. The way you handled that dispute over the estate was masterful—there's no other word for it. And your flame has been getting bigger, burning brighter."

"You're just saying that." He turned away, no longer willing to make eye contact.

"I can't force you to believe me."

"And I can't force you to wait for me to catch up with the others. Calina has always been so good with her bow, and Tulip chopped off that bandit's head in a single slice. That kind of power is just *wow*." He kept his gaze studiously fixed to the ground, but I doubted he was seeing anything. He'd lost himself again, and nothing in the real world could anchor him.

Still, I had to try. "You're pretty wow too, though, Rurik. You know that, right?"

He shook his head slowly, steadily, not unlike Amariel's metronome. "It's not enough. I'm not enough, even though I try so hard to do the right thing."

"Rurik, you are plenty. Some might say you're too much. But not enough?" I laughed here to lighten the mood, which was something we both really needed right about now. "No, I would never use those words to describe you."

His brow furrowed at this, and he met my eyes again at last. "I'm too much? I'm sorry. I try to—"

"That wasn't meant as an insult. Just an invitation to reconsider." Poor kid. I had no idea he beat himself up like this. It made sense, though. Rurik focused hard on achieving results, yet he hadn't grown in his magic for weeks—for as long as I'd known him, at least. I'd complimented his flames, hoping to make him feel better, but he was right. He wasn't making enough progress to keep showing up as a wizard.

He'd proven himself with the property dispute. He could battle well with words, but in combat? And especially against Maltherius and his undead hordes?

Were we dooming ourselves with this unfounded optimism? Was it kinder to dash his dreams before they grew too big for either of us to manage?

Now that he'd mentioned Zephyriel's prophecies again, I worried about her deadly decree. Someone would die. Maybe metaphorically, but maybe in fact. What if it were Rurik?

At the start, I'd wanted nothing to do with these annoying teens, but as we'd traveled together, they'd grown on me. I liked them and wanted them to succeed, but more than that, I wanted them to live. Rurik deserved to fulfill his heart's wish, to master magic, and become a mage of great renown. He couldn't do that if he died in some dank necromancer's dungeon.

Something flashed, drawing my eye. I looked down and smiled. It was the bracelet Brynlee had fastened to my wrist as the kids and I prepared to depart town. I traced an index finger over the glittering loop of gemstones and summoned her sweet face in my mind.

Brynlee was the very best person I knew, and she believed in me. She believed I could carry out my mission and keep the kids safe while I was at it. If she trusted me to get the job done, shouldn't I also be able to trust myself?

Yes, I should. And also...

"I believe in you, Rurik. In you and your magic."

"But after the run-in with the bandits, you expressly said you didn't. You said I should give up." He cast his gaze at the fire, revealing the beginnings of tears.

I nodded. "I did say that. Then. But now I'm saying something different. I have a right to change my mind, yeah?"

He considered this for a moment, then shrugged, sitting up straight again and raising the palms of both hands in confused surrender. "Yes, but that makes you even more likely to change it again later. You've made it very clear that you think I'm wasting my time with this wizard stuff, that we'd all be better off if I just accepted my fate and became a barbarian like my parents."

"It's not my choice to make."

"More and more, it seems like it's not mine either. Like fate already has it all figured out, and I'm just playing out decisions that were made long before I was ever born."

I sat down beside him and crossed my legs under myself, placing one hand on his arm in solidarity. "I can relate. Quite a lot, actually. But even if someone else is calling the shots, does that really change anything? We still have to live our lives the best way we know how, and for you, that means magic."

Rurik finally smiled. "And for you, that means protecting those you love at any cost."

"Wow, you really just read me like one of your books."

"Well, I had to leave them behind, so the only thing I have left to read is people." He smiled again, and it warmed me more than any fire ever could.

"And your favorite new bit of reading material is one, Ms. Thunderhoof," I said with a muted chuckle.

"What? Hu-how did you know?" Rurik straightened and glanced around in panic, worried I would reveal his "secret" to the others even though they weren't there to hear it.

"Relax. I'm just teasing you. Also, I'm pretty sure it's obvious to everyone except Tulip herself."

"You mean, Calina?"

I nodded. "Yeah, she definitely knows."

"I don't want to hurt her, but I can't help how I feel."

"I get that. And love can be its own gift, even if it's never returned. Hold on to that feeling because love is one of the most powerful forces in the whole world."

"You're saying I should channel my love for Tulip into my magic? That it will make me better at wielding it?"

"I am definitely not saying that. Mostly because I have no idea how magic works. All I know is that I feel better when I think of my secret crush and what she means to me. Sometimes it's the only thing that keeps me going."

"Calina's mother. She loves you, but not in that way."

I hugged my arms around myself and rocked back and forth with gentle bliss. "Ah, but she loves me. And that is more than enough."

"Do you think Tulip loves me too?"

"Bit too soon to tell, buddy. But you'll have your whole lives—or at least the rest of this journey—to figure things out." I yawned and stretched my arms overhead. It had gotten late, and I'd long since finished my tea—time for bed. "See you in the morning, champ," I said, rising to my feet and preparing to head toward the tents.

I gave Rurik one last glance before I turned away. He smiled and rubbed the stubble on his cheek. I recognized his new expression: one of hope.

I had said that love was the most powerful thing of all, but I knew that it was hope that would keep us going... even when it would be better to stop.

At the end of the day, I knew I would give everything I had to bring Gaaron back to his family. I just hoped I wouldn't be asked to surrender something that wasn't mine to give.

17

The following day, I woke to quite the surprise. Last to sleep, first to wake—that was my style. But when I emerged from my tent that morning, I found the rest of the camp had somehow disappeared as I dozed. The kids had packed up everything and then moved to a distant clearing to spar with one another.

I crept closer to their battle playground, stealthily staying out of view. But they were so enthralled in their current activity they probably wouldn't have noticed a herd of wild hordebeasts charging at them.

Rurik's voice boomed across the fields. "Calina, you're quick and light. Use that to your advantage. If you have to fight close range, be ready to dodge and get out of there as fast as you can. Find the high ground and rain arrows on your opponents until they drop. But, uh, try not to unload your full quiver into a single body. One arrow per foe. Two if they take too long to drop. As a general rule, shoot two more before returning to that first with a second arrow. Got it?"

"Battle is chaos!" Calina sang out as she dodged away from the gnarled branch Tulip was using as a makeshift maul. "There shouldn't be any rules, especially ones that involve math."

"Battle can be chaotic, but if you want to win, you need to apply a bit of logic. Fight with your brains and your weapons, and no one will be able to defeat you." Rurik grunted and grabbed hold of Tulip's forearm.

She huffed but let him keep his hold.

"Tulip, you swing with too much force. Your blows are powerful, but they exhaust you too quickly. Try a fast strike to throw your opponent off balance. It will slow her down, and then you can hit with all your might. The other guy—or, uh, girl—won't stand a chance."

Tulip leaned into his touch and batted her thick eyelashes. "I cut that orc's head off. Did you see?"

Rurik reflexively reached for his own neck but wore a smile rather than a grimace. "I sure did. And it was a thing of beauty."

The two held very still as they smiled at each other.

Was this even real? I glanced back toward my tent, half-expecting to see I'd left my body behind me and was experiencing some weird ethereal reality.

"Hey, Rur!" Calina called from several paces away, drawing everyone's attention including mine. As soon as Rurik turned away from Tulip, Calina fired her bow sans arrow. "Pow! How's that for a long shot? You're dead now, Tulip."

Tulip stomped. "I am no such thing!"

Rurik chuckled as he hung his head. "She got in that shot, but you aren't the type to be taken down by a single arrow. You're a barbarian. You fight close range. Close the gap!"

Tulip reared back and prepared to charge, and I went sprinting toward them to break things up before this escalated too far.

"Hey, hey! That's quite enough!" I waved my arms wildly overhead to make sure they were focused on me and not each other. "What's going on here?"

"Hold your fire!" Rurik called to the others and jogged my way. "Hey, Tilda. We were just sneaking in some training while you grabbed some extra sleep."

"Training?" I asked, blinking into the bright sun.

"Well, yeah. Our talk last night made me realize that I'm not progressing with my own studies, so it might be a better use of our time for me to teach the others. I prefer sorcery to swords, but that doesn't mean I can't pass on what I know to the others."

I wanted to insert some humor into the situation, but I'd learned that Rurik preferred to keep things literal. Also I was currently too stunned to call upon my signature wit. "What I just saw out there was mighty impressive," I said plainly, reverently. He was doing what I had failed to do all this time—and far better than I'd have been able at that. "How'd you learn all that?"

He covered his lower face with one hand and chuffed. It was clear he'd been practicing the gesture and had come quite a ways with it too. He dropped his hand and wiped it off on his trousers, then tutted at me for good measure. "You don't know much about orcish culture, do you? War is life. It's our whole reason for being. Everything we do is about training for battle. Work, play, even just relaxing at home. I didn't reject the family business without first giving it proper consideration. I trained and learned just like everyone else, and that's exactly how I know it's not for me."

Huh. I didn't know what to say to that, so I nodded and changed the subject. "Did you guys already eat your breakfast? Are you ready to get back on the trail?"

Calina came jogging back and playfully slapped Rurik on the shoulder. "Yeah, Rurik put us on a tight schedule. He ensured we did all the musts before we could start on the wants. Like training, which I would argue is a must, but that's just me."

"We've survived this long without training. Besides, we've already wasted time that we might not have. I wanted to make sure we were ready to get back on the path to Mystwood as soon as Tilda woke." He placed a heavy hand on my shoulder, causing me to stumble. This kid didn't seem to know his own strength—or my relative weakness. "Grab a tanuki cookie, Tilda. I'll break down your tent, and then we can go."

Well, who was I to argue with that?

We finished our journey steadily, stopping to return the mule and the horse to the impoverished farmer before ascending the plateau to the castle compound.

Amariel rejoined the party but looked exhausted from her work healing the gaunt old man. He, however, appeared nice and spry, almost as if he'd shucked off a few decades since we'd seen him last.

"What happened to her?" the old celestial

demanded with a brassy boom when she noticed Calina's limp.

"Thrown from her horse in battle," Rurik stated with a note of pride.

Amariel grumbled under her breath as she extended glowing hands toward the elf girl.

"I'm fine. It already feels better than it did yesterday," Calina argued and attempted to pull away.

"Uh, you should probably leave her to it," I warned, remembering the gruesome scene with the farmer the last time we were here.

"We have to get to the keep. We don't have time for this!" Calina argued and threw up her hands.

"Take my mule with you, and just leave him when you're finished," the farmer said. "There are no wild predators on the plateau. He knows how to get home to me."

And so Rurik lifted Calina onto the mule while Tulip took charge of Amariel. That left Rurik and I to guide the group, one walking ahead and the other walking behind to ensure nobody fell off. We switched positions occasionally to keep things interesting because when any of us attempted to chat, Amariel shushed us with an angry snap of the reed.

Relief flooded me when, at last, the keep's outer walls came into view. Had a part of me expected to fail so soon into our journey? Yes, I realized with sickening clarity. The largest part of me believed each step would likely be our last. But look how many we had already taken—and largely unscathed at that.

We could do this. We could really do it, especially now that Rurik was sharing his expansive battle knowledge with the girls. We had our healer back too. Yes, things were looking up for Team Tilda.

We continued our approach, and I spotted the hobgoblin guard amongst the others with no difficulty. By the time we reached the gate, I had even concocted a plan to get her alone.

"My companion was attacked by a bandit," I said tersely, motioning to Calina on the mule's back. "And before he died, he gave us a message." Out came the seal we'd received from Brugnor, which I flashed before the castle's security team.

My hob guard's eyes grew wide, and she muttered something under her breath that I didn't quite catch.

"He said it was for his sister and that we would find her here," I pressed.

"Well," the half-giant leader prompted. "Out with it then. The sooner you deliver your message, the sooner you can leave."

I clucked my tongue and shook my head. "He said it was only for his sister. Honestly, he didn't even want to tell us, but you don't always get to choose who hears your final words, seeing as we'd already stabbed him deep in the gut." I shrugged and glanced at the guards apathetically.

When nobody moved to offer the requested privacy, I turned back to the road that led down the plateau. "I did my part by coming here. If you don't want to hear his message, so be it. C'mon, team. Time to go."

Rurik and Tulip exchanged a confused glance but didn't argue as they fell into step behind me. Calina kept quiet as Amariel continued to send healing magic flowing through her.

One, two...

Frantic footsteps sounded behind us. *Three!*

"Wait!" the hob yelled after us. "You spoke with my brother? What did he say? Come back and tell me. I'll find us someplace private."

We let her usher us around the corner and into a private garden, remaining quiet all the way.

"That's Brugnor's seal. Is he really dead?" she asked, shaking her head in disbelief the entire time as she fought back deep, wracking sobs.

I stared at her, dumbfounded. I hadn't known many hobs in my day, but between Brugnor and his sister, they didn't seem to be the brightest cabbages in the patch.

"No, he's fine," I hissed, fighting the urge to roll my eyes. "You sent us to help him with the haunting, remember?"

"But you said..."

"We needed an excuse to spend some time alone with you, so when you return to your post, make sure to look extra sad. And you can have this." I passed the seal to her but decided to keep the map in case Calina and I needed to use it to write notes to each other again later.

The hobgobliness blinked back the last of her tears and sniffed. "So you helped him? The ghosts are gone?"

"There never were any ghosts. It was an artificer playing games with him," Rurik explained with far more patience than I had remaining. "It was quite a brilliant plan, and the craftsmanship—"

Nope, we didn't have time for professor Rurik right now.

"As you can see from the seal," I jumped in, taking back my control of the situation. "Brugnor was satisfied with the aid he received. And now it's time for you to deliver on your end of the bargain. Get us into the keep."

She stumbled back a step. "Come back in a few days, and I can—"

I took three big paces forward, getting right up in her face—or rather her belly region. "No, you will get us in today."

"I didn't expect you to return so fast." She stepped back again, and this time I stood my ground rather than following in close pursuit. "Or at all, really. But since you're here, it will be much easier if you wait for the weekend. On those days, the gates are open to anyone who wants to enter the keep."

"Did you really send us out on a job knowing that we could have achieved our payment for free?" Rurik demanded.

"We should stomp you into the grrrrrrounnnnnnd where you stand," Tulip neighed, sounding extra equine in her anger.

"Any last words?" Calina asked, hopping down from the mule, grabbing the dagger from my boot, and brandishing it with inexperienced hands. Noting this trouble brewing, the farmer's mule took off running down the hill. Well, that was one problem taken care of then.

This whole display, while unquestionably over-the-top, worked wonders. Good job, kids! While Rurik had now become their official teacher, it seemed I'd rubbed off on them a bit too.

"Mercy, please!" the guard cried. "I will get you in today. See, s-s-s-seee! Your quest was not wasted. I can get you in today. Otherwise, you would have had to wait."

"Fine," I snapped, motioning for the kids to settle down. "How are you going to get us in?"

She leveled her gaze at me, her jaw set hard like granite as she whispered, "The dragon wagon."

"The what now?"

"Regent Grimlock is expecting a delivery of juvenile dragons for his private collection, and their handler will bring them in later today. He comes every few seasons with a large wagon that hardly fits through the gate. There will be plenty of room to hold you lot as well. Even the big one." She hooked an elbow toward Rurik, but refused to glance his way.

"So you want us to climb into a dragon's hold willingly?" he asked, shifting his weight from one foot to the other and back again. "That's just asking for death or dismemberment."

"Yeah, and as you can see, my fine green friend here is already dismembered," Tulip interjected with a snort.

The hob hushed us and then dropped her voice

low. "It won't be long. Just long enough to move through the gates." The guard began to scribble on a scrap of paper she withdrew from her breast piece. "The handler's name is Shim. He's a friend. Give him this, and he'll let you into his wagon."

I nodded my understanding, but Calina grabbed my shoulder and spun me to face her. Her violet eyes were wide with fear, and that was something I'd never seen in them—or her before.

"Tilda, this is crazy. Are we really doing this?" She stood shaky on her feet, but apparently Amariel's work was now done. She was healthy of body, but not of mind. I'd never seen her look so afraid. I wasn't exactly thrilled about getting up close and personal with a clutch of untrained juvenile dragons either, but we also had to get into that castle by any means necessary.

So I acted like it didn't bother me, hoping my false show of confidence would calm the rest of my party.

"Yup," I said with an extra pop on the P-sound. "We're really doing this."

I marched back down the hill with renewed purpose, waving one hand above my head and motioning for the kids to follow. "All aboard the dragon wagon. Next stop: Mystwood Keep."

18

A well-known rule amongst adventuring folk was to never work with children or animals if you could avoid doing so. Unfortunately, these days, it seemed those were the only sorts I found surrounding me.

This so-called dragon wagon would surely be at least double the trouble it was worth, adding a lengthy yet unknown list of things that could go wrong. But right now, it was our best bet to get past those gates. And time was ticking past at a worrying clip.

The kids remained relatively quiet on our march back to the bottom of the plateau. I didn't care if it was because of fear or exhaustion because I also felt both to an alarming degree.

At least we were making progress. Soon, we'd

complete our mission and be free of Finnian Sly, ready to face down Maltherius and save the day. And I refused to wait even a second longer than was absolutely necessary.

That shifty hobgoblin guard had instructed us to find the dragon master Shim and hand him the note she'd scribbled down hastily before entrusting it to me. Any concerns I'd had about locating the mysterious merchant disappeared before we'd even half-descended the plateau. Shim stuck out in a pronounced way. After all, he was a human, dressed in flowing garish colors, standing next to an even more ostentatiously decorated wagon presumedly filled with young dragons.

As described, the wagon was so massive that I wondered whether it could genuinely fit through the gates and cross into the castle compound. I also wondered how the scrawny human would pull its massive bulk up the slope. No horses, mules, or even dragons were attached to the front. Did that mean he himself had magic?

Whatever. It didn't really matter how he helped so long as he did.

I marched straight over and thrust the hob's note at him while studying the enormous vehicle with growing distaste. Like Tulip's ill-fated conveyance that had carried us through the earliest part of our journey, this cart had no windows, although it did have one narrow door locked securely on its backside. The remainder of the cart sported a poorly drawn mural of many different types of dragons standing on their hind legs and holding hands as they appeared to dance amidst a field of flowers. The words *DRAGON WAGON* were painted in bright colors with bold, sloppy strokes. Additional script ringed the upper perimeter; I guessed that it was the same moniker spelled out in multiple languages.

"Well?" I prompted as the man continued to puzzle over the brief note for a needlessly long time. "You are Shim, aren't you?"

He nodded and sucked air in through his teeth, then crossed back to his transport, unlocked the door, and swung it open. Without even peering inside, he crumpled the small scrap of paper and tossed it into the cart's dark interior. "But are you sure you want in here? Really?" he asked as a burst of ice exploded from the wagon and shattered the note mid-air.

Welp, definitely dragons in the wagon. "We're sure," I said with far less confidence than I'd previously felt about the situation.

"It's just that juvenile dragonlings like these can be a bit unpredictable. They're still learning the way of the world, and their little bodies don't do a great job holding back all the magic they've got coursing through their veins. It will be..." He stopped speaking, sighed, and shook his head. "You know what? It's your funeral. If you want to climb inside without having me there to keep them tame... well then, I won't stop you. But I'm also not going to come crawling to your rescue. So do what you want."

Funeral? What the fig was that? Humans had such odd expressions and customs, and Shim seemed even more peculiar than most. For one thing, he had no hair. Anywhere. Not on his head, face, or the parts of his body I could see. Not even an eyebrow. What gave?

"Tilda, I don't want to do this," Calina said, yanking on my arm to pull me away from Shim and his vibrating container of critters. "Let's just scale the wall. It can't be that hard."

I ripped my arm away and turned back to the others. "Stop. We haven't got a choice."

"No choice, you say?" Shim's eyes suddenly glinted in a way that reminded me of my old master Finnian. "Pray, tell me, what's this little trip worth to you? At least five gold coin, I'd wager. Or that beautiful pink battle axe I spy."

Tulip neighed with rage but failed to form any words in common.

"We already paid our way by helping that conniving, little guard friend of yours. Let us on or—"

"Or what?" the man challenged, using his lanky frame to loom over me in a way I did not like at all.

My pulse quickened, even as I outwardly stood my ground. He was going to make this difficult, wasn't he? Another human with poor impulse control. Would we have to fight our way inside? The five of us could easily take on a single human opponent, but what if he brought his dragons out to play?

"You don't have hair," Rurik blurted out, and for the moment, I was grateful for his lack of social graces. "That's because of the dragons, right? Hair burns too easily. It would be an occupational hazard."

Shim chuffed. "You're right. This occupation comes with many hazards. Usually, I can whip the dragonlings into shape, but... well, you catch fire once, and that's enough. I'd rather be hairless than covered in nasty burns."

Tulip snorted and dragged a hoof menacingly through the dirt. "For your sake, I hope you don't honestly whip them."

The dragon master staggered back a step. "No, no. Of course not. Getting in there with them is dangerous, but it's survivable. I'm still here, aren't I?"

Tulip did not look satisfied with this answer, and

in truth, neither did I. But we also didn't have any other options. "Just so you know, nobody touches this axe except for me. If you try to take it, I'll take your hand—or your head. This beauty is really sharp. It can cut through pretty much anything."

Shim gulped audibly and moved behind me, like I could shield him from the peeved-off horse lady. He certainly shrank down to my size in a snap. "Fine, you've paid your way," he said with a voice that shook wildly. "I'll collect what I'm owed from the lady hob. On you go."

"Our chances of death or dismemberment are higher than fifty percent. I'm not exactly sure how much higher, but probably a lot," Rurik contributed.

"We will be safe in the conveyance," Amariel chimed, floating past us to be the first onboard the dragon wagon.

"She does know this is a different cart than before, right? That there are actual figgin' dragons on it?" Calina practically screamed. I found it endearing that she was now using one of my preferred curse words, but I agreed with her worries. How could I not when we were about to mount a literal death trap on wheels?

"If Amariel says it's safe, then it's safe," Tulip said with a stomp. "She's old and sleepy, but she's not stupid. So go ahead already." She shot another warning glance toward Shim, who'd already made himself scarce, having seemingly disappeared to the other side of the cart.

"After you, princess," Calina challenged with a big, sweeping wave of both arms.

"Figure it out or get left behind," I ground out as I passed them both. Pulling myself up the high steps into the raised wagon was a struggle, but it beat standing around while those two bickered. Besides we had a tight schedule to keep.

Amariel had already positioned herself in the middle of the cargo hold, asleep but glowing with barrier magic. She'd created a safety bubble for the rest of us, and I eagerly dipped into its shining embrace.

As the kids fought over who would board next, I surveyed our new digs. I had no idea how long we'd have to wait inside the hold, but I now knew we'd be safe—or at least safe enough, thanks to Amariel's peaceful magic. The wagon stood at least five halflings high. Cages were stacked two, sometimes even three high, covering every spare speck of three walls. The fourth wall was the one that held the door and a few scattered taming supplies. And, of course, nearly every-where were stains from either dragon breath or leavings from the other end.

"We are safe in the conveyance," Amariel said again,

with woodwind accompaniment, though I couldn't be sure she was actually awake anymore. All this made me wonder if our group would always be safe in all conveyances or if Amariel herself just had a particular fondness for this form of transport.

Rurik joined us in the bubble with big, heavy steps, then Calina crept in on quiet feet, and finally, Tulip clopped over to round out our group.

"I don't like seeing creatures in cages," the centaur whined. I didn't like it either, but I far preferred the cages to allowing the dragonlings to roam freely around us.

"Do you think he really whips them? That he hurts them?" she asked Calina, who simply shook her head with a pained look.

Shim's face appeared in the open doorway. "Everyone settled?" he called, not waiting for a response before he slammed the door shut, confining us to the near darkness.

A flame zipped to life beside me, so close to me that it melted a few of my arm hairs—just as Shim had explained when asked about his unnaturally smooth appearance. Amariel's protective barrier kept me safe from the fire-breathing dragon across the hold, but not from the bumbling half-orc beside me.

"Ack, you've got to be more careful," I cried and scooted away from Rurik.

Rurik shrugged and snapped off the flame. "You're the one who doesn't have night vision."

"There's still some light from Amariel's barrier," I answered through clenched teeth as I rubbed at my sore arm. "Give me a little while, and I'll be able to see things just fine. Besides, this whole wagon is made of wood. Having your flame out is way too risky in here."

"I doubt that. There are bound to be fire-breathers aboard, especially considering what Shim said about his hairlessness. It wouldn't make sense for the cart to not be warded against their flames."

He had a point. Still didn't mean I needed the orc melting a hole in my arm whenever the wagon jostled us.

"Oh my gods, this one is the cutest!" Calina squealed from somewhere I couldn't see, but it didn't sound like she was close enough to still be within Amariel's wards.

"Ouch!" she cried mere seconds later, and I was not at all surprised. "It bit me. It actually bit me."

"Can we all just sit still and keep our hands to ourselves? I don't know how long we're going to be stuck in here, so make yourselves comfortable and stop causing problems. Maybe take a nap like Amariel."

I was summarily ignored as Rurik left the bubble's protective embrace to study one of the specimens up close. "Fascinating," he murmured. "While all are dragons, no two are exactly alike. They are adapted for their specific, unique environments. And these adaptations also align with their magic types, like this one which seems to be from Sandsibar. It's small, close to the ground, and a light brown. It would be nearly impossible to spot racing across the dunes. It could sneak right up on you and—"

"Can we just not?" I asked with a groan.

"But dragons are the very embodiment of the elements, of the purest magic in existence. There's so much we can learn from them. What a treat."

"They're not books for you to study, Rurik. They're living creatures," Calina argued, having moved on to a different, smaller cage. "And I want to have one as a pet."

"Dragons aren't meant to be with people. They're supposed to be wild and free. Like magic itself." This came from Tulip, who was shockingly respectful when it came to creatures, even though she treated most people like crap stuck to the bottom of her hoof.

"Exactly," Rurik remarked, "But since we're here, we should—"

"Everyone sit in the circle and be quiet. This is

supposed to be a stealth mission, and I'm pretty sure even the most incompetent guards could hear us talking in here, so shush."

"But Tilda, we're not even moving ye—"

Calina's argument was cut short when the dragon wagon jerked to life. Nobody dared say anything after that, though I could still sense the kids ambling around the interior. We'd had far too short of a rest, but at least things were moving forward again—forward and uphill.

I still didn't know how this blessed thing was powered, but I knew better than to mention my curiosity to Rurik, provided I wanted to keep him quiet. I also didn't know what we'd do once we got inside the keep, but that was a problem for the future. Sure, that future was only moments away, but it was the future nonetheless.

I held my breath as the wagon stopped at the top of the plateau. A guard asked Shim a series of questions about his cargo, but those questions were quickly answered without a single glance inside. No one with half their wits about them would willingly climb into a transport filled with unruly dragonlings.

Yet, there I was. And happy for it.

However, a few scaled passengers grew upset as we stalled at the gate and began thrashing and throwing themselves against the cage bars. Despite my reassurances to the contrary, I still couldn't see much. Maybe that was a blessing.

A young rock dragon had already smashed through one of the bars and threatened to escape at any moment. It reminded me so much of the siphons we'd fought earlier that I had to suppress a shiver and swallow back bile as I recalled watching the rocky magic eaters hurl their heavy bodies against an unconscious Rurik.

I had thought I'd lost him, and I had thought it was all my fault. That was the thing about life. It was precious and fragile and indescribable all at the same time.

Rurik had survived the ordeal. He would live another day—hopefully another many days—so that he could help me kill a few select others who did deserve to die.

Yeah, life was strange. Death was stranger still.

The wagon started again, and I motioned for the kids to settle. Almost there, almost there.

Hopefully, this assassination mission would be completed quickly so we could return to our main quest. Gaaron was waiting, and I refused to let him down again.

19

"How much longer do we have to wait?" Tulip's startling vibrato awoke me from a light slumber, and I was not pleased. "I'm bored and still upset about that Shim guy whipping these poor dragons."

"*Shhhh.* What's wrong with you? Did you forget we're supposed to be hiding?" Calina was quick to correct the other girl, but unfortunately, she was just as loud. "Besides, I'm sure it was just an expression. He couldn't possibly hurt such lovely little creatures."

"If someone would help me with my magic, I might be able to cast a silencing spell," Rurik mumbled unhappily. Well, at least one of the kids understood what we were supposed to be doing here.

Amariel said nothing; the gentle tick-tick of her metronome told me she was still asleep.

I decided to go back to sleep, too. Maybe that would set a good example for the others. It hadn't been that long since Shim had shut us into the dark, dragon-filled wagon, but it had been far longer than I expected. Once we rolled through the gates, Shim had parked us somewhere and then disappeared for the better part of the day. He still hadn't returned. I was furious he'd forgotten us back here. More than that, didn't he need to perform at least a cursory check of his private little zoo filled with sensitive magical creatures?

I didn't know much about dragons. Just that they were rare and powerful, and thus very expensive. Wasn't he worried someone would break in and attempt to steal one of the less aggressive-looking beasts?

"This is ridiculous. And I'd rather—" Tulip stopped abruptly, letting out an ear-piercing neigh.

My eyes had finally grown accustomed to this dark, but I didn't like what I saw.

Because all around us, the dragons stirred and readied themselves for a fight. The rock dragon snapped off another bar of its cage, and even the water elemental looked like it would jump clean out of its tank, such was its agitation. I doubted its tiny little fin could do much against an enraged centaur, but I also didn't want the chance to find out.

"We are safe in the conveyance," Amariel chanted along with a flute's smooth, undulating notes. "We are safe, safe in the conveyance."

"What were you thinking with that?" I whisper-yelled at the horse girl.

"I'm sorry, I didn't mean to." Surprisingly, she sounded apologetic... and also in immense pain. It was almost enough to make me feel sorry for her.

"It's just all this sitting takes a toll," Tulip continued in hushed tones. "I got a Charley human, and it really hu—"

"A what now?" I couldn't let her say another word without figuring out what the fig she was talking about.

"A Charley human," she answered matter-of-factly, practically channeling Rurik with her no-nonsense need to educate. "Do you not get them? It's when a muscle in your lower flank seizes up, and it's one of the worst pains imaginable."

"I've had that feeling," Rurik confessed. "But we call them pains of peace. They are dishonorable because they are injuries not caused in battle. Though they are painful, we are not meant to show our upset. Only children who have never seen battles can safely cry out when afflicted with a pain of peace. But I know a trick that might help."

Tulip sucked air in through her teeth, then whispered, "It still hurts quite a lot."

I watched in a dazed stupor as the half-orc approached Tulip, reaching toward her palm first.

"I will help, then you will explain why they are known as Charley humans amongst the centaurs," he whispered gently.

"Here." Tulip pointed limply to her upper left flank. "It hurts here."

And then Rurik's hands were on her, rubbing strong circles into the knotted muscle.

Calina mumbled something under her breath. The only words I caught were "sweet Sylric," but she did not seem happy about this development. She continued to quietly hiss and curse as she moved out of Amariel's bubble and back to the same dragon who'd bitten her earlier.

My eyes followed her across the hold. The moment between Rurik and Tulip felt intensely private—and it also turned my stomach. I'd much rather watch Calina get mauled by a baby dragon than whatever was going on with our other two companions.

Dragons were rare and special. I'd always liked them... until I met Maltherius's partner, Cindara.

She'd once been a flame dragon but had been corrupted by necrosis to live an unnaturally long life. Because dragons never stopped growing and she couldn't die, she'd become impossibly large, almost akin to a small mountain—which is still pretty big, way bigger than they're ever meant to get.

I hoped we wouldn't see her again, but I knew we would. Our only chance at beating Maltherius would be to keep Cindara out of the fight or avoid a fight altogether, which was my current preferred option.

"You're such a good little baby," Calina cooed. The dragonling chirped and purred. Oh, sweet divinity, things just kept getting stranger and stranger inside the dragon wagon.

I glanced back at the other two and spied Rurik pulling one of his hands away while offering a satisfied nod.

Tulip sighed with relief. "I don't know about the rest of you, but your hands really are magic. Thank you."

Rurik removed his other hand but stayed close to Tulip's side. Remarkably, he wasn't even blushing. He seemed... right at home sitting beside the only thing he seemed to like every bit as much as books. "Thank me by telling me the story of the Charley human," he said with a single-tusked grin.

Tulip's cheeks darkened as if burning. When she spoke, her voice was soft and lyrical. "Well, many years ago, there was this guy named Charley. He was a human who had been disowned by his village and taken refuge with the centaurs."

"That must have been many, many years ago. No centaur I know would ever show kindness to a different race unless there was something in it for them," Calina interjected from across the way.

Ugh. Apparently, they'd all forgotten the need to be quiet, but what was I supposed to do? I couldn't exactly yell at them to shut up.

"Well, it just so happens the centaurs and Charley had a mutually beneficial relationship," Tulip continued, nonplussed. Her gaze was focused solely on Rurik. Was that because he was the one who had requested the story, or might there be some other reason?

Ick, ick, ick. I did not want to know. I squeezed my eyes shut as Tulip continued her tale.

"They protected him and gave him a home, and he brought knowledge of far-off places and taught new skills to the tribe. One day, following a particularly restless cold season, the tribe's chief—"

A booming knock on the door immediately silenced Tulip. I shrank as far into the shadows as possible without putting myself within claw's reach of a dragon.

The voice that met us was strong and stern. "Who's in there? I heard you talking. Per the official crossing documents, this wagon only holds dragons, but in all my many years, I've yet to meet a dragon who can speak the common language. Either that merchant is a liar, or he doesn't know you're back there. Frankly, I don't care much for either option. But I need to find out which it is so I can do my job. The sooner I do my job, the sooner I can go home and have a nice dinner. And my stomach is already grumbling something fierce. So, I'll ask you this one time and one time only: Are you going to come out, or do I need to come in?"

"Tilda, what do we do?" Calina asked in a pitchy voice somewhere between a cry and a pant.

"Tilda!" the man outside repeated, then laughed. He actually laughed.

I bristled at his obvious merriment. My name wasn't common, but it wasn't odd enough to elicit laughter.

"I once knew a Tilda," the guard continued. "Many, many years ago. She was the tiniest little scrap of a thing but had the biggest attitude I'd ever—"

He didn't get to finish his recollection because I

wasted no time emerging from the shadows, flinging the door open, and throwing myself into the waiting arms of my oldest friend in the entire world. This man was as good as family. Finnian liked to claim he was my father, but Johan had actually filled that role before I'd abandoned him for a thief's life.

"Tilda, it is you! I never thought I'd see you again once that Finnian fellow took you into his ring of merry little thieves. I thought I'd lost you." His eyes brimmed with tears, and I wasn't sure whether they were sad for our past loss or happy for our current reunion.

"I should have listened to you, Johan. You were right the whole time, but I was a stupid kid back then. I didn't know." I'd been so focused on my regret over losing Gaaron that I'd forgotten the many other missteps I'd made during my youth.

Johan had served in the city watch, and even though the guards were meant to arrest the street urchins at the first sign of wrongdoing, he often looked the other way when it came to me. He would forgive my crimes, provided I at least pretended to listen to his advice.

He'd tried so hard to set me on the right path, to convince me that my sorrowful beginnings didn't need to amount to a sorrowful—or early—end. But I'd fallen in with Finnian at the first opportunity, choosing his extensive network of spies as a surrogate family when I'd already had Johan as a ready and willing father figure. He'd been amazing to me, and I'd betrayed him at the first opportunity. Stupid, stupid.

"You still look like a kid to me, Little Foot. Just with a few gray hairs to keep things interesting, eh?" Johan's eyes twinkled as I took in his weathered countenance, the pale white skin, the long white beard, the even longer white hair. He looked like some kind of winter-time wizard, all hoary and flowing.

And all mine.

My dear, dear friend. He was still alive after all these years and was here with me again. I was so happy that I started to tear up, too. What a beautiful moment.

"Tilda, who is this man, and how does he know you?" Tulip demanded as she leaped from the wagon, avoiding the down ramp entirely.

Johan set me on the ground, swiped away his tears, then sniffed and changed back to his stern guard voice. "I didn't realize that centaurs were now being classed as exotic pets, but I guess that makes sense. Our majestic regent—long may he live—sometimes likes to adjust the rules to better fit his glorious vision, and this is a magnificent specimen of—"

"I'll stop you right there," Tulip said, reaching for her bedazzled battle axe like a security blanket. "I am, indeed, magnificent, but I am not a pet. Neither are these dragons."

"I don't disagree with you on any of that," Johan sputtered, his earlier bliss draining rapidly. "But I am not meant to have my own thoughts or opinions. I am only meant to aid in the glory of our majestic regent—long may he live."

This man no longer sounded like my old friend. Speaking of old...

"Shouldn't you have retired years ago?" I asked, blinking up at him.

"I did retire, but our majestic regent—long may he live—called me and many of my brothers and sisters out of retirement to bolster his guard. So I live to work another day, it seems."

"For how long?" I demanded, already livid on his behalf.

"I live in service to our majestic regent, and I will die in service to our majestic regent," he declared, then leaned close to my ear and whispered with the same jovial spark I remembered from my childhood, "But since it's you, Tilda, I'm willing to look the other way for old-time's sake."

"Ahh, I see here there was an error on the paperwork," Johan announced loudly, even though there wasn't a speck of paper to be seen anywhere—or for that matter, any other people. "I'll just adjust here and here. There! Now everything is as his majestic regent— long may he live—demands. Since that matter is settled, would you and your centaur companion care to join me for dinner?"

"As long as my half-elf, half-orc, and celestial companions can also join us." I nodded vigorously because I wanted more time with the old guy and longed to fill my belly with something besides our sweet, dry rations. Tanuki cookies, *blech*.

"I don't know that I have enough food to accommodate the appetites of an orc—even if he is only half —but I will share what I have. And did you say you had a celestial in your group as well?" He stared intently at the wagon, almost as if he could see through it to find what was inside. I knew his old human eyes could do no such thing, but that didn't seem to stop him from trying anyway.

"I did. And she's the only person I know who is even more advanced in years than you, you old walrus." I snapped my fingers so Johan would look back toward me. For some reason, I felt a bit jealous. Maybe a part of me was getting back in touch with the kid I'd been when Johan had looked out for me.

For the first time on this journey, I felt it might be okay to take a little break and spend some unplanned downtime. Maybe Johan could help us get to Eldrin Grimlock—*not* so long may he live—but even if he couldn't, an evening in his company would be an evening very well spent.

I needed this and hoped the kids would stop complaining long enough for me to enjoy it. Because first thing tomorrow, we'd need to enact the next part of our plan—and that, of course, would be actually making one now that we had successfully infiltrated the keep.

20

Johan led our group farther and farther away from the dragon wagon, weaving through the castle complex's multiple dark alleys as he navigated the maze-like layout. Judging the size of Mystwood Keep from the outside had been difficult. I'd seen that it was big but had no idea it was practically the same size as the town we'd left behind. The size, however, was the only thing Briarhaven and this place had in common.

Back home, everyone was friendly and happy—besides the centaurs, but they mostly stuck to themselves rather than bothering the rest of us. Here, however, there were hardly any people out at all. Those we encountered refused to make eye contact and quickly darted away. It was almost like they were afraid of Johan... or like there was an axe hanging over everyone's head. Whatever the case, it gave me an unsettling feeling. Like we might be walking straight into a trap.

Of course, I knew my old friend would never hurt us, but my gut kept screaming otherwise.

At one point, Rurik offered to light his flame, but Johan quickly rejected that idea, stating that an unidentified half-orc wielding mysterious magic would raise more questions than we wanted to answer.

So we quietly followed him in and out of alleys and up two flights of steps until he finally stopped outside a stone door and fumbled his keys onto the step below.

I stooped down to retrieve the keyring, noting how Johan's old hands shook when he finally managed to fit the desired key into its place and push the door open. He was far too old for this type of work—for any work, really—and I was furious that the regent had forced him out of retirement in this enfeebled state.

Johan smiled kindly as he motioned for us to enter ahead of him. "Please, please come inside. My home is humble, but you are welcome to all I have."

Humble was putting it far too kindly. We could hardly close the door once we'd all entered.

I, of course, wasted no time stating my displeasure. "What gives, Johan? I thought you were going to retire to the forest. Live out the rest of your days beside a gurgling creek? That's what you always said. It's what you dreamed of."

His face twisted in agony, and I worried that I'd misspoken. "I had... until the regent came for me."

Now that our party had moved into private quarters, the required "long may he live" was notably absent.

"You had your dream! Why would you give it up?" I placed a hand on my hip and stared up at him, much like the sassy child I'd once been. After I'd joined Finnian's ring of child thieves, I'd only ever seen Johan a handful of times—and from a distance, at that. I realized now that I was mimicking the movements and behavior of when I'd last spoken to him. I'd been a child then and felt like a child again now. I also felt like I might throw a tantrum over all this injustice. Eldrin Grimlock needed to be put in time-out. Maybe this initially unwanted side quest had been just what I'd needed after all.

Johan shook his head and looked down. "I tried to refuse him, to explain that I was too old and wouldn't be much use to him anyway..." His words trailed off, and he choked on a sob.

I placed a comforting hand on his arm; all the while, my stomach churned with dread. This was not okay. Johan was a good man—among the best I knew.

Whatever Eldrin had done to him, he'd also done to countless others. He deserved the death that had come for him.

Finally, Johan was ready to speak again. He placed his hand on top of mine and squeezed it fondly, meeting my eyes directly as he said, "He burnt my cottage to ashes, leaving me no choice but to join him. He garnered my wages to punish me for my insubordination. I make a pittance. I can barely afford to feed myself, let alone find any time to actually live my life. I sometimes even go so far as to pray for death."

"That's awful," Calina spoke up, anger reflecting in her pale purple eyes.

"There's privilege, and then there's cruelty," Tulip added, her nose wrinkled in disgust. "The Briarhaven centaurs don't much care for the other races, but we don't actively harm them either."

Calina looked like she wanted to argue with this, but then, realizing the two were on the same side, she kept quiet for once.

"An unjust ruler doesn't deserve to keep his throne," Rurik said in such a way that made it clear this line was being recited from one of his books. But wherever the sentiment came from, I heartily agreed. Usually, I wouldn't get involved in politics, but here I was, already deep in and glad for the opportunity to set something right for my friend.

"Yeah, no wonder Finnian Sly wants him dead." This came from Calina.

I shook my head as I thought through the situation. I still didn't know why Finnian hated the regent enough to send us here, but I knew it wasn't because of the truths Johan had just tearfully revealed. "Finnian wouldn't care what Eldrin did to Johan. He may not even know. The tanuki serves his own purposes and only his own purposes."

"I was one of many forced from their homes, and it's not just the guards." Johan's voice came out smoother and stronger now. Apparently, it was easier to speak of the present than to reflect on the past. "Eldrin has forced many workers from retirement. He pays them poorly and taxes them mightily."

"And he keeps poor, beaten dragons as pets," Tulip added with a huff and a stomp. "I can't wait to murder him."

Johan sank onto his narrow cot, eyes wide as he asked," Is that why you've come here? To kill the regent?"

"We're on orders from Finnian Sly," Rurik confirmed matter-of-factly.

"Finnian?" Johan spat this word like a curse before

251

his voice cracked on the rest. "You mentioned him before, but I had hoped it was only in passing. Tilda, I thought you had broken free of his grasp?"

He'd wanted better for me and tried to help me get it. The regent wasn't the only one who had stolen something important from this old man. I was guilty, too, in a different way, but still. I owed him an explanation, an apology, but the right words wouldn't come. Still, I had to try, so I sputtered an awkward string of whatever excuses I could find. "I had. I mean, I have. But—"

Calina grunted and started gesturing wildly, sliding her index finger across her throat. Right, the comm-stone he'd thrust upon me before we departed the celestial treasure room. Finnian was listening to everything. If I betrayed him now, it all would be for nothing. How far we'd come, all that we'd accomplished, and all the time we'd devoted when we had other, even more pressing matters to attend. Yup, all I had to do was say a single sentence the tanuki master thief disliked, and our group would be named next on his hit list.

I couldn't allow myself to make foolish mistakes just because I was getting emotional.

No. I needed to play this carefully.

"Finnian is right to want Eldrin Grimlock dead. It

seems all of Mirathane would agree," Calina provided smoothly, coming to my rescue once again.

Yes, that's how we'd handle this. I picked up right where Calina had left off. "Indeed. If what you say is true, then folks will look at Finnian as a hero. A savior, even."

My half-elf companion began to rummage through our supplies with one hand while twirling the other in a fast circle to indicate that I should keep talking to buy her some time.

I left her to her riffling and turned back to my old friend. "We're here to help take out the regent. We just don't know how we're going to do it yet. Can you offer us any aid?"

"The more I learn about this guy, the more I look forward to chopping his head off with my snazzy axe," Tulip added with a wicked grin. It looked good on her.

Johan said nothing. He appeared too shocked to form words, a reaction I understood completely. We weren't talking local gossip or preferred drink orders here. This was a matter of life and death—and not just Eldrin's.

Rurik watched Calina intently but appeared to be listening to my conversation with Johan even though he did not remark upon it.

Somehow, even Amariel remained awake and at

attention. Our entire adventuring party was on the same page for the first time. I didn't know what book we were reading exactly, but I liked that we were doing it together.

I kept talking, ticking off idea after idea on my fingers, even though I knew none of them were any good.

I had just suggested that we drown our target in wine from his own cellar when Calina finally found what she was looking for. She grabbed both the guard's map and her enchanted quill from the sack, then, for lack of a better place, she rolled it out on the floor, keeping it face-side up to hide our previous conversation from the others.

Speak carefully. JS is listening through a comm-stone.

She wrote, then pointed for everyone to look.

Johan's eyes grew wider still, almost like he might never blink again.

I gave him a concerned nudge. "Are you all right, old friend?"

"Eldrin will not be an easy target," he said at last. "And when you are found out, he will do far worse than take your lives. He will torment you. Tilda, it's too risky. You can't do this."

"I understand your concern, Johan, and I appreciate your caring. But we don't have a choice. We have to do this."

"Tilda, all these years, I'd thought I'd lost you, and now that I have you back again, I can't let you knowingly walk into a trap. I can't stand back and watch as you get killed."

That was it then. Finding my old friend had felt like a miracle, a good omen. And his sudden rejection cut deeper than any dagger ever could.

"Then look away," I said, my voice hoarse and heartbroken.

"I'm not trying to upset you, Little Foot. I'm trying to save you." Johan placed a hand on my shoulder, but I shook it off with a dissatisfied snort. "He knows something like this is coming. Why do you think he's bolstered his guard? You won't make it within twenty paces of him before you're taken. And then you will wish for death, every day and every night, just like I do."

"Our chances of success would improve greatly with help from an inside source," Rurik pointed out, ever the skilled logician.

"No. No." Johan shook his head as fat tears

splashed onto his trousers. "But not enough. Never enough."

"Will you not help us only because you think we'll fail or because you think it's wrong?" Rurik asked, appearing genuinely curious about the answer.

"It's not wrong to kill a tyrant," Calina answered quickly.

Tulip nodded her agreement as she slid one smooth finger along the blade of her axe.

Amariel, however, blared her disagreement. "It is wrong to end a life, even one poorly lived."

"Not this again," I mumbled.

"All life is sacred. It is not for mortals to end it," she continued to trumpet.

This was not a concert I wanted to attend. Amariel could heal us and create protective bubbles, but she was useless in all other situations, and right now, she was actively hindering our cause. It made me furious with her.

"But you aren't a mortal," I pointed out, hoping that would be enough of a gotcha to keep her quiet. "You could save us all this tiresome moral quandary by doing the figgin' job yourself, Amariel, but I'm guessing you'll refuse to get involved, as usual. Why don't you just go back to sleep and let the rest of us handle this?"

"We made a deal with Finnian. We have to get rid of Eldrin. Otherwise, we won't be able to rescue my dad." Calina got down on her knees and shook her joined hands at Johan. It was all a bit dramatic, but it also had the intended effect on its target. Johan's tears came even quicker now.

"He said death was preferred but not strictly required," Rurik clarified, glancing around the room nervously. He didn't like excessive displays of emotion, especially not coming from his dearest friend. Calina was usually the strong one in their duo, but she had come undone in her desperation. And I was right there with her.

"Killing Eldrin and ending his rule is the right thing to do. With him out of the way, someone good can take the throne, and all of Mirathane will be better for it," she continued to argue, briefly unjoining her hands to swipe at freely flowing tears.

Gods, we were all crying now.

I decided to step in and offer my support. "She's right, and we'll do much better with you both on our side. Johan, Amariel, can we count on your aid?"

All was silent until the sound of Amariel's metronome filled the cramped room with its gentle tick-tick.

"How could she fall asleep at a time like this?" Calina spat.

But I kept my eyes glued to Johan. He'd helped me so many times before. Surely, he'd help me again.

He shook his head and moved farther back on the bed, unwilling to meet my gaze. "Tilda, I can't. Don't you understand? It would be helping you into your grave."

"Then I guess I will have to get there by myself. Goodbye, Johan. C'mon, kids. We're going."

"Going where?" I didn't know which of them asked this, but it also didn't matter much in the greater scheme of things. As always, we were taking our journey two steps forward and one step back. And the whole thing with Johan had been a giant leap in the wrong direction.

"I don't know. Somewhere that isn't here," I said as I moved toward the door.

"Please don't do this, Tilda. I beg of you. It will not end well." Johan's voice followed me, but I refused to look back at him. I would never see him again and had to be okay with that. He'd made his choice, and I'd made mine. This was goodbye. This time forever.

Tulip scooped up Amariel, and the kids followed me down the stairs and onto the main level of the keep.

"Are we going back to the dragon wagon?" one of the girls asked.

"No. No. We'll see if there's a temple. Clerics are obligated to take in weary travelers. It is their calling to help," I informed them, inwardly recognizing that our pseudo-cleric almost always refused to help when we needed it. Maybe at the temple, we could trade her in for a newer model, someone that would actually be useful in our upcoming death mission. "Keep an eye out. The sooner we find a temple, the sooner we can all rest, regroup, and plan for what comes next."

Everyone was silent as we searched until, at last, Rurik piped up with a question that I could tell had been on his mind for quite some time. "Tulip, will you tell me the rest of the Charley human legend?"

21

I had a hard time paying attention to the Charley human story, and not just because it was boring. After all, someone had to remain alert to any dangers lurking nearby. Like I'd learned early on in my training. There were four dangerous Ds of thieves. Daggers, dogs, do-gooders, and drops. But someone also had to locate the temple in the maze of alleys. And as usual, that someone turned out to be me.

From what I could gather, though, the human named Charley often experienced painful muscle spasms because he had difficulty keeping up with his half-horse comrades.

Now, because he was so beloved, many of the centaurs broke traditional naming conventions to honor their favorite human pet, and thus, a generation of Charley centaurs was born. The centaurs found Charley's pains funny until one very long winter when they started to experience the spasming leg cramps for themselves. And whenever they did, they'd shout and curse Charley for bringing this affliction upon the tribe. Once the brief but intense pains dissipated, they would forgive him for the blight, but for the few minutes those cramps lasted, they hated that man with every fiber of their beings.

Still, so many little Charley centaurs were running around that the elders' pained curses led to more than a few tearful children wondering why their parents suddenly hated them with such vitriol. To avoid any further confusion or upset feelings, this special kind of cramp was officially dubbed "Charley Human" after their originator.

Huh, I guess I'd paid more attention than I realized. It was a stupid story, but listening to it did help to pass the time as we roamed the labyrinth inside the keep. Plus, I knew Rurik well enough by now to know that he would keep asking until his craving for this particular bit of knowledge was satisfied. Come to think of it, maybe I could start referring to my curious interludes as "Rurik Half-Orcs." That was just as stupid as Tulip's original story, but perhaps that was also the point.

Hey, sometimes it was nice to bug the kids back. It kept me from thinking of the hollow look in Johan's eyes as we said our goodbyes. As it turns out, I'd much rather be petty than haunted, so I focused on the Charley Human story and used it to bore myself into a fragile state of peace.

Somewhere between Rurik's tenth and twentieth follow-up question, we found the Mystwood temple. It took a moment to recognize because the holy symbol on the temple was blank. Either it sat abandoned or perhaps served Simon, the god of silence, death, and peace. I found this particularly disturbing, given what we'd learned about the regent. Choosing Simon as his patron deity was quite obviously less about his own piety and more of a maneuver to subjugate his followers. It made me sick.

I'd never been much for religion, but whenever I needed help from the divine, I tended to invoke Shi, the mother deity who oversaw luck and destiny. I firmly believed I could do whatever I needed myself... except for the times when luck seemed to actively work against me. In these types of cases, a quick call out to the luck keeper or a shouted "sweet divinity" set me back on the right path again.

I probably owed Shi a prayer of thanks for getting us this far. Maybe even an offering to formally request that she grant us swift and true steps toward our end objective. It was generally considered gauche to pray for outside deities in assigned temples, but as the mother of the pantheon, lady Shi could be worshipped anywhere.

Besides, I would never pray to Simon, whether his temple provided us aid or not. It's not like you could get an answer from the Silent God. And yet, we needed a place to stay. The chances of Mystwood Keep having a second temple were slim, especially considering how long it had taken us to find this one. That meant we'd have to take up with Simon for the night. We just didn't have any other choice.

"Look, we found it." I pointed to the unassuming stone building. "Let's head inside."

Amariel snapped awake with the rattle-clink of a tambourine—a new one for her—and zoomed past me toward the temple. She appeared to be pulled by an invisible string straight through the doors. I'd never seen her move like that before and doubted I would ever see it again. The unexpected burst of energy caught the kids' attention, too. They all exchanged confused glances before following her inside.

That made me the last to enter. The temple wasn't likely to be trapped, but I did wish they would be more careful. I'd have to lecture them about proper entry procedure later.

Almost immediately, an elven cleric appeared to greet us, offering a slight dip of her head in acknowledgment.

"Whoa, what is this place? It's so cool!" Calina gasped, her voice ricocheting off the high walls. The temple's entrance started at normal room height but lifted at a sharp angle as it approached the rear altar. This amplified any noise made inside, and my kids always made a lot of noise wherever they went.

The cleric shook her head and motioned to her own closed mouth, then lifted one finger to her lips to indicate we should remain quiet.

"This temple serves Simon, the god of si—" Rurik began but was similarly cut off by the not-so-welcoming cleric.

She raised a hand with her palm straight out to us, indicating we should wait, then stepped away without turning her back to us. She kept her eyes on us the entire time before bending slightly at the knees to grab a stack of papers and silks. When she returned to the entry vestibule, she tied one of the strips of silk over her mouth, handed the others to our group, and waited for us to copy the motion.

Amariel, Rurik, and Calina immediately complied,

but Tulip and I flatly refused—although for different reasons I'd suspect.

The cleric shrugged and then handed a pamphlet to Calina. And we all packed in tight to read over her shoulder or, in my case, from around her hip. The papers said:

You have entered a temple of Simon.
All are welcome here so long as they honor him with their silence.
Please feel free to offer your prayers or take refuge for the night. You are welcome as long as you continue to observe the requisite peace and quiet.
Praise be to Simon!

Right, this was not going to be easy for our group. Not one bit.

Perhaps we should have gone back to the dragon wagon after all. I glanced around at the kids, narrowing my eyes at the others to convey that goof-ups would not be tolerated.

But almost immediately, a muffled voice broke our brief, strained silence. I almost slapped Calina in the back of the arm, but then I realized who was actually speaking out.

My eyes zipped to Amariel just in time to see her remove the silk gag she'd only just fastened to her face. All eyes were on her, not just mine.

"It is good to see you, old friend," she chimed, her expression went blank for a moment, then began to shift unnaturally from one extreme emotion to the next. She looked happy, then sad, then something I had a hard time even identifying—back and forth like a children's flipbook with no easy transitions between one face and the next.

The cleric removed her gag next, eyes wide and unblinking. "Is she speaking with Simon himself?" she whispered so slightly I could hardly hear it. It made me wonder how long it had been since she'd last used her voice... If, as a supplicant of this temple, she was able to speak outside of it or if her vow extended past these four walls.

I didn't get the chance to ask because Amariel continued her disturbing, one-sided conversation despite appearing completely unhinged and unnatural.

"Too few honor you these days, my friend. The mortal realm does not recognize how badly they need peace and stillness. Instead, they turn to your brothers and sisters in pursuit of pleasure, wealth, knowledge, and love, or they ask your mother to rewrite their destiny. But silence is the garden in which the rarest and most beautiful flowers can grow. I understand, and I honor you, my friend. Today and always."

"It is Simon," the cleric hissed, a bit louder now. "Do you think he's speaking back to her? He's never spoken to me. Not in my near decade of service. Who is this woman to so boldly command the attention of the gods? And who are you to accompany her?"

I just shrugged and listened to Amariel. It was the most I had ever heard her say in one go. Witnessing this exchange left me a bit dumbfounded. Stunningly, not even the kids had anything to say. We all just watched and waited to see what would happen next.

"I am glad to have found you, sweet Simon, for I am facing a time of great turmoil. My tranquil heart is scarred and bleeding as if it has suffered war despite devoting my entire existence to peace and peace alone. Simon, I pray that you will show me the true path. I fear my eyes have grown hazy and my mind troubled. Only you can bring me the serenity that is needed to know what is right."

And with those final words, she collapsed onto the cold marble floor. Her face continued to flash exaggerated expressions, but the rest of her had grown eerily still. Whatever had happened, I knew she wasn't asleep.

Her metronome didn't accompany her gentle snores. In fact, she made no sound at all.

For the first time since we'd entered the temple, it was completely quiet.

We all stared at her for a while, unsure of what to do. Even the cleric looked out of her element, which was probably not a great sign.

Calina was the first to act, and she did so by rummaging through our supplies until she found her enchanted quill. Grasping it firmly, she used the bespelled instrument to write something on the pamphlet the cleric had provided to communicate the temple rules.

Is there someplace we can put her to rest for a while?

Calina scribbled, then held it up for our host to see.

The cleric nodded and motioned for our group to follow. This confused me. Could she speak or not? Had she taken a vow of silence in reverence to Simon... or not?

This was a big part of why I didn't do religion. The rules meant everything, until they meant nothing—

and I had a hard time understanding the point at which this balance shifted.

Calina and Rurik followed our guide deeper into the temple, but Tulip hesitated, shuffling her hooves gently as she stared at her restless chaperone. "I've never seen Amariel like this," she confided in me as close as she could get to a whisper in the place. "I'm afraid to move her."

"I think it will be okay, but we need to get her somewhere more comfortable, and we all need a good night's sleep."

"I'm scared, Tilda."

I thought about the many possible responses I could give to assuage this rare show of frailty, but in the end, I decided the truth would be best.

"Me too," I answered simply, meeting her vulnerability with an equal exchange of my own. "Me too."

22

I awoke the next morning to the comforting caress of hot, fragrant steam on my face. Wildflower tea, it had to be!

But I couldn't even remember falling asleep. Last I knew, we were inside Mystwood Keep at a temple that served Simon. But I only made wildflower tea while camping, and other than Gaaron many years ago, nobody else had ever prepared this brew for me.

As much as the tea's presence comforted me, it also worried me. The only thing I could do now was to sit up and open my eyes.

And so I did, immediately coming face to face with the same silent and strange cleric we'd met the night before. She pushed the mug toward me again, a finely polished silver with a padded handle to keep it from getting too hot to hold.

"Your name's Tilda, right?" she asked with the slightest of smiles. It sounded like she had a croaker stuck in her throat.

I nodded dumbly, keeping my hands in my lap. Clerics were generally trustworthy, but I also knew better than to accept a drink I hadn't made myself. The kids were nowhere to be seen besides, and that increased my apprehension.

"Eight and a half years, I kept my vow of silence. And then last night..." The cleric set the steaming mug on a small side table, then leaned forward and tugged on her long elven ears. She winced in pain, but I couldn't tell whether that pain was physical, emotional, or perhaps both. "Your friend walked right in from off the street and was immediately granted an audience with the god himself. All these years I've served, only to be ignored."

I shrugged and wiggled my toes beneath the quilt, eager to be on my feet again. "The gods have always played favorites," I said with a shrug. "Plus, Amariel probably knew Simon when he was mortal," I added under my breath.

"I thought I was favored, but now I see I've wasted the better part of my youth, and for what?"

She let go of her ears and threw her hands in the air, then bit her lip and made a guttural noise somewhere between a groan and a growl. Her agitated movements made me nervous. Her mysterious tea made me nervous. This whole thing set off my danger radar in a big way. I needed to get out of there—and fast.

"Look, I can see you're going through something, and I'll happily get out of your hair, but I can't leave without the rest of my party. Where are they?"

She tipped her chin toward the table, then studied me with side eyes. "Drink the tea, and I will catch you up."

"Respectfully, no. You have your rules, and I have mine."

Now both hands were on her chest as if forcibly trying to keep the air inside. And yet a lengthy gasp escaped anyway. "You think I'd poison you?"

I crossed my arms over my chest, refusing to fall for whatever act this woman was trying to pull. "Simon is also the god of death, is he not?"

The cleric chuckled at this, then gasped again. "Wow, laughter. Ah, ah ha ha ha! It's been so long. Too long. Thank you, Tilda. I needed that." She then took a long drag of the tea herself and sighed with pleasure. Finally, she appeared to relax a little, slowing her movements and just existing in the space like a somewhat normal person.

She took another sip, appearing thoughtful. "Maybe I'll serve Rubessa next. If there's no guarantee the gods will return my affection, then I might as well serve the one that honors pleasure and fun."

"Yeah, you have to live your life for you, first and foremost. Now please answer me this time: Where are my kids?"

"I hadn't realized they were your children. You look nothing alike." She laughed again, this time a full-out guffaw.

I refused to smile. "You're not supposed to laugh at your own jokes... *you.*" I realized too late I hadn't gotten her name, which led to my awkward verbal fumble. I didn't know her name, and I didn't care to find out, either. I needed to get out of here.

Putting on my meanest mug, I started over. "Tell me where they are, or I start breaking things. First, it will be that teacup, but it won't take long to get to your fingers."

The cleric yelped and rushed to the other side of the room. Once she found the farthest corner from my bed, she yanked at the pointy parts of her ears again and curled forward into herself. "Don't hurt me," she squealed. "I wasn't trying to hide anything. I was just so excited to have someone to talk to. Do you know what it's like to say nothing for almost ten years?"

I shrugged at that. "Actually, I kind of do. Tell me where the kids are, and then we'll talk." I swung my legs over the side of the bed, ready to chase her down and show her that I meant business. This woman was pathetic. I'd feel bad hurting her, but nobody stood in the way of me and the quest—especially not so far as those kids were concerned.

"Stop right there. I'll tell you, okay? Like I said, I wasn't hiding anything on purpose!" She removed her hands from her head and placed them flat on the wall, pressing her back to it as well. Clearly, this woman had found other non-verbal ways to communicate during her long vow of silence. I didn't much care for the theatrics, but at least I could tell when I was making progress. The bigger the gesture, the more it meant my words had landed as intended.

"The orc never went to sleep," she continued, shaking her head rapidly, then pausing briefly and switching to a vigorous nod. "He told me he doesn't really sleep and asked if the temple had a library. I showed him where it was and haven't seen him since. The elf and centaur woke up about an hour ago. The centaur was worried about the old lady—she's a celestial, right? I've never seen one before. In fact, I thought they were—"

"Extinct, right. I know. Keep talking about the kids." I made a fist with one hand and then covered it with the others, eliciting a satisfying series of cracks from my knuckles.

The cleric rose high on her toes and pressed her cheek into the wall as she squeezed her eyes shut. *"Ahhh, uhhh,* the centaur... She was worried, but the elf got her to calm down enough to head out to the market square. I think they mentioned shopping."

Okay, this I hadn't expected. I needed to make sure I'd heard her right. Slowly, I rose to my feet and took a small step toward her. "They? The two of them? They left... together?"

She tried even harder to burrow into the wall. "Yeah, about fifteen minutes ago. After they left, I made you that tea, and now here we are."

I took another step forward, clasping my hands behind my back to offer some reassurance that I wasn't currently planning on hurting her. This woman served the god of death, and yet she was afraid of a sleepy halfling? Something wasn't adding up. "What about the celestial?" I pressed.

"She's the same as she was last night. Not awake, but not exactly asleep. I've never seen anything like it."

She raced past the open doorway and to a farther-off corner of the room. Oh, brother.

I stood still, hoping that if I calmed her, she'd offer me the information I needed faster. "You're a cleric. Can you heal her?"

"I could try, but I also broke my vow when I spoke last night." She wilted in front of me, all her vim and vigor gone at once. As she spoke her next words, she slowly sank to the floor. "I'm no longer favored by Simon, if I ever was."

"Meaning?" I came to stand beside her, and this time she didn't try to creep away. She hardly reacted at all.

She acknowledged me with a small sigh. Her voice came out flat and hollow. "My abilities will be significantly dampened. What your friend has isn't some run-of-the-mill head cold. It's really serious. She would need someone at the top of their game to heal her, if what she has is even curable."

I chuffed at this. "She'd need someone like herself. Well, that's completely not helpful."

"I'm sorry. It's the truth, at least as best I know it. Maybe I should take up service to Wissandor. Knowledge is a particularly useful domain, and once learned, it cannot be unlearned. Wissandor wouldn't forsake me as Simon has." She lifted her hands to tug on her ears, but caught herself and stopped before she could make contact. This woman was a wreck. I hadn't exactly chosen to become a rogue. It was more like the thief life had chosen me. Still, I was immensely glad that I hadn't chosen the religious track. The gods could create, but they could also destroy —and the woman before me proof of the latter.

"Look, I don't know much about the gods, but maybe Amariel could put in a good word for you with whomever you choose to serve next. It was clear she had an audience with Simon last night. She may still be with him, which is why she isn't waking up. But, as I said, I don't know much about the gods. And based on everything you've told me so far today, maybe you don't either. But I still think we can help each other."

"By having your friend put in a good word for me, provided she ever wakes up?"

"Yeah, something like that. You help me now, and I'll help you just as soon as I'm able. Fair?" I reached out a hand to shake on it, but the cleric refused to meet my grasp.

"May Antar smite you if you are speaking in deception," she said with a grimace, as if she couldn't choose between a smile and a snarl, so she settled for some disturbing expression in between.

I dropped my hand and raised an eyebrow. "Antar's

justice, right? Or was it love? Anyway, I'm not lying. The whole reason I'm even at Mystwood is to keep a promise I made to someone else."

"Go on." She perked up at this, straightening her spine so that she now sat taller against the wall as she studied me intently. I'd never been much for books, but I was a pro at reading people. And this person had just made one thing exceptionally obvious: she couldn't be trusted. Not by me, anyway.

I had to be really careful as to how I revealed my hand. Johan had warned that Eldrin Grimlock had already set traps, knowing the assassins would come, that he was ready to defend himself. Given that bounty hunters were the most likely to attempt such a high-profile murder, he would be looking for an adventurer... like me. And when adventurers rolled into a new town, they almost always found their way to either the tavern or the temple... like I had done.

Fig, I'd practically heralded my arrival here.

The regent probably already knew we were inside his compound. He'd probably also sussed out our ties to Finnian. What if this cleric was the one to alert him? What if all this vow of silence stuff was little more than a ruse on her part? A cover for her sudden yet inevitable betrayal?

I bit my tongue to keep from saying anything until I calmed down.

My companion noticed.

"Tilda, Tilda, is everything all right? You got real quiet all of a sudden. Do you not think your friend can help me?" Her movements were smooth, fluid. She believed she had the power now, and that was not a good sign for me.

"I'm not sure. Maybe it's better if we wait for her to wake up first. Can you take me to the girls?"

She shook her head in a controlled way, unlike her exaggerated motions from earlier. "I can't leave the temple. Even if Simon has shunned me, I'm still paid by the glorious regent. Long may he live."

Well, it looked like I was right about not being able to trust her. Good thing I had realized her true allegiance before it became too late for me to untell any dangerous secrets.

"Can you take me to the orc, then? You said he was in the library, right?"

"What about the celestial? Don't you want to see her?" She tilted her head to the side as if in thought, but I could see the gesture was forced. This woman was not the great actress she thought herself to be.

"There's nothing I can do for her other than wait for her to wake up, but the kids need me to help keep them out of trouble." I only hoped they hadn't already blurted out our intentions. For all I knew, they were already wasting away in the castle dungeon.

"Please. It's my job to look after them. Just as it's your job to stay here and help people in need, I'll let you get on with your job as soon as you help me get on with mine. Take me to Rurik, and he and I will find the girls together. And if Amariel wakes up, I promise you, I will ask her to help you with your little god problem, okay?"

She offered a firm nod, then whispered—perhaps of old habit. "Okay."

23

As soon as we left the sleeping quarters dedicated to strays and wanderers, the cleric fell quiet. Apparently, her broken vow of silence was intended to remain secret to all who hadn't directly witnessed it. She moved with swift, efficient movements as she guided me through a series of hallways, finally delivering me to a small room with no windows. Here, Rurik sat cross-legged, surrounded by many carefully placed stacks of old books.

Having fulfilled her duty, the cleric offered me a curt nod and motioned for me to enter ahead of her. Once I was inside, she clicked the door shut between us. Not a single word was spoken, but that suited me just fine. Rurik was the most likely of my companions to say something that would be better left unsaid, and I was glad he'd busied himself all night away from her. I was also pleased that she'd granted us our privacy, although we'd still need to be careful about what we said inside this temple. Voices carried quite far here.

I watched Rurik for a moment, trying to figure out whether he'd even noticed me enter. It didn't seem like it. He was so absorbed in his impromptu studies that nothing else existed outside his reading selection.

Deciding to have a bit of fun, I crept over, grabbed an especially thick book, and slammed the cover shut, creating a resonant thud. All this time spent in the company of teens was causing me to regress a bit, or maybe it was because of spending that tiny bit of time with Johan. Whatever the case, I knew my actions were childish, but they also felt right. I shouldn't have to be the only person responsible for our party. Even I needed a break from time to time.

Rurik jumped to his feet, knocking over the already precarious stacks and sending books scuttling everywhere. "Tilda! What were you thinking?" he cried. "The books. Oh, the books!"

Well, now I felt bad. The books appeared no worse for the wear, but I did my part to help regather them as Rurik moaned and tutted over each one like a newborn baby needing nourishment.

"It could have been worse. Your flame cantrip could have flared up by accident, right?" I offered by way of apology.

Rurik stared at me with his jaw slack and his single tusk quivering in disbelief. "You thought that was possible and still decided to scare me?"

"Sorry. I guess I just don't revere books the same way you do. Besides, it's a temple of Simon. How much help are these things even providing?" I'd worried the cleric would come running back to investigate the sound, but nobody came. We were alone, as far as I could tell. Still, I had to be careful, though.

Rurik shook his head slowly and then sighed. "It's true. The best learning would be from Wissandor's temple, given that he is the god of wisdom. But I have a feeling I'd find what I most need at the altar of Frikis and Morkan."

I stared at him blankly.

"They're the twin gods of magic," he tried, and when I continued to show no interest, he added, "Tilda, this is all fundamental theology. How could you not..."

He turned away and returned to his books. "You're not very pious, I take it?" he muttered as he caressed the spine of an especially thick leather-bound tome.

"I know enough to know it's not for me. And honestly, I've never met a cleric I like."

Rurik glanced at me briefly before flipping the book open and trailing a stout finger down the table of contents. "What about Durgan?"

"He was a paladin, and only just barely." I picked up the book he'd been reading when I entered and glanced at the title: *Inner Peace, Outer Power*. Oh, brother.

"*Huh*. Well, Frikis and Morkan are the only ones who might be able to help me unblock my magic. I gathered in these texts that my mind and body are not one. They do not exist in peaceful harmony, as the Simonites would say. And until they do, I will never get any better at magic. I'm lucky I'm even able to make my flame."

"That's rough, buddy." I set the book down and began to pace circles around the room. I wasn't anxious; I just needed something to do while we talked, something to keep me from getting bored. "I know it's not what you wanted to hear... or read. Maybe you're misinterpreting, though. I know it's hard, but you can't just give up. Not after all you've been through, after all we've been through."

His face twisted into an odd expression as he said, "Orcs are built for might, not magic. But that's only half of my biology. Pat had the right idea when he gifted me this shield."

Rurik glanced around the room until his eyes landed upon the long shield he had propped in the corner near the door. "I need to nurture my human side. That's the part of me where the magic lives. But half-orc is just as good as a whole to anyone born outside the tribe. They see me and assume I will fail, and I think I've internalized that."

"So people underestimate you. They do that to me, too. But you don't have to let them define who you are and what you can do. You get to decide those things for yourself, right?"

He slapped the book shut and sighed. "In theory, yes. In practice, it's been a struggle."

"C'mon, you've had a long night. Some fresh air will do you good. Let's take a walk. You can help me find the girls."

Rurik shook his head sadly. "No, Tilda. I don't think I can. I need more time, more answers."

"And you think these books will have them?"

"No, but I need to make sure." He found *Inner Peace, Outer Power* in the spot where I'd abandoned it and picked the odd book up, clutching it to his chest like a dear friend.

I backed slowly toward the door, giving the kid

time to change his mind, but he'd already buried his nose in the bowels of that book, shutting me out completely.

All righty, then. It looked like I'd be leaving him behind. Amariel was still sleeping it off in the monastery, so our party was already split. The best thing for me to do would be to find Calina and Tulip and to bring them here.

It was easy to find my way outside. Simon's temple was simplistic at best. The place felt more like a tomb than a place of worship, and I was eager to escape it. Somehow, it reminded me of Maltherius's lair, the place I thought had claimed Gaaron's life all those years ago. With Maltherius, everything was dark and creepy. Simon—or at least his followers—liked big, plain spaces. Or, in the library's case, small, plain spaces.

I liked being in the open; finding and escaping trouble was easier there as the need arose. Once outside, I filled my chest with as much air as I could fit inside. I hated having been cooped up for so long. Camping would have been preferable to a night in the monastery, but we hadn't had a safe space to set up our tents.

Now that I was back in the larger complex, I noticed the air stank of smoke and sweat—a marked difference from the night before. But why? I followed the scent, which was soon joined by the low murmur of a crowd. Was there a festival on?

As I drew closer, the rest of my senses engaged in puzzling out the mystery. This wasn't a festival; it was Shim, delighting the residents of Mystwood Keep with a dragon show.

He'd brought his wagon into the center square and had climbed on top of it. With him, a trio of dragonlings struggled against thick iron collars that bore equally thick iron chains. Shim had one in his hand, fastened with a leather grip, while the other two were anchored to the wagon's roof.

"Ladies and gentlemen, now that you've met our top three contenders, I encourage you to place your bids on which the regent will choose to enhance his collection. Remember, odds are ten to one that he'll choose our fire-breathing friend here." Shim yanked on the chain, and the little dragon belched a few sparks.

The crowd booed until Shim tugged on the chain once more, and this time, the flame dragonling spewed a long and steady stream of fire. Several observers had to jump back to avoid getting torched.

"Are you enjoying the show?" he asked, clearly already knowing their answer.

The crowd roared their approval as expected. They

were playing right into his greedy hands, and Shim was basking in a warm glow that had nothing to do with the fire-breather at his side.

"You'll enjoy it even more if you join our betting pool." He paused and tossed an exaggerated wink the crowd's way. One dwarven lady swooned from the attention, but her friend caught her before she could fall.

"I see you, sweetheart." Shim shifted his speech smoothly. "I see you all. You're people who know a good deal when you see one. Some of you would like to make easy money with our best bet, little Sparky here. Some of you will go for a long shot to win big. Well, we have plenty to choose from. There's the perfect betting choice for everybody, and that's a fact I'm very sure of. So whether you choose Rocky or Sandy, who you see with me here, or one of the fifteen other fabulous choices inside my wagon, you're choosing right!"

I searched the crowd for even a single spectator who wasn't falling for Shim's flimflam act but failed. I seemed to be the only one immune to his charms.

Shim hooted and made a broad gesture I was unable to interpret.

The crowd still ate it all up, then asked for seconds.

"Remember, I will offer private tours today and

tomorrow for just four coins per person, with a minimum of three per group. You can also pay ten for a private tour. See, folks, it pays to have friends—or, in this case, it saves!"

Shim paused to allow for the crowd's laughter.

"Find your best buds and tell them to join you for a delightful tour. There's no guarantee I'll be back this way, so this may be the only shot you've got to see these fearsome dragons up close. I promise you it is one hundred percent safe and one hundred and ten percent marvelous. Place your bets and purchase your tour vouchers right now. Don't forget that you can also purchase tickets to the choosing tomorrow evening inside the castle itself. See if your bet paid off while enjoying another truly unforgettable experience. Are you ready? Of course you are! Come, come. Shim is waiting!"

The people gathered about the square surged forward, each eager to be swindled by the odd human I now assumed was some kind of legendary mercantile thief rather than an even-halfway competent beast master.

I remained rooted to the spot as best I could, but a few folks jostled me as they pushed past to get first dibs on being taken by Shim's con. The more I learned about this guy, the less I liked him. No wonder Tulip and Calina had been so bothered by our first encounter. Seeing him handle the dragons firsthand was proof enough that "whipping them into shape" had been much more than a simple figure of speech.

I hoped they ate him alive one day—either the dragons or the crowd. It didn't matter just so long as someone was dispensing justice. It couldn't be me, though. I already had too much to do and too little time to do it. With one last scan of the crowd, I turned to look elsewhere for my missing party members.

"Hello... Hello..." A far-off voice called from somewhere I couldn't see. I stopped, growing stiff as I tried to figure out who had spoken and from where. It was a wonder I'd even heard the voice in this torrent of excited people jostling about the wagon.

It was silly of me to panic. The voice probably belonged to someone shy, trying to find some new friends to split the cost of a dragon wagon tour.

Yeah, that had to be it. Shim's ridiculous circus drew the focus of the entire square, sucking in every single person except me. Feeling good about my explanation, I hurried away from the pulsing throngs in search of one missing centaur and one missing half-elf. They couldn't be far and shouldn't be this hard to find, either.

I'd made it a solid ten paces when the same far-off

voice called out again. Unfortunately, I couldn't ignore it this time, and I couldn't write it off as belonging to Shim's crowd—mainly because it addressed me by my own blessed name.

"Tilda? Tilda Quickthatch? Can you hear me?"

24

I spun where I stood, glancing around as I tried to pinpoint the mysterious speaker. The square was flooded with activity, but none of it seemed to include me. Everyone was either busily engaged in their activities or moving swiftly toward Shim and his dragon wagon.

Well then, who had spoken to me? Who here knew my name?

"Hello?" I mumbled cautiously. "Who's there? Show yourself."

"I can't show myself because I'm not there," the voice answered with amusement. "Not yet, anyway."

What? His response made absolutely no sense.

A giant sigh shook the air around me. Or was that just my imagination?

"Check your pocket or your boot, wherever you put things for safekeeping," the unknown speaker commanded.

Suddenly, the obsidian comm-stone weighed heavily within the fabric folds of my trousers. I reached in and drew the object out to examine it up close. Nothing had changed about the stone's appearance. Whatever magic was happening here, it wasn't something I could discern.

"Did you find it?" This voice didn't belong to Finnian, but I'd heard it before. All at once, the last piece clicked into place.

"You're that kid," I spat out. "The snake shifter. What do you want?"

"I shifted into a snake once. *Once!* I'm not a snake shifter. I can take any form I want. It's just that one time I chose a snake, okay? Fin—"

"Stop," I shouted loud enough to cause several people to turn and study me with confused expressions before carrying on their ways once more. "We can't speak freely. I am... exposed."

"Then find someplace to hide because I have a lot to say, and I need you to listen."

"I'm working on it." I pushed the comm-stone back into my pocket, knowing I could hear it perfectly well from there and that it wouldn't accidentally be jostled from my grip by an errant passer-by.

"Just speak my name when you're ready to continue," the boy said.

"Sure thing, but what is it again?" It had only been a few days, but a lot had happened since we'd left Mirathane. This kid was little more than a footnote in our story so far, which meant I'd had no reason to remember his name.

"Leviath," he eagerly—perhaps a bit proudly—provided.

Levvy, right. I remembered now. "Okay, I'll let you know when I'm ready to speak more."

My legs pumped quickly as my mind spun. Where could I go to honestly speak freely? I didn't want to be overheard by the wrong people, and right about now, there were so many people around that at least one was bound to be the wrong sort.

I couldn't go back to the temple. I trusted that cleric just about as far as I could throw her, and as a halfling, I couldn't throw anybody any distance, even if I mustered all of my tiny might.

The dragon wagon was out because it was the most crowded place in Mystwood Keep at present.

That left a single location, and I doubted I'd be welcome back to it. Still, needs must. I ducked into the first alley and followed a twisty web of back roads until I finally started recognizing my surroundings. Moving as fast as I could without possibly rousing suspicion, I traced my way to Johan's meager living quarters.

I even said a quick prayer to the luck keeper. While it was true I didn't put much faith in the gods, they'd been front and center in my mind lately, and, well, it didn't hurt to whisper a few words to Shi, especially if she was listening and could help me out here.

"Almost ready," I said once I found myself in front of Johan's door. After a quick rap on the frame confirmed that nobody was inside, I grabbed a lockpick from my boot and got to work.

Deep breaths, Tilda, deep breaths. I kept my motions steady even though they were out of practice. I hadn't successfully picked a lock since *before* the whole kerfuffle in Maltherius's dungeon. There was no need while laying low as a tavern wench in Briarhaven.

Something clinked inside the mechanism. I squinted, bit my tongue, and delicately lifted my wire tool up and slightly to the left.

Click. Pause. *Click.*

And just like that, I was in. *Yes, this old girl's still got it!*

I pushed the door open and slipped into the cramped room, pressing my back to the wall and taking a moment to get my breathing back under control. "Okay, Levvy. I'm ready."

"I'd prefer you call me Leviath. Levvy is the name he insists upon, so we all match."

"Sure, whatever. It doesn't matter. What matters is why you contacted me. So spill."

He tutted at this, and I was surprised by the guttural sound carried through the stone. "It does matter. Names have power, especially a name like mine."

"Okay, sorry, *Leviath,*" I overemphasized his name, hoping we could move quickly past this point. I'd served many a year as Tilly, so I got the kid's frustration, but it was bad enough having to stroke Finnian's ego. I didn't have time to waste on this entitled kid, too.

"Can you please tell me why you reached out?" I asked while settling myself upon Johan's unmade bed. "I didn't know these comm-stones could send and receive."

"Most can't. The one he gave you is special. Just like you were."

"Were?" I scoffed, taking the stone from my pocket and tossing it in the air before catching it again. "I'm still here, you know."

"And still special, too?"

I stretched my legs out on the bed, luxuriating in loosening previously tight muscles. "Obviously, Finnian thinks so, or he wouldn't have worked so hard to hunt me down, right?" I couldn't help but boast. I didn't want the tanuki's adulation and especially didn't want his favor... but I still liked lording it over his newest charge. Old habits die hard, after all.

He groaned through the stone. "You're taking too long. That's why he's sending me to help."

I bolted upright in bed, ready for a fight—even if it was only with words. "Too long? It's been like three days!"

"He's been waiting decades for Eldrin's demise, and he can't risk letting you screw it up in the final hour."

"Wow, that's a bit harsh. We're really close." I rolled my eyes, even though Leviath couldn't see me. At least, I assumed he couldn't see me.

"Is that so? I see, I see. So, then, what's your plan?" It did not escape my notice that this child took on the speech patterns of his master. It made me wonder if Finnian was nearby, telling him the exact words to speak.

"We're close, but not that close," I confessed. If Finnian Sly was lying in wait, I had to be careful about phrasing things. For the love of the blessed mother, it felt like I couldn't trust anyone lately. As reluctant as

I'd been to accept their company at the start of this journey, they'd become my only lifeline. And right now, two out of four were missing. I needed to finish whatever this was with Finnian's servant and then get back out there so that I could reunite our fractured party.

"That's what he figured, which is why he's sending me in."

"And you have a plan?" I challenged, blinking up at the ceiling in disbelief.

"I do. Tilly, you were his favorite then, but I'm the favorite now. He should have just sent me to begin with. I tried to tell him, but he wouldn't listen."

"Look, I don't care who does the deed, just so long as it's done and Finnian gets me and my party to Maltherius as promised. Now, spit it out. What's your plan?"

"Well, as you pointed out, I can shift. Not just into a snake, but—"

"A dragon!" I sputtered excitedly. Yes, yes, of course!

"Yes, and I can incorporate others into my shift. It will just mean that whatever creature I become will have two heads. Did you see any dragonlings in the wagon with two heads?"

"I'm not sure, but—"

I stopped speaking as soon as I heard footsteps approaching from outside. "Levvy, shush. Someone is coming. I have to hide."

"I told you, it's Leviath," he spat as I hopped off Johan's bed and wiggled beneath it.

Before I could pull the last of my limbs into hiding, a firm hand wrapped around my ankle and refused to let go.

"Don't make me pull you out of there, Tilda. I've got a bad back, and I don't feel like making it any worse."

Yup. Johan had found me. Hopefully, he would forgive the intrusion, even though he'd made it clear he was not on board with my mission.

"Tilda, what's going on?" Leviath implored through the comm-stone I'd hastily shoved back into my pocket.

"There's more than one of you under there, huh?" Johan ground out. "Well, you'll both need to show yourselves."

"Let go of me, and I will." I could have kicked my way free, but I didn't want to risk hurting my friend. He was so frail that a solid blow could knock him over. He could hit his head and then never wake up again. *No, no, mustn't think like that.*

As soon as Johan removed his grasp, I rolled out

from under the bed and stared up at him from the floor. "It's just me. The other voice is coming from the stone. Here." I yanked it from my pocket and handed it to the old man.

He widened his eyes in surprise as he studied the cooly, shining obsidian. "This reeks of a certain tanuki we both know and hate. Who've you got on the other end? Another of that crook's child slaves?"

I nudged Johan with my foot and shook my head. Didn't he know to speak carefully? That he could get us both in big trouble if he wasn't careful here?

"I work with Finnian of my own free will," Levvy corrected with evident pride, even though all three of us knew this had to be a lie.

"Yeah, of course you do." Johan bent to offer me a hand, but I refused it. Instead, I pushed my palms flat into the floorboards and then popped back to my feet with my own power. "Tilda, you broke into the home of a guard. If anyone other than me had caught you, you'd already be serving time in the dungeon. I can look the other way this time. For old-time's sake. But I won't be able to save you if you go through with this terrible plan of yours."

"It's not her plan. It's my plan," Levvy said, once again letting his hubris slip out.

"Even worse," the old man grumbled. "Wherever you are, stay put. It's not safe here. For either of you."

"It's too late. I'm already on my way up the plateau. You have to get me in."

I watched as my friend's face twisted, first in shock and then in outrage.

"Johan, be reasonable." I touched his wrist to draw his attention back to me. "He'll be safer with you than with anyone else."

"But then you'll take him directly into the beast's maw. I know Finnian Sly has a soft spot for children, but the regent does not." Johan closed his eyes and took in several slow breaths.

I could tell he had more to say, so I waited.

"He'll torture you both, and then he'll kill you. I've seen it happen before, more times than I care to confess."

"I can't turn back, and I can't fail. Finnian is doing me a big favor by trusting me with this. He doesn't think I can do it," Levvy added with a quavering voice. His confidence had finally worn thin. "If I prove him right, he'll never let me out again. I'll never get another chance. Tilda, Tilda's friend, please."

Johan wore a pained expression as he lifted the comm-stone to his mouth and whispered, "I'll sneak you in after dark. If the guards at the gate figure out what you're up to, they'll imprison you immediately. At least you'll have a chance with me. Be it a very, very small one."

I gave my old friend the biggest hug I could offer. My arms didn't wrap all the way around him, but my heart sure did. "Thank you, Johan. You won't regret this," I practically cried with relief.

"I already do," he said, remaining stiff in my embrace.

25

Johan did not return my hug; in fact, he grew even stiffer in my embrace. "I'm having my lunch. Get out of here. I don't want to see you ever again, Little Foot. I mean it this time. I meant it last time, too."

I let him go but smiled wide as I spoke. "Thank you for helping Leviath. When you get him inside, bring him to—"

"No," Johan barked at me. "I will help him inside, then it's up to the two of you. Use your comm-stone. I don't care what you do. Just leave me out of it."

I held up my hands and backed away. "Fine, I'm going." It was better to leave now than risk him rescinding his aid. He'd already given more than he wanted, which would have to be enough. I could do the rest, filling in the blanks as we went.

My thoughts raced with all the possibilities as I rewound through a few alleys until I found myself in the main social square. The "dragon master" Shim was deep into giving his tours and had a line that wrapped a couple of times around. I scanned the crowd once again for the girls but came up short. If Tulip were here, she'd be easy to spot, which meant she and Calina were both somewhere else.

"Hey, no cutting in line. You'll have to wait your turn like the rest of us," someone shouted when I got too close to the wagon for their comfort.

"No pushing!" another person shouted at the first one.

Solstice was fast approaching, which meant the days were long and hot. Folks were also impatient, waiting for their turn at Shim's spectacle, and that led to big tempers. I noted this all with interest. Then, just to add to the chaos, I made sure to stomp on a cranky gnome's toes as I passed by.

And just like that, a tussle broke out.

I hurried along my way, leaving them to their misery as a fresh wave of hope swelled within me. Our plan could work. With Levvy's shifting capabilities, he could bring me close to the regent. We could pose as one of the dragons at the choosing ceremony. Even if there weren't any two-headed dragons on the cart, only Shim would know that for sure. One of the kids could distract the snake oil salesman just in case, and the others could create chaos amongst the crowd. I'd just proved how easy that was to do.

Once everyone was adequately distracted, we could unshift, and I would slice Eldrin's throat to finish the job. It was all remarkably simple, proving that, with the right party, you really could do anything. Or at least I could. That's why rogues were the best. Although even I had to admit, the plan wouldn't work without our newly acquired shifter.

It was midday now, and Levvy wouldn't be inside the keep until nightfall. That left me the rest of the day to inform the others of our plan and prepare them for what would happen next.

I just had to find them first.

I kept my eyes peeled for Tulip and Calina as I made my way back to the Simonite temple but failed to locate them. It wasn't easy to lose a centaur, yet I'd managed to do it twice since we first embarked upon this adventure. I doubted the Genesis Crest was involved in Tulip's disappearance this time, mainly because the artifact was currently tucked safely beneath my tunic. What else could this old thing do? If things went wrong with the assassination, would it find a way to help us out of trouble?

These were the thoughts swirling around my head when I re-entered the temple—this time without any fanfare. The cleric wasn't there waiting to welcome us, and not a single worshiper congregated around the altar. That suited me just fine. Going through the whole silence-is-golden schtick again would have irritated me to no end. I didn't need piety thrust upon me. I just needed to regather my party.

Now that I was inside, my first stop would be the windowless room that served as a library. Unlike the larger keep, the inside of the temple was relatively easy to navigate. I found the library again with zero difficulty, but when I entered, I saw all the books set meticulously back in place with no half-orc to keep them company.

Huh.

Refusing to give up so quickly, I shuffled to the monastery to check on Amariel. I didn't know where the cleric had set her up, but I figured the celestial would be easy to find.

And this time, I was right.

I just had to follow the voices down a long white hall and open the door, flanking the wall at the end. I found everyone I was missing inside that far room, including the Simonite cleric. She sat in the corner, watching the others as she rocked gently back and forth.

"Hello," I said because it seemed like the polite thing to do. I didn't want her to know that I found her untrustworthy and dangerous. That would just make her more of the latter, and we already had plenty of danger crowding in on us.

The cleric stopped rocking and raised a finger to her lips, having apparently resumed her vow of silence. That saved me from having to offer her any aid, I guessed—and that would save me a little bit of time and frustration.

Good, good. Everything was going well.

As I approached, I saw that Amariel had woken up. Although she remained lying back on the bed, unspeaking, her eyes were now open, and she appeared to be taking in her surroundings.

"Oh, there you are, Tilda," Calina said with a quick nod of acknowledgment. "We were wondering where you'd gotten off to."

I chuffed at this. "Me? You and Tulip were the ones who disappeared even before I'd had the chance to wake up."

"Shhh," Tulip said with so much extra verve that she splattered Rurik's face with spittle. He didn't seem to mind, though. "Can't you see Amariel needs her rest?"

I glanced at the old woman again, watching her eyes dart about the room. Was she seeing things we couldn't? Was she really even any better than last I'd seen her? I found her current state deeply concerning. What if she never got back to normal? I knew Tulip would refuse to leave her behind, which meant the celestial would become an almost literal dead weight, an enormous liability. And if she couldn't wake up, then she also wouldn't be able to heal. This was really, really bad.

I tried to hide my concern from the others, saying, "I won't force her to get up, but we do need to find a place to stay for the night."

Rurik's brow furrowed in confusion. "But we already have a place to stay. Right here."

I widened my eyes at Calina, willing her to understand.

"Tilda's right. We can't impose on Simon any longer. He and his faithful have already been more than generous enough." Calina had become incredibly reliable as of late, and I wondered whether it was because Finnian had arbitrarily put her in charge or for some other reason. She reminded me of her parents in the best possible way, and somehow, she still reminded me of myself, too. At first, I thought her desire to become an adventurer was silly and foolish, but now I see that she was always meant to be a part of this. She was born for it, perhaps even more than I had been.

"We are safe in the conveyance," Amariel spoke without any music to back her up.

"Is she okay?" I asked, suppressing the shiver that threatened to overwhelm me.

Rurik answered, "She's been working through our journey since she woke up. It's like she's reliving the past week at rapid speed."

Hope rose anew. "And she just got to the part where we boarded the dragon wagon? Does that mean she'll be back to normal soon?"

"No, not that part," Tulip said with a sad sigh. "The first conveyance."

"The first conveyance! How long has she been up?"

"Since late morning," someone said.

Oh no, this was not good.

"We need her to be at her best. Is there any way we can speed up this process?" I asked the kids as Amariel appeared to fall into slumber. Was she really asleep or just reenacting her earlier sleep? None of this made any sense. I hated it so much, especially what it might mean for our fast-approaching mission. Either we succeeded in assassinating Eldrin Grimlock, or he'd

have our heads. At least one person would die tomorrow, and I couldn't let it be any of us. How fitting we'd
found our way to Simon, to his temple of stillness and
death.

Once we left here, I would never be back. This
place gave me the creeps.

"Well?" I prompted again upon realizing no one
had answered.

Rurik glanced at the cleric, who shook her head
and began to tug at her ears in distress. Was this
because she couldn't help or simply that she wouldn't?
Neither answer would surprise me, but both made me
furious at her.

"We need to go," I decided at once. We really
couldn't stay here—not another minute. "Tulip, can
you carry her?"

"Yes, but is it safe to move her?" Tulip turned her
full attention to me, her blue eyes shining as she waited
for me to give my answer. One corner of her mouth
tugged slightly, but not enough to make a smile. She
wore a completely new expression that took me a
moment to identify, having never seen it before.
Respect.

She and the others were counting on me. More
than that, they trusted me. I had to make sure their
faith was well-founded. I had to, and I would.

"It's safer than leaving her here. Let's go."

"Okay," Tulip answered uncertainly, but already, she was hoisting the unconscious celestial into her arms without hesitation. If you're sure."

I wasn't, but I couldn't let that slow us down.

26

We rented two rooms at a small inn tucked a few streets away from the temple. Mystwood Keep seemed to have everything you'd expect to find in a large population center. Strangely, this complex had initially been built as a military outpost. It was later updated to house the district monarchy. But neither of those purposes gave it any right to be so large and well-equipped. I wondered if it had always been this way or if Eldrin had rapidly expanded the keep's footprint once coming to power.

If Eldrin was the one behind it, then it was likely that the various shopkeepers and townspeople were incredibly loyal to him. I knew at least one guard who disapproved of the regent's policies, but I also knew that Johan was too afraid to challenge him.

If Eldrin himself had created new jobs and gathered everyone here, the people would assuredly want to protect their benefactor. And that could mean dodging the revenge of an entire population if we were to succeed in our mission... and if anyone noticed.

Stealth would be paramount. Stealth and a swift escape.

We needed Leviath. He was our surest bet to best this challenge, and thankfully he was on his way to us now. Now, I just had to explain all that to the kids. As soon as we'd paid our coin and settled in the space, I gathered them in one room to catch them up on the broad strokes of our newly formed plan.

"The druid who could incorporate others into his shift," Rurik stated the very moment Levvy's name had left my mouth.

I nodded, quickly continuing before Rurik could lead us too far afield. "Yes, we met him in Zephyriel's throne room. He reached out to me through the stone, and he's coming to the keep. Johan has agreed to help sneak him in by dark."

"We don't need anyone else in our party," Calina huffed and crossed her arms. "Especially not some random child."

"Yes, yes, we do," I argued patiently. "And we need him specifically. He's going to be the one to get us close enough to Eldrin to act."

"By shifting into a dragon," Rurik finished for me. Well, at least someone got it. Perhaps he could explain it all to Calina later when she was more willing to listen.

I pointed to him and nodded in confirmation. "Yes."

"Ooh. At the choosing ceremony tomorrow?" Tulip asked, eager to be included. She glanced at Rurik for approval, but he looked more confused than proud.

"Yes," I answered, biting off the end of the word to make it snap. "How do you know about that?"

Tulip's eyes grew dark and narrow. "Calina and I were there this morning, checking up on the dragons. That man Shim is terrible. Those poor dragons are just big bags of coin to him."

"We have to help them," Calina agreed, repeatedly slamming her fist into her hand as if she were already actively engaged in this freedom fight.

"Calm down, would you?" I grabbed Calina's fist and forced her to still before saying more. "I agree he's not the nicest guy, but we already have a lot on our plates, and I can only fit so much in my stomach, you know?"

"What?" Tulip shouted and stomped, shaking the floorboards beneath us. "Are you saying you won't help these poor creatures in need?"

Someone on the lower floor of the inn shouted for us to "cut out or get out." Yikes, we had to be more careful. If Tulip brought her hoof down hard enough, she could stomp a hole straight through the blessed floor.

Rurik raised one finger in the air. "It's a metaphor. But yes, it seems she's saying she won't help."

"Not that I won't. Just that we're too busy already," I tried to explain.

Tulip stared at me and willfully stomped again.

"Cut out or get out! Last warning," that same aggravated voice called up.

"You have got to stop. If we get thrown out of here, we'll have nowhere else to go. We need to lie low and finalize our plan; this is not just our best option. It is our only option. So, *cut out*, I guess."

Tulip spun so that she was facing away from me, but at least she didn't stomp the floorboards again.

I stayed where I stood as I tried to reason with her. "I'm sorry. I get that you're upset, but if we waste too much time here, we won't have enough to finish our main quest. You know, the part where we save Calina's dad?"

She spun back to face me, rage burning in her bright blue eyes. "How could you even imply that it's a waste to—"

"No," Calina interrupted softly as her arms finally fell back to her sides. "She's right. We have to save my dad first, then come back to help the dragons. It's the only way. Right, Tilda?"

"Yeah, sure. Anyway..." I had no intention of adventuring with this crew once we'd finished up with Maltherius. There were still strong chances we wouldn't survive, and if we did manage to make it out alive, I would happily get back to my retirement and put this whole thing behind me forever.

"I'm going to check on Amariel," Tulip said before exiting abruptly.

"I need to reach out to Levvy... Uh, Leviath, and tell him where to meet us once he's inside. What will you two do?"

"I have some books," Rurik answered eagerly, not needing to say a word more for the rest of us to get it.

Calina let out a long sigh. "I guess I'll go for a walk."

"Fine." I moved in front of her before she could dart away. "Just make sure you're back here before nightfall. Once Leviath is here, we'll eat a big supper, discuss tomorrow's plan, and get a solid night's sleep so we have the strength and clarity to enact it."

"Yes, Tilda. I understand," she sang snottily, and then she was gone.

I stayed at the inn for the rest of the day to keep the kids from wandering off. I checked in on Amariel several times. When last I'd left her, she thought she was tending to Rurik as a swarm of siphons attempted to smash him to death inside that doomed mountain pass town.

She chanted words in a strange language as her eyes stared blankly ahead.

Sometimes, she would become lucid and join us in the present moment, asking for a drink or for Tulip to hold her hand, but mostly, she was stuck revisiting our adventure so far, reliving each moment as if for the first time.

Calina returned from her walk shortly before sunfall and seemed in higher spirits than before. I tried to ask her about it, but she appeared distracted and only offered clipped answers to my many questions.

The cloak of night descended, and I sat waiting in a seat by the window, the comm-stone placed on the sill beside me. After an hour without updates from Leviath, I became worried and tried calling him through the stone. But the magic had to be activated from his side of the connection, which meant I got nowhere.

So I continued to wait.

Until, at last, a furious knock sounded at the door. "Tilda!" Johan's haggard voice cried. "I know you're in there, and I've got a bone to pick with you."

Oh, fig. Johan had said he wasn't coming, that I'd never see him again. And now he was here. And angry. Had something gone wrong? Was Leviath not coming after all? How did he find us?

No, no, no. We needed him.

I jumped from my seat and flung the door open, revealing a red-faced Johan and an exhausted but happy Leviath.

"I thought you said I'd never see you again," I mumbled dumbly.

"That was before I realized you were keeping a half-dryad child inside the city. Don't you realize that it's killing him?" Johan pushed past me into the room and immediately sunk onto one of the beds to catch his breath.

Levvy skipped inside the room, appearing happy and spry to me. I watched him prance circles across the floorboards and then turned back to Johan with a bemused expression. Whatever fatigue he'd picked up on the journey had disappeared in an instant, and now he appeared to be brimming with boundless energy.

"He feels better because he's been in nature on the walk over," Johan explained as he shook his head at me in apparent disappointment. "He probably feels better than he has in years. But he's going to fade and fast."

"I'm sorry to hear that. But I hardly know this kid. I've only met him once before now. He works for Finnian, and, for the moment, so do I. That's all."

"You can't send him back to Mirathane. It's the worst possible place for him."

Rurik put down his book and stumbled, tripping but quickly catching himself. He didn't say anything helpful or even anything at all.

That left it to me then. "I'm guessing Maltherius's lair is even worse," I hissed at my old friend. "And that's where we're headed next. I can't keep him. You can if you want."

"Hello, I'm my own person," Levvy sang while

prancing in big, looping circles. "I decide where I go, and right now, I've decided to be right here."

Rurik grabbed the skipping child by the arm, forcing him to stop. "You're part dryad?" he asked with his lips tight and his single tusk steady.

The child yanked his arm away and grimaced at the half-orc. "Yeah, so what?"

"Dryads are servants of Cardis, living people sprouted from trees. And I thought they reproduced through a type of self-pollination. But, they aren't meant to travel so far from their groves," Rurik said, then brought his face closer to the child to examine him.

Leviath attempted to back away but was stuck in the stronger person's grip. "Well, I don't know what to tell you because I've lived here my whole life."

"You're only part dryad, I don't know the split though, and you work with Finnian Sly. How does that happen? Did Finnian help create you? Or because you're only part dryad, does it mean you're an orphan? Or are you like your own half-brother?"

"I don't like you or your questions," Levvy spat, literally spat at Rurik.

But still, the aspiring wizard hung tight to his newly discovered specimen.

"Rurik, leave him alone," I commanded. I was too

tired for this, and we had no time to spare. "He's here to help us with... you know. Not give you a genealogy lesson."

Rurik loosed his grip but remained focused on the druid. "What is the rest of you? Is it human, elf, or halfling? I can't tell."

"Rurik, stop. You're being rude," Calina warned from her place across the room.

But he wouldn't listen, not when there was something so enjoyable for him to learn. When the child began to flit around the room again, Rurik lumbered after him, wanting to remain close. "Yes, it must be. That's why you can incorporate others into your shift. And if Cardis created dryads, that would make you at least partially a demigod. Wonders of Wissandor, you're quite possibly more powerful than any mortal. Even Finnian."

Now Leviath seemed interested. He stopped and turned to face Rurik head-on. "More powerful than the master? Really?"

"Dryads are demigods created by Cardis after Shi gave her dominion over nature. And dryads, self-replicate. If I knew the breakdown of your lineage, we'd know just how demigod you would be."

"A god, really?" Levvy laughed and then initiated

what appeared to be a weird victory dance. "You're kind of stupid, but I guess I like you after all."

Rurik danced with him, too, trying to copy the child's moves but doing a very poor job. "You're different, special. And because of that, it doesn't matter what else you are."

"Did you just learn an important lesson?" I asked, recalling our conversation inside the Simonite library.

Rurik stopped dancing, returned to his corner of the room, and returned to his books with fresh insight. The entire time, he wore a broad, complacent smile.

"Kid, can you just stop moving for a second? You're making me dizzy," Calina interjected, which was funny since she was generally the prancer of the group.

Johan chose this precise moment to re-enter the conversation. "Tilda, you have to get this child to safety. And I guarantee you safety cannot be found with your old tanuki master, Finnian."

"If you're so worried about him, you can help. I already told you I have other plans. Besides, don't I have a big enough nursery school as it is?" I motioned to Calina and Rurik in their respective spots across the room. Tulip was still in the other room, tending to Amariel.

Rurik nodded his agreement while Calina shouted an impassioned, "Hey!"

Johan kept his eyes glued firmly to Leviath as he mumbled, "But I'm a prisoner here. I must serve the regent until the day I die."

"Or until the day he dies. Which will be tomorrow, by the way." I waited for him to smile, to argue, to do something. He didn't.

"Now, will you help us?" Calina asked in a way that refused to be ignored.

"I..." Johan began, stopped, and then tried to start again. "I... I don't... I can't..."

"It's fine, Big Foot. We've got this. Go home. Get some rest." I helped him from the bed, pushed him toward the door, and then pushed it open for him, too.

He stepped out into the hall, keeping his back turned to the rest of us. After standing there, tall and still, for several moments, he finally said, "If you succeed, I will help the child. My old home, the bubbling creek."

"Yeah, that will be nice, Johan. You deserve it. You both do." I smiled, even though I knew he wasn't looking. Still, I felt too happy to restrain the expression, even if it was only for myself.

He nodded and took off down the hall with slow, measured steps.

This was it, then. Perhaps I'd seen the last of my

old mentor and friend, but now I knew we would part with fond memories. If all goes well tomorrow, then...

No. I surged down the hall after Johan and stopped him with a gentle touch of his hip.

"There's no if about it," I said to him and to myself. After all, we both needed to hear it. "We *will* succeed."

27

"This itches. Why does it itch?" I moaned for what must have been the millionth time that morning.

"You aren't used to wearing scales," Leviath said from beside me, while echoing *within* me. We were currently sharing the body of a two-headed toxic-blood dragon. Since we were but an imitation of the actual creature, we had no poison, which was probably a good thing, as we also had no immunity to said toxicity.

I'd reasoned that anyone watching Eldrin Grim-lock's choosing ceremony play out would pay less attention to our presence there if we shifted into a dragon that was a bit more... unassuming. We couldn't help the two heads, but we had chosen a dragon type that Shim hadn't publicly deemed a "best bet."

Leviath and I had crept into the unlocked dragon wagon before the sun started its ascent for the day. Once inside, we found an empty cage and slipped inside.

Thankfully, Leviath was happy to follow my instincts when making the plan. Unfortunately, he couldn't stop moving, and since we currently shared a body, I had to grit my pointed teeth to keep from yelling at him. He'd retained some of his manic energy from the night before but wasn't quite as spirited, which was both good and bad as far as our next steps were concerned.

I needed him alert, ready for whatever happened once we entered the throne room. But until then, I really needed him to stop tapping his claws against the cage bars and bobbing his head like it was the most excellent song that had ever been played. He paused to sigh, pant, and rebuild his strength every now and then, but he always started up again before too long. Johan had been right about the city setting dampening his health. I hated seeing it but was glad the druid's magic had held steady thus far.

The last thing we needed was to get caught because of a flickering shift.

Stealth was the name of the game. That and waiting.

The choosing ceremony was scheduled to begin after the regent took a lavish private breakfast, and my grumbling stomach begrudgingly reminded me that I'd missed my morning meal. I'd been too nervous to eat. Of course, Rurik had been happy to help himself to my tanuki cookie cast-offs. That boy's stomach was a bottomless pit. After a week of traveling together, I had yet to see it reach its fill and doubted that I ever would.

I'd instructed the half-orc and the rest of our party to remain behind and purchase their tickets to the ceremony at the doors whenever they opened to the public. Tulip attempted a half-hearted argument about spending her coin, but even she knew that we had to play by the rules here until we broke them in the worst possible way.

It was bad enough that Levvy and I were sneaking about as this fake two-headed dragon thing. There was no possible way we could effectively hide a massive centaur, a clumsy half-orc, or an unconscious celestial. Calina at least more-or-less blended in... well, so long as she kept quiet. Which she never did.

I'd assigned them each a station to take up once inside. Planning this hadn't proven easy, given that we hadn't gotten the chance to view the throne room in advance. So, regarding this part of the plan, I had to work off my memories of other castles and the group's best guesses about what this one might hold. A part of me wanted them to wait it out at the inn, but with so many things that could go wrong, it was better to have them close.

Calina was to be my eyes. She had no specific station but was meant to move around and keep ahead of any possible trouble. We'd agreed that if she spotted anything she was unequipped to deal with, she would shout, "Look at Sparky's thing. It's just the cutest I've ever seen!"

The word "thing" was to be replaced with varying dragon body parts depending on where the problem was located relative to the throne. Last night, Rurik devised a clock system to divide the space and assigned a code word to each of the twelve ticks. He'd grilled Calina mercilessly until he was sure everyone understood. And I had to hand it to him; his pedantry occasionally came in handy. I still hoped our plan went off without a hitch, but I knew better than to expect a smooth go.

That's why I'd ordered Tulip to hang out near the back of the crowd while she kept hold of Amariel. If we needed to make a quick escape, she could charge a path for the rest of us to follow.

That left Rurik. He was to get as close as possible to the area where Shim would be showing off the dragons. This suited him well since it's what he wanted to do anyway. Ostensibly, he was there to study the creatures up close, spewing off various smart-sounding facts about every dragon in attendance *except* the two-headed poison barb. However, my true goal was to ensure he stayed close to me and Leviath in case we needed extra muscle in a pinch. I kept this motivation to myself, betting Rurik would channel his might through his fists if the situation demanded it. I'd seen him do it with farmer Dewglen's giant locusts in Briarhaven, so I knew he had the potential.

He also seemed to be changing somehow. All that reading and reflection had gone to his head, and I didn't yet know whether that was a good thing. Had he found the answer he needed to unlock his magical growth? Or would he soon give up on trying everything together? Rurik was a smart kid, and I trusted him to figure out what needed to be done, both today and in any days yet to come.

Indeed, I didn't know much else about what would go down during the ceremony, only that we'd finish it off with a dead regent, thus keeping up our side of the bargain with Finnian Sly. Then it would be on to Maltherius, and that's the mission that mattered.

Yes, infiltrating the castle and committing murder in a highly public place would be a challenge. But if we couldn't pull this off, we had no hope against the far more deadly necromancer we needed to face next. Either we'd survive, or we'd be done. I didn't hate either option. I probably should have been more afraid of death, but I'd encountered too much of it, I guess. It no longer felt sacred or even final. It just was.

This thought unnerved me as I prepared to end the tyrant's reign. What if somebody brought him back? What if he returned more powerful and more pissed off than ever before?

That wouldn't be good for us.

Sometimes, I wished I lived in a world where magic didn't exist, that time couldn't be unwound, and lives couldn't be unborn. Sure, none of these things were common, but they were always possible. And that made victories less certain. It made me infinitely more anxious to think that all our hard work could simply be undone with the wave of someone's wand.

I'd never met anyone that powerful... other than my very next opponent, that is. I gulped down a knot of dread as I envisioned Maltherius, growing ever angrier for each second he awaited my arrival. Unlike

Eldrin Grimlock, Maltherius knew we were coming. He'd been preparing for years, and—

Tip-tip-tap-taaaap. Leviath stretched his foreleg forward and scratched a new tune on the cage bars, shattering my icy wall of fear.

Okay, I was psyching myself out. I needed to stop panicking and focus on the current mission. I let out a slow breath through my weird dragon's snout and attempted to ground myself back in the present reality. Unfortunately, that created other problems.

"Are you used to these itchy scales?" I asked Leviath, feeling like I was beginning to lose myself to madness. The longer we waited, the worse it would become. I hoped the ceremony would start soon. Anticipation was only helpful when there was more to learn and more plans to be laid. But here I sat with nothing left to do other than to get on with it. My mind spun in circles while my portion of this odd, foreign body remained rigid and still.

Oh, but it itched. I raked my claws across my neck, willing the discomfort to end. "I don't know how much more of this I can take," I confessed to the kid. Even though, to me, it sounded as if I were speaking normally, Leviath had assured me that nobody could hear me except him. Since dragons didn't naturally speak, he'd explained, our shifted form also couldn't speak common. We, however, communicated with each other because we were sharing a body... or something like that.

It didn't make sense to me, but I wasn't used to wielding magic. I also wasn't used to standing on four feet or coordinating my steps with a second brain that controlled half of my new reptilian body. That's why I flatly declined when Levvy suggested we attack the regent in our dragon form. I had no idea whether our strength was up to the task, and we couldn't risk the time it would take to find out. What if we wasted our only opportunity with an anemic swipe that led to raucous laughter rather than a gushing artery?

No, definitely not worth the risk.

Instead, we would approach Eldrin as the dragon and then exit the shift. I had my dagger waiting in my pocket, which Levvy assured me would still be there once I turned back into my halfling self. We even practiced merging and unmerging a few times at the inn the night before, so I knew what to expect and could act fast once I was exposed as my true self.

"Every body feels a little different. Just ignore the itch," Leviath answered in my head as the wagon began to roll forward with us inside.

"Sweet divinity, it's time. This is happening, and it's happening now. You remember the plan, right?"

"Of course, I remember the plan. We've only been over it a thousand hundred times." The druid's answer reminded me just how young and inexperienced he was. Sure, he stole, but had he ever taken a life? I felt like the world's worst babysitter for tying myself to this youngster on a life-and-death mission.

"Humor me one more time. After you shift us back into our normal bodies, what will you do?"

"Run and hide."

"And?"

"And do not get involved, no matter what." He sniffed and craned his neck awkwardly to meet my eyes. "It's fine, Tilda. Murder is just stealing a life. I steal stuff for Finnian all the time. This is really no big deal."

A shiver snaked through my limbs as I recalled the boy's master saying almost the exact same words. They were so much worse coming from the lips of a child. I may not have cared much for the gods, but some things were meant to be sacred—childhood chief among them. My heart ached for Leviath and all that he'd missed out on. It ached for the child I'd once been, the one I sometimes still felt stir within me.

I'd missed my chance, but Leviath still had his.

Johan had said he'd take him to the forest and give him a proper life. It helped to focus on their happily ever after. I was still far from my own if I was meant to have one at all. Right now, my best possible scenario was keeping all the people I cared about alive and reuniting the little family of three I loved so dearly. That was it.

Once they were happy, it would be enough. I'd probably go back to work at the tavern, serving up drinks and keeping Durgan from imbibing so many he couldn't walk home to his husband, Pat.

Tulip Thunderhoof was obsessed with ensuring she was the main character in life. She wasn't, but neither was I. At best, I was a loyal sidekick. I'd never stopped fighting for Gaaron, even when I thought he was lost for good.

I didn't have the energy to want anything more, especially not for myself. And when you want nothing, you also have nothing to lose. I was going to give my all to our mission today, and then tomorrow, I would wake up and do it all over again, with a different foe but the same end goal.

The people I loved would be safe and happy. They would be together and free.

And that was it. That was all I needed for my happy ending.

As for this? This was only book two, and I was so ready to turn the page to a new chapter.

The wagon stopped rolling, and a moment later, the door swung open, emitting a blast of light that caused spots to appear in my eyes. When the dark specks burned away, I saw Shim's lanky form hurrying about the cargo hold.

"He's unlatching all the cages," I told Levvy inwardly. "Get ready for things to start happening."

We hung back in the darkest corner of our cell, hoping Shim would not notice the unexpected addition to his traveling zoo.

"Don't you dare embarrass me out there," the showman hissed and wagged a finger at one of the cages before popping it open. "One more wrong move, and it's off to Sandsibar with you, Frosty. And believe me, you don't want to discover what happens to an ice dragon in the desert. Suffice it to say, it's not good. So you better be. Got it?"

The dragon did not answer, and Shim moved on, muttering to himself.

But a moment later, I watched with wide, lidless eyes as the whitish-blue frost dragon popped his head out from the cage and bared its fangs while staring after his cruel master. He swung his lean face back and forth and tasted the air with a slow, flicking tongue.

And then he saw us, or at least the poison barb we were pretending to be.

The corners of his mouth pulled back in a very personable smile—an unsettling thing when coming from a dragon.

"What's going on with this one?" I asked Leviath, panic mounting.

"Dunno."

We both watched with coordinated heads; mine stretched higher with the druid kid's dipping low. The ice dragon moved back into the cage, disappearing from our line of sight.

A moment later, Shim marched back through the open door and bent down to tug at a leather handhold as he exited. I watched in horror as a thick iron chain rose from the floorboards. One by one, the dragonlings emerged from their cages, getting pulled along by the complex system of shackles.

The ice dragon popped its head out again and hopped down, shaking itself happily to show it bore no fetters. This was good for Frosty but even better for us.

"Leviath, we need to search his cage for that collar," I hissed. My voice sounded odd as if I was beginning to fuse with the ruse. Blessed hell, I hoped that wasn't the case. My happily ever did not include being stuck inside a dragon's itchy skin for the rest of my days.

When we find it, you need to put it on," I pleaded. There was no more time to waste. The waiting was finally over.

Levvy swiped at me with one of the legs he controlled, but my thick skin absorbed the impact. "What? No way," he argued and attempted to swat at me again. "I'm not wearing a collar!"

"Stop fighting me, and just listen," I argued back. "People will notice and say something if we don't fit with the others. I've got my lock-picking tools in my boot. As soon as I kill Eldrin, I'll free you. I won't leave you, I promise."

He sighed, and suddenly, all remaining fight leaked out of him as if he'd been drained at the base. "I don't know why, but I trust you," he muttered, already moving us toward the abandoned cage. "Fine, I'll wear the stupid collar."

Show time.

28

Leviath and I marched in line with the other dragons, a chain gang of magical creatures on display for the amusement of the wealthy and bored. Once he'd ensured all paying spectators had found their way inside, Shim had pulled the wagon right up to the castle doors for ease of transport. Apparently, he didn't trust anyone else to touch his "beloved" pets, which made tethering us all together the best—and only—option as far as he seemed concerned.

Shim now paraded us through the throne room, singing a peppy but tuneless song to delight the crowd.

"Eighteen dragons," he crooned as he approached the raised stage at the far end of the room where the regent sat waiting to make his choice. "Soon to become seventeen, once your great and glorious sovereign makes his selection."

"All hail Eldrin Grimlock. Long may he live," the people cheered and waved their fists in the air.

My stomach churned, and every part of me itched, especially the part that would soon be holding a dagger to the throat of that vainglorious villain. I kept my eyes focused ahead, even though we were still too far away for me to make out much more than the blurry shape of the fellow sitting upon the throne. Our shift was nothing more than a visual dupe, which meant we hadn't gained the dragon's superior vision.

That was okay by me, though. The only thing I had to do inside the disguise was get close enough to unshift and unalive my target. We lumbered slowly forward as Shim turned every step into a spectacle and took every opportunity to pump up his audience.

Fig, this was taking forever!

With nothing interesting to keep my attention and a poor vantage point for sussing out the crowd, my mind began to wander once more. I hadn't seen the missing ice dragon since he'd escaped his cage. I hoped he'd made it somewhere safe to evade recapture. Thanks to that little trickster, the count remained accurate. Shim had eighteen dragons, just as expected.

He just didn't know that he'd swapped frost for poison.

As we moved, I took stock of the other dragon youth in our line, noting that Shim already had a poisonling. This one didn't have two heads, which meant we were still a special part of the collection so far as the unwashed masses were concerned.

"This is your last chance—last chance!—to place bets. The regent is about to take his pick of these fine creatures. May his choice make you rich, friends. Come, come. Don't be shy. My dragons won't bite so long as you don't get close enough to let them." Shim laughed heartily at this, moving one hand to clutch at his stomach as part of his peculiar pantomime.

A few of the spectators chuckled along awkwardly. Others appeared concerned more than anything, and rightfully so. Dragons were dangerous, not just when they were halfling assassins in disguise.

A family of elves approached to place their bets and join the game. As they passed, a child reached out and attempted to pet Levvy on the head. My druid accomplice hissed and bit down firmly on the errant hand, causing the little elf to cry out in pain.

Nobody seemed to notice, though. Not even the parents. Such was the chaos of the moment.

"What are you doing?" I ground out irritably.

"Acting like a dragon. We don't want to raise anyone's suspicions."

"You can't bite kids!" I thought back to all the times I'd inwardly yelled at myself over wanting to hit my kid companions and the one time I'd actually done it. But thwapping Rurik in the thigh had practically broken my hand, and he hadn't even noticed.

"Eh, I just soft-mouthed her," Levvy's response came. "Scared her more than anything."

We stood, waiting in place, while Shim continued taking his last round of coin. All this stop-and-go almost made me miss Leviath's stupid tapping from earlier. Why did everything have to take so long? Granted, I hadn't been back in the adventuring game for long, but it seemed like all we did was wait for things to happen. I wanted to *make* things happen, and I wanted to do them right now.

"Sweet Sylric, this sucks." It took me a moment to realize I'd invoked Calina's minor trickster deity. Every member of our party was rubbing off on the others. And I'd assumed I was too old to change. Huh. Soon, we'd all sit around the campfire holding a traveler's book club with Rurik. He would like that far too much. As for me, I'd like anything that wasn't this.

C'mon, Shim. Keep it moving!

Finally, *finally,* we started forward again. *Almost there, almost there. Just no more stopping!*

I spotted Rurik upfront, a few paces away from the throne itself. With a quick backward snap of my twisty head, I noted Tulip and Amariel near the doorway. I couldn't see Calina, but I trusted she was somewhere close by.

At the far end of the throne room, just beneath the dais, Shim took a sharp turn to the right, crossing to the adjacent wall and anchoring his leather handhold in a predetermined place. He then turned back and cavorted theatrically to the other end of the room, grabbing a second hand loop at the other end of the dragon chain, which he then fastened to the opposite wall.

His beasts were secure, so Shim stopped before the center stage and bowed low to the regent. "Eldrin Grimlock, as promised, I have brought you eighteen of my finest dragons so you may choose one to add to your royal collection. Your people have gathered, eager to support your choice. May I present them to you so you may select?"

The slender dark elf stood, and it was as if all the air had been sucked from the room. He took soundless steps forward, his fine silk clothing reflecting light from the chandeliers that hung high overhead. I imme-

349

diately recognized him from Finnian's impression: his cold, calculating gaze and counterfeit smile. There was no doubt that this was the guy I'd come for.

Eldrin stopped at the edge of the stage looming tall, which only added to his immense sense of power, and looked down upon the human merchant-posing-as-a-dragon-master who had approached him.

The crowd quietly awaited his decree. The local Simon temple seemed to have done a good job spreading its message of silence. I wasn't sure how that worked, but that would have to be a question for another time. Right now, I had other far more pressing matters to attend to.

Shim took off his hat and held it to his chest as he bowed again. "Your majesty, is there a problem?"

Eldrin's dark eyes narrowed as his lips pressed into a thin, tight line. He took his time before answering, and every second that ticked past unanswered only thickened the sense of power in the air. "You say you have brought me eighteen dragons, but I only see seventeen. Count them again," he said at last.

What the fig was going on? Oh, I did not like this. I did not like it one bit.

"Be ready," I whispered to Leviath, even though I knew no one else could hear us. "Something big is about to go down."

Shim straightened back to his full height and walked to the far left, pointing at the first dragon in the procession. This was Sparky, the fire-breather, his best bet to win. The master of ceremonies had lined us up according to our odds, I realized then. Leviath and I were near the back, where the frost dragon should have been—a weak bet.

Shim counted the dragons one by one, pointing at each as he passed. "Fourteen," he said as he stopped before a wingling. The creature hopped up and attempted to fly away, but the chain choked the dragon, causing it to fall back to the throne room floor.

The crowd oohed and ahhed, and I hated them for it. Couldn't they see this creature was suffering? That it was not meant to be stuck inside a city or, worse, confined to a tiny cage as it traveled across all of Verandel for these shows?

"Fifteen," Shim announced, glancing down at us and finally noticing that we didn't belong. He sucked in a sharp breath and cleared his throat but then quickly recovered, offering a smile as he crooned, "Twofy is the newest addition to the dragon wagon, a rarity such as most have never seen."

I chuffed at this. Of course, no one had ever seen a two-headed poison barb. They didn't exist outside of our current ruse.

Shim carried on to the next specimen. "Sixt—"

"Stop," Eldrin cut in. The single syllable echoed through the long room. "Go back a pace."

Shim shimmied his shoulders and hopped back, drawing laughter from the crowd. "Ah, Twofy. He really is quite spectacular. Is he the choice you've made?"

"You say there is a dragon here," the regent responded coldly, "but I see a half-human and a halfling crouched beside you. I wonder why that is."

Shim turned back to us and blinked hard. "Your Highness? I do not see it as you describe."

"Look at Sparky's nose. It's just the cutest I've ever seen!" Calina shouted from somewhere that felt closer than I would have expected.

Nose meant trouble at two o'clock, precisely where Levvy and I stood. Gee, thanks, Calina. Super helpful.

The crowd began to murmur. Some challenged Eldrin's claim, while others heartily agreed in a misguided attempt to win the ruler's favor.

The regent tutted and descended the stage with slow, steady steps.

"Tilda, he sees us. What do we do?" Levvy implored. Half of our body began to shake violently as the child's fear overtook him.

I kept still and murmured, "Just be ready."

"How? I'm wearing a collar. I'm stuck!" Now, he was crying. Oh, sweet divinity, we'd really stepped in it now.

No, no, it would be okay. The time we'd all been waiting for had arrived, and I was good under pressure even when the plans suddenly and irreparably changed.

"Did you forget that I could see through magic, or was it simply that you did not know?" Eldrin challenged the dragon master. He now stood only a head above the hairless human, but still, his presence was much larger.

Wait, there was something important there...

Eldrin Grimlock could see through magic, of course!

Finnian had been sparse on the details when presenting this mission, but he had shared many facts I'd impatiently deemed unimportant. Like the story of how he and his nemesis had first taken up with each other:

"I found Eldrin Grimlock on the outskirts of Sandsi-bar. Or rather, he found me. I'd been wandering the desert for many long days and nights by then, wearing the skin of a beautiful orcish maiden I'd met many moons ago in a small coastal town. Eldrin, for all his guilelessness, saw straight through my disguise. He asked who I was, allowing me to take my true shape for the first

time on my long journey through Verandel. We became companions after that. Eldrin and I were outsiders looking for a place to belong, so it made sense that we could belong to each other for at least a little while."

Eldrin could see through magic. Our plan had always been doomed to fail. Shi had cursed me for my impiety. The luck keeper had betrayed us in our hour of need.

"Your g-g-gr-graciousness?" Shim sputtered and gagged beside me.

Eldrin hooked an eyebrow as he rounded on the other man, a cobra ready to strike. "Were you trying to deceive me with a bad deal?"

"No, no. I did not know. I do not see it. I believe you, but I don't..."

"Look at Sparky's toe. It's just the cutest I've ever seen!" Calina shouted again, even closer than she'd been before. It was the last thing I heard before utter pandemonium erupted in the throne room.

The wingling beside me took flight, but it was not yanked back to the ground this time. It flew higher and higher until it brushed the ceiling. I watched it float away slowly, slowly, as if time no longer moved at all.

And then the other dragons broke away from the chain joining us all together.

"Tilda, what's happening?" Levvy demanded as he

tugged and fought but remained hopelessly stuck in place.

"Unshift us. Unshift us right now!" I screamed. We didn't have a second to waste.

Leviath obeyed, and I found myself crouched on my feet a moment later. My hand was already in my pocket, going for the dagger. Eldrin was so, so close. I could end this right now.

The crowd gasped. Someone screamed a terrible shrill sound that wriggled into my brain like a hungry grub.

Elves, dwarves, gnomes, humans, and other odd assorted races dispersed as the newly freed dragons tore toward the only exit in the place, the door from which we'd all entered.

"Guards, seize these imposters!" the regent cried and pointed at Leviath. But I had already fled my previous position.

I had to act fast and then get the kid. I couldn't leave him in peril, but our mission would fail if I didn't go for Eldrin first. We'd all die—well, almost all.

There was only one death I wanted on my conscience, and I was ready to take it right now.

I lunged forward, dagger extended. I would plunge it into any part of the dark elf's body that I managed to reach—an eye, a groin, or, best of all, his cold, cruel heart.

For a moment, I flew through the air, a halfling on a mission. The mayhem around me became a blur as I focused all my senses on the dictator ahead of me, moving closer and closer and closer still. I drew so near that a waft of strange perfume hit my nostrils. I realized it was Eldrin's imported bath oils. Maybe there would be time to raid his collections of luxuries before we left the castle, a nice reward for an honest morning's work.

Eldrin spun toward me without a weapon, unable to ward off my fatal blow. This would be easy, almost too easy. And best of all, I'd be able to look him in the eyes while I drained the life from his miserable husk. Justice would be served at my hands, and it felt great.

I pumped my legs harder and kicked off the ground for one last burst before...

Johan grabbed me around the waist and pulled me into his chest, stopping me dead in my tracks.

"No!" I cried and kicked. I didn't care if I was hurting my geriatric friend, not anymore. How could he? I knew he wasn't planning on helping, but to actively thwart us?

"Little Foot, it's too late. You've been caught out.

Don't make things worse for yourself," he warned as I wrestled against him. Fig my tiny, weak body!

"Go! Free yourselves!" Calina shouted as she jogged into view, encouraging the last of the dragons to escape their bonds.

Rurik stood near the throne as initially assigned; it seemed he hadn't moved since the first time I'd spotted him. "Calina figured out how to talk with the dragons. She told them she'd free them, but they had to wait for her to give the command before they fled. That was the deal."

What? How did Calina communicate with the dragons? And when had she worked all this out?

Tulip galloped forward, racing wide circles around the gathered attendees and herding them toward the exit. She didn't have Amariel with her, but I knew the celestial must be nearby. Her charge would never abandon her.

"Rurik, what's going on?" I demanded and kicked Johan in the knee with all my might.

The traitorous guard dropped me, and I scrambled away before he could capture me again.

"This is the backup plan. We came up with it this morning," Rurik called after me. I reached into my boot and tossed my thief's tools to Rurik, who was still not moving from his assigned spot. "Get Levvy out of that collar and get him someplace safe."

To my surprise, Johan scooped up the lockpick and made a beeline for the child. Was he on our side or not? This constant back and forth was giving me whiplash.

At least Leviath would be safe, which meant that part of my job was done. Now for a little light murder to end things strong.

I spun, searching the room for Eldrin Grimlock. I spotted him sneaking off behind the stage, absconding his party in pursuit of safety.

Think again, loser. There's no place you'll be safe from me.

I took a deep breath, gathered all my might, and then threw myself after him, dagger extended. As they said, the second time was the charm.

At the last moment, the regent shifted, pulling a saber from his side and lunging toward me with equal vigor.

"Tilda, noooooooo!" Rurik shouted and threw himself between us. How? When had he moved? And where was his shield? Did he plan to...

Everything went white.

29

I stood in a blizzard of pure light. I saw nothing, felt nothing, *was* nothing.

Is this death? Had Simon claimed me even though I refused to claim him?

It had come upon me so suddenly. I'd been flying, ready to stab Eldrin Grimlock with everything I had in me—all the love, the hate, all that had transpired on my journey so far. And then he'd... He'd pulled a hidden saber, ready to deflect my blow and land a fatal one of his own.

And then...

Then...

Rurik.

As soon as I recalled his presence, he appeared

before me. The regent's posh silver saber stuck straight into his chest and poked through from the other side.

No!

I tried to run to him, to help in whatever small way I could, even if that was just standing vigil as he stumbled his way toward the next life.

I pumped my legs furiously, and yet I did not move a pace. "Rurik, I'm here!" I called out, but my voice stuck inside my throat, unwilling to swim the short distance to my fallen comrade.

But he had not fallen. Instead, he was floating in the vast nothingness that enveloped us. Looking down, I realized that I was, too. I tried to cut through the void with my limbs but could not propel myself or escape my current position.

Where were we? How did we get here? And how could we get out? All of these questions seemed equally important, yet none could be answered.

Would this be it, then? What could this be if not death itself?

Wind chimes tinkled despite there being no breeze to enliven them. Finally, an answer. Only what did it mean? Was I meant to understand?

"Hello?" I attempted to call out, but my voice would not come. The gently clinking chimes were the only sound in this blank, featureless void.

Rurik did not speak, move, or give any indication of life or understanding.

Was he really here with me? Or was I alone? Had I merely envisioned him because I didn't want to be stuck here by myself?

Huh. When we'd started this journey, I'd have done anything to go it alone. Yet now my heart was breaking at the prospect of being separated from the others. They were my party, my family. Together, we lived, and together, we died. Or at least Rurik and I had.

I thought.

I didn't know, don't know.

Time weaves around me—past, present, future—all overlapping. I didn't know where I was. Now I don't know when I am. I desperately cling to the who. That's all I have left, if anything remains at all.

You are Tilda. You were brave. You will be reunited with those you assume you lost.

Who was speaking? Was it my inner voice? There was so much I didn't understand.

And then, a young woman materialized in the distance. She floated forward with long, wavy hair that appeared spun of moonlight or magic—maybe both. Her snowy garments blended into the void as if they were a part of it. Behind her, wings.

A celestial, then. Was this Zephyriel the same

blessed being who had bestowed prophecies upon our group via an old crown and an honored kobold? I tried to remember what she had predicted for me. She'd said that nearly all I desired would be mine but had also said that two lives would be lost in pursuit of our victory.

Mine and Rurik's.

That meant the others were still okay. At least, I hope it did.

"Come, do you not recognize your old friend, Tilda?" the celestial spoke. A triangle tinged with each syllable before shifting to a soft trill of a piccolo. "Although I suppose I do not look so old to you now."

Amariel? How?

"So you do know me," she answered my thoughts.

Where are we? And Rurik, is he okay? I thought the words, for I still could not speak them.

"He will be. I shall make sure of that." She glanced at him with a sad smile before returning to me. "As to where we are, this is the space between."

What does that mean?

"We are neither here nor there. Not the mortal plane or the ethereal realm, but also not among the fae. We are in the absence of space. It is here that I came whenever you assumed me sleeping. It is a conveyance of such, and thus it is safe."

Again, with the conveyance schtick. I would have sighed if I could.

The maiden Amariel tittered. "This place will deliver us to where we need to be. Or rather, it will deliver you and Rurik."

You had a way to teleport us this whole time, and you didn't?

"I can enter freely, but this place was never intended for outsiders. I have broken one of my kind's most ardent rules in bringing you here. As such, I can no longer accompany you on your journey. My time in the mortal realm has reached its end." She approached Rurik with one hand outstretched and fingers splayed in a wide fan. I recognized the gesture she used to transfer her healing magic, although no light emerged from her fingertips.

We were in a space of pure light already. There was nothing more she—or anyone—could add.

Amariel pulled the saber from Rurik's chest, instantly dissolving it with her touch, then leaned forward to caress the gash the regent's weapon had been left behind.

She hummed and pulled away, and when she did, Rurik's eyes popped open, all his life returning at once.

"Amariel!" he gasped. "Am I dead, or is this the space in-between?"

Why could he talk and I couldn't? That hardly seemed fair. Also, how did her healing magic work so quickly? It usually took hours to heal even minor scrapes, yet suddenly, she could bring a person back to life within a blink. Nothing about this place made sense. I had half a mind to—

"Shush, child," Amariel said, not to Rurik but to me. *To me!*

She circled him with careful concentration. In search of more injuries, I assumed.

When Amariel was satisfied, she stopped between us. And closed her eyes as if each word drained the last dregs of her energy. I, on the other hand, felt nothing. Not tired, nor awake. Not good, bad. Just nothing.

"We are in-between. I will rewind a few moments, but you won't have long. Doing so will force me from this realm, returning me to the ethereal plane. I will be with you no more."

"You're going to die," Rurik summarized with a pained expression. His lone tusk quivered as his dark eyes grew glassy.

I never cared much for Amariel, but I felt like I might cry if I could move, speak, or act. But I remained powerless, only able to watch the other two or communicate with the celestial when she chose to hear my thoughts. Did Rurik even know I was here with him?

Amariel kept all her focus on the young half-orc. "I cannot die," she explained softly, and for the first time, her words held no music. "But I will not be allowed to return to your realm for many years, if ever. I will no longer be with you on this journey."

"Tulip needs you," Rurik argued, appearing genuinely aggrieved.

Amariel blinked slowly a few times, then placed her hand where the wound on Rurik's chest had just been. "I made a vow to protect her, and now I transfer that vow to you."

I imagined a spark of light passing between them as if the vow was a literal object that could be bandied back and forth. I also imagined that said duty would now fall to me, as I was responsible for the entire party, including Rurik and Tulip.

Great. From now on, I would have to protect the kids without any healing magic as a backup. We weren't dead, but we may as well have been. Our chances were not looking good here.

I expected Amariel to tell me off, but she ignored my inner monologue, focusing on the inquisitive young half-orc between us.

"Young wizard, do you remember what you asked of me the first day we met when we rode in the first conveyance?" Her eyes remained half-lidded. I half-expected her invisible metronome to fire up again, but the only music now was the sound of her voice.

Rurik's words lacked a pleasing melody, coming out panicked and discordant even as he kept his responses simple. "I asked if you would help me with my magic."

"And what did I say?"

"You said I couldn't become magic because I was not born of a magical race but that I could be taught to wield it."

"And?" Amariel's hair lifted off her neck in soft curls. Still no wind.

"And that you would give it your best." Rurik sniffed and rubbed at his eyes with his fists. We all knew this was goodbye.

Amariel nodded, her eyes firmly shut now. "Indeed, I shall give you my all. Rurik Bane of Briarhaven, the two halves of your being are mired in conflict. Heart, head. Orc, human. You are a series of parts, but you are not whole. You must find harmony within yourself. It is the only way. And only then will magic flow through you."

She reached for him again, putting a pale hand on each of his green cheeks and bending forward to press a kiss to his forehead. Her long white hair whipped wildly around them as if to warn that our time was coming to a bitter end.

"I am leaving this place," Amariel confirmed. As she continued to speak, her words broke apart because of gasps and cracks. She had to fight for every single word. "I am leaving, but my magic shall remain. It will be yours, Rurik. Find your inner harmony, and become a conductor of the divine. You will no longer be half-orc, half-human, but rather the first of your kind, something truly special, just as you were always meant to be. I believe in you. Now, all you must do is find a way to believe in yourself." Amariel's lips murmured against Rurik's forehead as she said all this, and when she'd finished, she pulled back.

Once their contact was broken, the blank space collapsed in on itself. One second, I was floating in melancholic nothingness, and the next, I was embroiled in the chaos of Eldrin Grimlock's embattled throne room.

Nobody moved. It was as if we'd been returned to a portrait of the moment rather than the moment itself.

And then all five senses slammed back into place at once. The panicked shouts and stale sweat of the crowd, my pain as I struggled against Johan's iron embrace.

Rurik stood a few paces away near the base of the dais, just as he had before Amariel took us into that hidden mystical space. The celestial, however, was nowhere to be seen. I wondered briefly if she ever finished retreading our journey via her strange semi-coma or if she'd known it would take her away. There was an even briefer moment when I considered how many questions I'd forgotten to ask Amariel. The answer was... many.

"Rurik?" I called out, and this time, my voice worked.

He opened his mouth to answer me, and a blast of light rent the air with a boom as if he'd just belched thunder. All around him, it swirled before enveloping the young wizard in a pillar of star shine.

The scene played out around us, everything exactly as it had been the first time... except for Rurik. His newly bestowed power surged so ferociously that he couldn't contain it. The floor beneath his feet fractured, sending long splintering cracks in every direction.

I had never experienced an earthquake, but I imagined this could be described as one. A chasm appeared down the room's center aisle, along the same course Shim had marched his dragons. When the cracks reached the edges of the floor, they began to climb the castle walls.

Stones and chunks of plaster began to rain from overhead. Oh, sweet divinity! The entire place was crumbling around us. If we didn't get out of here fast, we'd find ourselves buried alive.

Johan released his grip on me, and I fell forward from losing his support. To be honest, I'd somehow forgotten he'd taken me hostage in the first place.

"Tilda, help!" Leviath's scared voice cried out.

Fig, he was still chained in place. Amariel had rewound time just long enough to threaten him anew. I didn't know if this was the moment she most thought could change things or if it was as far back as she'd been able to take us. Whatever the case, I needed to act fast.

"Johan, help the kid." I tossed him my lock pick and ran for Eldrin.

"Tilda, you have to get out of here, too!" Johan called after me while rushing forward to free Leviath from his shackles.

"Calina! Tulip! Where are you?" I scanned the room but couldn't find either. Most of the people had already scattered before Rurik's magical explosion, and the rest had hurriedly dispersed once he'd started bringing the house down.

At this precise moment, I found myself with a choice to make.

I could go after Eldrin as planned, finishing our mission so that we could move on to the more pressing matter of visiting Maltherius, so that I could finally do what I'd set out to do in the first place, to free my friend and make up for my past mistake of unwittingly abandoning him. Killing Eldrin as ordered was the next step on that journey. Without it, I'd be stuck serving Finnian Sly until he deemed my side of the bargain fulfilled. And by then, it could be too late to save Gaaron.

Yes, finishing this thing with Eldrin Grimlock was the obvious choice.

But Rurik needed me, too. That obnoxious, know-it-all kid who had a knack for testing my last nerve had already died once today. Amariel had brought him back, but the power she'd bestowed upon him was too much. And now he remained trapped in a cyclone of magical chaos. His expression remained neutral, placid. I couldn't tell whether he'd returned with me or remained stuck in-between, but it was clear he could not break the spell he'd found himself unintentionally casting. If I didn't escort him out of here, he would surely entomb himself in the rubble.

I didn't know whether I could help him. More

than likely, I couldn't. I lacked the physical strength to move his much larger body against its will, and if he were still wrapped in that pocket dimension, I wouldn't be able to reach him at all.

Eldrin was the sure bet. I knew I could take him out, just like I'd promised. And yet...

"Figging fig!" I shouted at the top of my lungs before tackling the teen.

30

I slammed into Rurik with my arms spread wide, ready to force him to the ground. Given that he was more than double my height and quadruple my size, this maneuver did not have the intended effect. Instead of knocking Rurik from his trance, I bounced off him and fell back onto my butt.

A wooden beam from the ceiling crashed down, hitting so close to me that I had to roll out of the way to avoid being crushed. Just like the in-between space before, the throne room seemed to be collapsing in on itself. Stone, wood, decor, it was all violently dislodged by Rurik's magical earthquake.

The swanky, shining chandelier that hung over Eldrin's dais fell next, sending splinters of glass scattering in all directions. A particularly nasty hunk of crystal gouged Rurik's cheek on the opposite side of his missing tusk, making his face appear even more out of balance than before.

Still, he did not react, even as bright red beads of blood dripped violently from the cut.

I yanked on his arm with all my might, but my efforts amounted to nothing more than a light breeze in the middle of a hurricane.

One of the decorative pillars fell from its station by the wall, sending out chunks of marbled debris from the point of impact. The crystal glass of the windows shattered, raining down shards like a hailstorm. I didn't even bother trying to dodge them all. What mattered was getting through to Rurik before the tempest buried us both.

Thunder sounded from below as a massive crack snaked through the floor.

We were out of time.

Rurik had become an immovable statue, and I had done my best to rouse him. But it wasn't enough. I was out of my element, and he was just plain out.

Try as I might, I simply couldn't save him from this. I couldn't leave him behind, either.

So, was this it? Had Amariel rewound time to give us a few extra moments to die, this time for good?

I silently cursed whatever god had played a hand in

this cruel, redundant fate. Just like when I'd lost Gaaron in Maltherius's dungeon all those years ago, I'd failed my mission. Almost impossibly, today's failure would be even worse than the one that had haunted me for the past decade. It would be worse, and yet I'd never get the chance to set things right.

I reached for Rurik to wrap the big lug in one final hug. We might have started rough, but he'd wormed his way into my heart. And I wouldn't abandon him now. At least we were tog—

"Rurik! Tilda, I'm coming!" Tulip's voice carried over the din. There was a battle cry like a whinny as she appeared through the flying debris like a beam of ethereal light. She dodged through rock and wood with ease, leaping over a pillar as it fell, her forelegs tucking perfectly like she was just hopping over a simple stone fence. Tulip's gait and speed never faltered as she sped toward us, and despite the chaos of the moment, my mouth hung open in sheer amazement. Honestly, she was a wonder to behold.

She swept in like a battering ram, smashing into Rurik with a fearsome front kick, knocking him prone before she scooped his unconscious body up and onto her back in one fluid motion. "Tilda, don't just stand there!" she shouted as she tore off toward the hole where the doorway had once stood. "Get out of there!"

Right, right. Rurik was safe, but I wasn't yet out of trouble. I had a tough time dodging the rubble and debris, but I did my best, pumping my little legs so fast they would likely be a blur to any onlookers. But, of course, I was the only idiot still inside.

Another pillar fell, blocking my path. It was too tall to climb over, and there was no way around it. I tried leaping, but I didn't have the strength to clear it.

Really?!

No! I would not go out like this. I refused. Rage built inside my chest, my stomach, my everything. It filled me from the inside, making me strong. But would it be strong enough? Well, it had to be. I'd run out of any other—

"Tilda!" Calina's voice, a sweet song of salvation, rang out as she effortlessly vaulted my obstacle, bow still grasped in one hand. She positioned herself at the base of the pillar and cupped her hands. I nodded, ran to her, and placed my foot in her hands. With a bit more oomph than I expected, Calina tossed me like a half-filled sack of barley.

If I hadn't also jumped simultaneously, my landing probably would've been fine. But after a midair flip, I tumbled and rolled as the ground came at me too quickly to adjust my stance. I hit the floor with a snap that I heard just as much as I felt. Pain bloomed in my wrist quickly as I thanked my lucky stars that both legs were still in working order. They're what I needed to get out of here. Gritting my teeth, I clutched my wrist to my chest and ran. Fresh waves of hurt rippled with every step, but I kept crashing forward, nonetheless.

Together, Calina and I hurtled through the gaping maw of what used to be the doorway and out into the square where the rest of the spectators had gathered at a reasonably safe distance. I collapsed, or rather, fell into Calina's arms. She held me up as we both struggled to regain our breath.

And like a cliff being dragged into the ocean, the castle crumbled, stones and debris sloughing out along the break in the keep's walls. Then, with a stuttering sigh, like a dying behemoth, it was... gone.

Okay, it was more like a monstrous crash, but I hardly cared at this point. Against all odds, we had made it. We'd escaped... and so had Eldrin Grimlock. Fig.

"Over here," Tulip shouted, waving at us as she knelt at a distance, cradling a semi-conscious Rurik's head to her belly.

Calina skipped ahead, but I moved toward them slowly, my energy spent on the mad dash for survival.

Passing through the dumbstruck masses, I spotted Johan speaking with Leviath. His posture reminded me of when he'd first caught me as an urchin trying to lift the purse off a newly recruited guard. He was stooped, perhaps more than he had been in the old days, but he didn't look angry.

Leviath was fully engaged in this conversation that I couldn't quite overhear, animatedly responding to whatever my old friend was telling him. I started to wave, but I could see they were so engrossed in their conversation that they wouldn't notice me if I were riding on the back of a griffin. Would my old mentor make good on his promise to adopt the dryad orphan even though I hadn't succeeded in deposing his despot of a boss?

We'd destroyed a whole figgin' castle, but that murderous dark elf had slipped away in the chaos. I'd failed. Again. This seemed to be turning into a habit, much to my chagrin.

But if I were really being honest with myself...

I'd also succeeded. No, *we'd* succeeded.

Our party had come together. We'd looked out for each other. Amariel had asked Rurik to look after Tulip, but it was she who had rescued him when it really counted. And Calina had saved me, even though it was at great personal risk to herself.

I had a feeling none of us were done saving each other yet. This wasn't the end, nor was it the beginning, but we'd turned another page on our journey. An important one.

At last, I finished my slow trek across the square and caught up to the others.

"Is he okay?" I asked as soon as I was within spitting distance, gesturing to Rurik with my injured hand and hissing in pain.

"Are you okay?" Calina asked with a raised eyebrow, her mouth drawing in like her mother's did when she got worried.

"I will be," I said. I tried to force a smile but was too tired to do much more than endure another moment.

Rurik's eyelids fluttered open. He parted his lips and belched another wild spell, an icy swirl of exploding snowflakes that thankfully missed hitting anyone head-on, as that would have stung.

"Don't talk. Not until you get ahold of that magic," I warned, then sighed. My chest burned from the effort, and I coughed. "Tulip, be ready to tackle him again if he starts anything dangerous."

"Like an earthquake inside?" Calina quipped with an exhausted sigh of her own. She quickly rearranged her face into a grin. "That was pretty epic, Rur. You literally brought the house down. But next time, wait until we're outside."

Rurik raised a finger.

"No, you don't. No talking at all. I mean it," I insisted. Calina had said he'd collapsed a house when really it had been a throne room. I knew he wanted to correct her, but I also knew that opening his mouth would likely invoke something dangerous. "I will get a gag for you if that's what we need to keep you quiet."

Rurik rose on unsteady feet, using Tulip's outstretched arms to brace himself. With a walk more befitting a drunk, he approached me.

"Don't say a word!" I yelped, admittedly, momentarily afraid of him. Keeping that trap shut was practically impossible for him under the best of circumstances, and we were currently all too tired to be making good choices.

Rurik didn't speak. He just shook his head and grabbed my wrist. The injured one. With both friggin' hands.

White-hot pain shot through me, and stars exploded behind my eyes. I howled in protest, trying to yank away in reflex, but the young orc's hands had me clamped in place.

Rurik's eyes closed, and thankfully, he kept his mouth closed. A thrum I felt deep in my chest vibrated me, and I realized he was humming. The simple tune was deep and almost primitive in nature, but a light built in his fingers as this melodic resonance built. The glow burst from his interlaced hands and then sunk languidly into my skin, disappearing from view.

Warmth radiated through my hands into my wrist and up my arm. And just like that, the pain vanished.

"You... You healed me?" I asked in disbelief as he released my wrist and pulled away. I moved my wrist, poking and prodding it with my other hand.

He nodded and smiled with his eyes since he was still too afraid to move his mouth.

"Thank you," I murmured, rubbing my newly recovered wrist. "That was much faster than Amariel ever did it."

"Is she..." Tulip cut in, her blue eyes brimming with tears.

Rurik returned to the sorrowful centaur and wrapped his arms around her, holding her as she sobbed. Nobody needed to answer her question. We all knew.

"Hisssss ahhhhh!" a delighted gasp sounded behind me, and I turned to find the missing ice dragon rolling back and forth on the patch of ice Rurik had accidentally conjured. Its belly faced the sky as the little creature twisted and wagged its tail in delight.

"Does that feel good, boy?" Calina asked, reaching down to stroke the dragonling's scaly belly.

"Shhhhhash shiiiiiiii!" it appeared to respond.

"You're welcome," Calina answered with a smile. That was right. She could talk to animals now, *huh*. That just might come in handy as we moved ahead to whatever came next. We needed to regroup. Our party had a lot to catch up on, but where to start?

Shrieks rose from the crowd, followed by vigorous mumblings. I glanced around until I found the source of upset—a blazing fire.

"Haaaa shih haaaa!" the dragon—I now remembered Shim had called him Frosty—cried, flipping over and jumping up and down in apparent merriment.

Just outside the hulking pile of debris, the newly freed dragons had gathered around their former prison, the dragon wagon. The fire-breather, Sparky, blew a twisting inferno at the vehicle, stoking the flames higher and higher. His friends danced and chattered animatedly. Some used their unique strains of magic to further aid in the destruction of the transport. The rock dragon, for instance, was pummeling the wagon's wheels with balled fists, unaffected by the burning wood—or at least uncaring. The flighted creatures flapped their wings to feed the flames, and the others simply looked on in bliss.

"What's all this now?" Finnian Sly appeared with a wing scout flanking each side. He wore no disguise today, appearing as his natural, furry self. "Celebrating a successful mission, I hope?"

One of his mercenaries studied the crowd while the other narrowed her eyes at me. I recognized her, the cruel human fighter who had ripped out one of Rurik's tusks in cold blood.

He spotted her, too, and nodded in acknowledgment.

"You're still alive," she said, then hit a fist against her chest twice. "Respect."

"He got away," I admitted between clenched teeth.

"No, Tilda. Look." Calina grabbed my arm and pointed to the opposite end of the crumbling castle. There, a single dark hand emerged, followed by a black and bloodied face. Sure enough, it was the regent himself pulling free of the collapse. It seemed he had lost the use of one arm but was still very much alive.

The tanuki sighed. "Why do I have to do everything myself these days?"

"I'm sorry—" I began, but he wasn't listening.

"Dayna, would you kindly finish that for me? Thank you, " Finnian ordered his lackey. He did everything himself, *right*.

The one-eyed scout immediately set to task, almost lazily drawing her swords before walking over to Eldrin and removing his head like she was harvesting a crop.

"Tilly, Tilly, Tilly..." Finnian pinched his snout with his claws and shook his head while tutting unhappily. "I'm disappointed, but unfortunately not surprised. I do so much for everyone. I even sent you my best little boyo to help you out when it seemed like this quest was too much for you, and still, you couldn't manage to finish the job. Dear, dear, I fear you are losing your touch, that you've probably lost it already, if I'm being honest."

He dropped his hands and studied me with sharp eyes, then heaved a massive sigh and continued, "But we shall persist as this little party of yours is currently my best option for what must happen next. Destroying the keep was a nice touch, at least. It had Pa's flair for the dramatic, and he so enjoyed the show even if you conveniently forgot why we staged this little charade in the first place."

"Leviath is okay, in case you were worried about that."

"Worried? Of course, I'm not worried. After all, he had you, and as I told you so many times, my dear Tilly, you were always my favorite. Levvy is powerful, so I had no doubts you two would come together to create something... acceptable. Truth be told, Levvy has always been far, far, far more trouble than he's worth. Do you know what it takes to look after a fae-

384

touched child? In the city, no less? Too much. Anyway, we have other more important matters to tend to, yes, yes. Now that Eldrin..." Finnian took a moment to spit on the ground, "is no more, and even though I was forced to intervene, I still need to hold up my end of our arrangement. It's time we pay old Maltherius a visit and relieve him of the Genesis Crest."

"Why do you want it so bad?" Calina challenged.

"Why do you care why I want it?" Finnian challenged right back.

"You sent us to our deaths and won't even tell us why."

"That's funny, Cally, because you still look very much alive to me. Don't worry about why I sent you after Eldrin. He needed to be disposed of, and now he has been. It's not very becoming, fixating on the past like this. Reflects poorly on your skills at leadership. Indeed, the past is behind us. Let us focus instead on what stretches out in front."

"And that's getting the Genesis Crest. Why?" This challenge came from me. If Finnian insisted on accompanying us to Maltherius's lair, then I at least wanted to understand his motives.

"Come now, you've got to stop focusing on things that are not the task at hand. Hasn't Cally taught you that? Suffice it to say, I will have what I want, and you will have what you want." Finnian picked at some invisible piece of lint on his trousers. "I'm sure you're still itching to retrieve dear ole Gaary from his prison crypt, yes? Yes, yes, of course you are. We both know how disappointed your little protégé will be if she never gets the chance to meet her father, if you fail her yet again."

The wing scout—Dayna—returned before either of us could respond to that. She cleaned her blades before resheathing her swords. The other wing scout held a leather satchel in his hands, the bottom of the bag darkened by dampness.

"Ah yes, excellent. Now we're ready with the teleportation spell, yes?"

Rurik made a guttural noise drawing everyone's attention to him. Once he had our eyes, he closed his, placing one hand on his chest and the other on his forehead, where Amariel had transferred her magic with a kiss. "The spell... It needs more casters to work properly. Eight would be best. Four as a minimum... Could cause a rebound otherwise." His voice was halting, and I could see the effort it took not to use all the words he wanted to. But no errant spells escaped when he spoke, and for that I felt immensely glad. Proud, too. Indeed, I was duly impressed by this quick progress, so much so that I had only just begun to process the content of his speech when Finnian spoke up derisively.

"Pish posh," he said with a dismissive wave of his claws. "Cast it."

Bolts of energy engulfed the rubble-strewn court-yard, and for a moment, I could've sworn I saw Brynlee in the light. After that, I lost consciousness.

My eyes fluttered open under the harsh light of midday. But something was off. Like some of the colors had been drained from the world. A sharp poke in my ribs brought me back to consciousness, and I found myself atop a mound of cobblestones, just like the last time that stupid spell was cast.

"Shhhhhaaaa?" the ice dragon seemed to question as I pushed myself into a sitting position. Its teal eyes practically burned with curiosity as it tilted its head and stared at me. Great, a stowaway. Frosty must have been nearby playing on that ice when we teleported, which got him sucked into the spell, too.

Okay, so I wasn't alone, but then where was everyone else?

The one-eyed wing scout sat crouched nearby,

fingers in the dirt as she sniffed at the air. Somehow, our landing hadn't been quite what it was before. She stood and straightened, dusting her fingers off on her feathered cloak. This battle-hardened mercenary didn't seem frightened or even disoriented. She just looked angry. But then again, that's how she always looked to me.

I followed her gaze from the ruddy brown dirt over to the dried scrub brush on the horizon. Death and decay surrounded us. Animal skeletons, bleached by the sun, stood in stark contrast to the ground. Especially where burnt sections of land trailed out from the distance. Chunks of rock and dirt floated over an immense canyon not held in place but free-floating as if by magic. Definitely by magic. I didn't have to see beyond the floating rubble below to know what lay beneath it. Nothing. Absolutely nothing. A never-ending abyss had been created in this place when the world trees were destroyed during the Fae War.

We were at the great chasm.

And sure enough, across the chasm were the black spikes of the Precipice. Maltherius's lair gripped the edge like a skeletal hand, with most of the structure hanging out over an abyss. It made his fortress impenetrable. Or so he'd thought until ten years ago when Gaaron and I had let ourselves in.

Despite the rough landing, Finnian had brought us to Maltherius as promised.

I checked my surroundings. It seemed like not all of us made it.

"Wing scout," I called, stumbling as I approached her from behind. "Dayna, that's your name, right? Dayna? Where is everyone?"

Without turning, she spoke, her voice deep and sounding nearly as scarred as she was. "Orc kid was right. We needed more casters. The spell went wrong. Rebound, he called it."

"What do you mean went wrong?" I grabbed her hip and tried to spin her toward me.

With a snarl, she rounded on me, stepping into me and using her size to push me off balance. Yup, this alliance was not off to a great start.

"Rebound, like your orc said," she growled, her voice sounding more like a weapon being dragged over a whetstone. "Spell didn't hold together. Now we're here, and no one else is."

"Is it just us? You, me, and the dragon? Where are the others? Are they back in Mystwood? Or did the spell rebound them to Briarhaven? Or have they been thrown into the Void? How are we supposed to find them? Oh, sweet divinity, are they dead? Do we—"

"Too. Many. Questions," Dayna barked, a glint of

metal in her hand suddenly as a dagger appeared almost out of thin air. "The elf child is close. Still unconscious. But alive. That's all I know right now. And now you know it, too. So don't ask again." The dagger flew over my head only to land close to Calina's foot, marking her location for me.

"What about Rurik? He hasn't gotten control of this new magic yet. He needs help, and it's not like he can shout for us. He'd blow himself sky-high. And Tulip, she just lost one of the most important people in the world to her. She has a lot to process emotionally, and—"

Dayna lunged at me, her sword flashing out and landing flat side against my neck. My heart boomed in my ears, and each thump made me feel the razor edge of the blade. "Ask one more question, halfling. One. More."

I lifted my hands in surrender and waited for the sword to move away.

"We're near our objective. And your emotions aren't about to complete our mission, are they? So, if you want to build a little campfire, sing songs, and hug, you do that. I'm sure the necromancer won't even notice. And while you're being tortured to un-death, I'm going to find that little tanuki bastard and then finish this mission so I can get paid."

"Don't you know rule number one of—"

Dayna glared at me, narrowing her view through that one good eye. She didn't even need to speak to deliver that threat. *No questions. Understood.*

"Rule number one of adventuring is to never split the party," I explained carefully. As much as the kids had irritated me, I missed them terribly. They'd been far better company than this brute. I shrugged as I continued, "I know you probably don't care, but I'm responsible for those kids. I need to find them first before we do anything else. After that, we can go in as a team and finish the quest. Do that for me, and you can keep Finnian's coin. All of it."

Dayna appeared to contemplate this for a moment before raising her lip in a snarl. "Look around us, halfling. This isn't some storybook adventure. We're here for a job, and the sooner we finish it, the better. Wake the elf, let's go."

I swallowed hard, nodding my understanding. I needed to keep Dayna placated. Otherwise she'd make things more difficult than they needed to be. I still planned to find Rurik and Tulip first, but I also had to make sure my new ally didn't charge in without me. She didn't know what we were up against, but I did.

I'd faced it before.

And soon we would all face it again.

Failure was not an option, but that didn't stop it from being the most likely outcome.

I took a deep breath of the stale air and marched toward Calina's prone form. A plan had begun to form, one that was so crazy it had to work. At least, I hoped that was true. We needed to reunite the party— *the whole party*—and that included someone who had been missing for a very long time...

"Wakey, wakey," I mumbled as I gently shook her shoulders. "It's time to meet your dad."

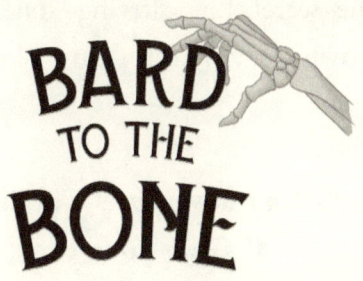

BARD
TO THE
BONE

I'm just a halfling rogue. Saving the world was never in the job description...

Ten years ago, I failed. I watched the greatest evil in the land capture my partner and barely escaped with my life. I've spent every day since trying to forget the secrets buried in that cursed fortress.

Now, I'm going back. With a spitfire half-elf, her chaos-loving ice dragon, and a mercenary who doesn't trust me, I'm marching back into the heart of the Void. We're seeking the Genesis Crest, an artifact of unimaginable power.

But the fortress is not as I remember it. It's guarded by a beast of smoke and shadow, and the necromancer himself is waiting. He knows I'm coming. And he knows the secret I'm carrying—one I've kept even from my own party. This isn't just a heist anymore; it's a reckoning.

The party's next adventure is available and ready for you to read! Grab your copy, then turn the page for a sneak peek of the action.

When real life feels a bit too crazy, you can always find comfort in the fantasy realm!

Yup, this feels like the exact right time to send you the first of my monthly slice-of-life stories starring Durgan Stoutbarrel, dwarven tavern owner and everybody's favorite guy.

I hope you'll enjoy learning more about his backstory and witnessing the meet cute with his half-giant husband Pat.

I'll write a new story about Durgan each month and deliver it exclusively to my newsletter subscribers. It's my version of giving you a warm, mead-drenched hug. *Awwww.*

You can sign up at www.LunaRAuthor.com/ subscribe to start reading the first delicious slice-of-life instantly. Enjoy!

WANT EVEN MORE?

If you loved this book and want to go deeper into the world of Verandel (or just collect shiny things), here are two ways to keep the adventure going...

SHOP THE LEGENDARY LOOT

Signed books. Special editions. D&D campaign adventures. Swag fit for a Chosen One (or a tavern wench with good taste).

Find it all at my official shop:
www.LunaRyderBooks.com

JOIN THE SECRET SCROLLS SOCIETY

Want to:

- Read new books *as I write them*
- Unlock exclusive lore and magical backstory
- Vote on plot developments and future projects
- Possibly become a character in a future book?

Then my Patreon is the place for you:
www.patreon.com/LunaRauthor

Your support helps me keep telling stories that are gloriously weird, queer, and chaotic... and I'd love to have you along for the ride.

Thanks for reading. Stay strange. Stay brave. Stay bard to the bone.

— Luna

ACKNOWLEDGMENTS

Bringing a book to life is a weird, exhausting, exhilarating magic trick—and doing it three times in a row? That's basically necromancy. I couldn't have done it without the incredible cast of characters in my *real* life, whose support made this trilogy possible (and who, luckily, didn't insist on being paid in gold pieces or bard songs).

To my kiddo—first Phoenix, now Vincent—thank you for being a daily reminder that it's never too late to discover who you were always meant to be. These books echo your spirit in every chapter, in every character who defies expectations to become something new. You opened my eyes to the world I was already living in and gave me the insight to write rainbow characters like Tilda, Durgan, and even Finnian Sly with love and authenticity.

To the LGBTQ+ community and my fellow neurodivergent creatives: our big, beautiful brains don't work like everyone else's, and that's kind of the point. We deserve to be heroes, weird and wonderful and unapologetically ourselves. Your stories matter. Your endings matter. And yes, you're allowed to skip around in your own life like it's a choose-your-own-adventure.

To my best friend and ride-or-die Bethany: thank you for being a cornerstone through it all. To the rest of my ride-or-die adventuring party—Mallory (x2), Jennifer, Russell, Kaitlyn, Becky, and everyone who's championed me—cheers to you.

To Dayna, who started as an ARC reader, became a close friend, and then lent her name, soul, and beautifully ruthless instincts to a one-eyed mercenary. We swapped plot twists over waffles, screamed about character arcs, and somehow made magic out of late-night chaos. You're not just *my* Dayna. You're *our* Dayna now.

To Megan, who dared to ask, "Um, are you an author?" while fixing my house, then showed up for sunrise coffee chats like it was no big deal.

To Crystal, editor of my soul and slayer of ellipses —you helped me wrangle the chaos into clarity and kept me sane-ish when the words refused to behave. To SJ Gautreaux, whose bold cover art and brilliant title helped shape the heart of the series. To Luca Strati and

Lucy Loo, whose character illustrations made it feel like my party was right there with me. And to the amazing Soundbooth Theater team—possibly the coolest people alive—you gave this series its cinematic soul.

To my therapist Sarah (and her four-legged counterpart Sky Princess, the world's most legendary three-fourths Chihuahua), thank you for helping me navigate the dark to find the story.

To my beloved ARC gremlins and the 148 Kickstarter backers who made these books possible: Major Payne, Matt D, Ella B, Emily Labes-Royce, Phoebe Ravencraft, Mallory Rock, Bethany Pratt, Becky Muth, Carol Kather, Cole Parker, Kate Hutson, Horatio Astor, Kassie Ziegler, Rachel Brown, Robert Forson, Suzanne Gochenouer, and Dandy Fielding— you are forever part of Verandel.

To the cats: You knocked over just enough stuff to keep me limber and blocked my keyboard when I forgot to rest. You're jerks. I love you.

And to you, dear reader—especially if you started with *When Life Gives You Legends* and are now blinking in disbelief at the end of *Bard to the Bone*— thank you. You didn't just read this story. You *lived* it with me.

If you ever feel like the world is too dark, too twisted, too far gone... show up anyway. Justice is real. Hope is stubborn. And weird little heroes can save the world, too.

Just ask Tilda.

www.ingramcontent.com/pod-product-compliance
Lightning Source LLC
Chambersburg PA
CBHW020525110726
47899CB00004B/1257